FINDING CUPID

BRIDGET E. BAKER

For Pansy Richardson.

You are loved, you are missed, and you are not forgotten.

I
GEO

Paisley has been my best friend for eight years. I'd leap on top of a bomb for her, but sometimes I really wish she came with a mute button. I know that sounds terrible, but all she's been talking about for the past two weeks is her friend Mary and the guy her friend's marrying, Luke something or other.

I'm sick to death of hearing about how ridiculously, absurdly, disgustingly cute they are. Since I'm about to see Pais, I brace myself for another onslaught of the same.

I've met Paisley for breakfast at the Rise-n-Dine almost every Saturday morning for more than six years now, a sorority tradition that we maintained, even though our sorority sisters peeled off one by one. It's a good thing the diner's sweet potato pancakes are so good, or I'd have been sick of it years ago.

Or maybe I still insist on coming here because I value familiarity more than your average person.

"Geode!" Paisley's smile almost cracks her face in half when she sees me.

I walk the last few steps and slide into our normal

booth. The wood's worn smooth and the tables are shiny. Blue glass bottles full of flowers decorate the shelf that wraps around the wall. Some people might argue it needs a refresh, but I think the décor gives it the same homey feel it had freshman year. I missed home then, and I still do today.

"I ordered your pancakes already," Paisley says.

I lift one eyebrow, but I can't summon any irritation. It's not like I was planning to order anything else. I always order what I like, and Paisley knows me well enough to know what that is. "Thanks."

Paisley on the other hand hasn't ever ordered the same thing twice. If there's a special, she'll eat that. If there isn't, she'll ask them to mash something together for her. Cookie dough pancakes. Bubble gum milkshake. Lemonade French toast. If someone thinks of something wacky, Paisley's sure to try it.

"I don't usually beat you here." Paisley wiggles her eyebrows. "Late night?"

I roll my eyes. "Not like you mean. Charity auction for a client."

Paisley drums her shiny, magenta polished fingers on the table. "Please tell me you at least took a date."

"You know my rules. But I knew you'd badger me for going alone, so I took a friend."

"Rob doesn't count."

I scrunch up my nose. "Why doesn't Rob count?"

Paisley ticks things off on her fingers. "He's hot. He has a great job. He thinks you're amazing. He comes whenever you crook your little finger." She bobs her head. "Taking Robbie Graham should be a date. But you utterly lose any credit I'd give you because—" she leans forward and drops her voice. "Does your heart rate spike when you think about kissing him? Do your toes curl at the idea? Does your breathing speed up, and do your hands get clammy?"

I grimace. "My hands never get clammy."

She huffs.

I force myself to think about kissing Rob, and bile rises in my throat. "Uh, no. Not exactly."

She leans back. "You should be dating. Your rules are stupid."

"I'm happy, so you should be happy for me." I didn't expect to miss talking about that dumb wedding.

"How long has it been since someone made your heart race, Geo?"

I shake my head. She shouldn't need to ask me this stuff.

She crosses her arms and leans back against the booth bench. "You can't tell me you haven't even been a teensy bit excited about anyone in more than three years. Clients, vendors, hotel or venue owners? You meet more people in one week than I do all year." She lifts one eyebrow.

When I don't offer anything, she doggedly continues.

"It's almost four years now, girl. It's time. Take the blinders off and look around. I ignored your insistence on those dumb rules because I thought they were like a cast for your heart. They kept you safe. But casts come off sometime, and in this case, I'm the doctor. It's time to cut that stinky cast off." She picks up her hands and mimes using a chainsaw.

I roll my eyes. "Don't be stupid. It's not a cast. My rules keep my life ordered and happy. I love my job, I like my friends well enough. Most of the time."

She shakes her head. "Not good enough. You should want more."

"Why?" I ask. "Because you do?"

She sighs. "No. Because you do too, and you just won't admit it."

I look pointedly around the diner and Paisley follows my gaze. A group of guys slump in the booths next to us, their hair a mix of tangled, curly mops hanging in their faces and man buns twisted into wads on the back of their heads. I turn toward another table, this one full of of preppy guys who look about fifteen years old. Everyone else in the room is female. "Uh, even if I take my blinders off, in case you haven't noticed, it's slim pickings out there. Maybe you're seeing something different?"

She shrugs. "Not in here, goofball. This is a college hotspot. But the good guys are out there. My friend Mary—"

I groan. "If I have to hear about your *boss* Mary and her perfect fiancé one more time..."

Paisley throws her hands up in the air. "She's amazing, okay, and she had given up too, just like you have."

I lean toward her. "Do you really think it's fair to say I gave up?"

Paisley sighs. "No, I'm sorry I said that. But Mary had given up, okay? And then BAM! Just like that, this guy shows up at a bar. She had borrowed a dress from me, so she dazzled a little more than usual. It was outside of her normal comfort zone, but thanks to that, he noticed. You have to be willing to try new things, and look in places you might otherwise ignore. If you do, well, it's more likely you'll spot him."

"I'm happy for Mary, I really am," I say. "I'd like to meet this Mr. Perfect one day, actually. Because he's probably hiding a smoking habit, or he's got a big old pot belly. In my experience, the good always exists right alongside the bad."

Paisley beams at me. "I am so glad to hear you say you'd like to meet him. In fact." She stands up and waves.

My stomach sinks, and I whisper-yell at her. "Who are you waving at?"

"Okay. Don't get mad, okay? I know you never ever *ever* plan weddings. Believe me, I know. I told Mary like five times. But they are really not handling the planning very well on their own and I knew you needed the money right now, and they need someone super competent with just the right touch for people, and well, I might talk about you a lot. And I just sort of mentioned we came here on Saturdays."

When I glare at her, she pokes my ribs and whispers. "I mentioned it by accident, I swear."

Paisley's a big mouthed liar.

I barely have time to struggle to my feet before perfect Mary and her flawless, and definitely not potbellied, fiancé are standing in front of me. I force a smile onto my face and glance down at my Emory sweatshirt, yoga pants and Ugg boots. Hardly an appropriate outfit for meeting a potential client. Not that I'd ever plan a wedding, no matter what ambushes Paisley orchestrates.

Never mind how badly I need the extra money. It's not like one wedding would be enough anyway.

Mary's wearing dark jeans and a beautifully cut and delicately painted leather jacket. Her hair's shiny and perfectly highlighted. Her boots rise in a sleek line to her knee and when she smiles, perfectly pink lips part to display sparkling white teeth.

"You must be Geode." Her voice sounds surprisingly normal, coming from such a polished exterior.

"Please, call me Geo. My parents couldn't have come up with a more obscure name, but you'll get used to it. They chose it to remind me it's what's on the inside of people that counts and I should worry about what really matters."

The tall man next to Mary is wearing a battered leather

jacket, his jeans aren't dressy and his plain blue t-shirt dresses it down further. They almost look like a mismatch. He holds out his hand. "Your parents sound pretty intelligent to me. I named my kids plain old Amy and Chase. Now I'm thinking I should've given their names a little more thought. My name is just as boring. I'm Luke. Nice to meet you, shiny on the inside Geode." He has a faint accent. I'd guess Australian, but he's been here a while and has tried hard to blend in.

"Wonderful to finally meet you both," I say. "Paisley talks about you all the time."

Mary grins at Paisley. "I'm sensing a theme. She's been telling me about her dear old roommate from Emory for years now. I can't believe I only just found out you're an event planner."

My grin nearly slips from my face, but before I can explain that I never do weddings, Paisley pulls me around next to her and gestures at the bench my bum was formerly warming. "Please, sit. Their pancakes are legendary."

"Or at least, they're reliably good," I say. "I prefer the sweet potato ones, unless you're sick of yam affiliated food now that we're post holidays."

"I always enjoy yams," Mary says. "I'm glad to be getting some recommendations from you already. As I'm sure Paisley has mentioned, Luke and I are getting married."

I scrunch my nose. "I hate to be the one to mention this, but I really never—"

Mary closes her eyes. "Don't say it. Pais told us you almost never do weddings. I get that, I really do, but she also told me you're amazing at dealing with people and planning for every contingency. And I'm going to level with you. I need that, badly. See, I'm running an office now, and it's new for me." She looks down and taps the table nervously. "If I'm honest, I'm barely hanging on with just that. I recently brought in a monstrously large client." She glances sideways at Luke, who meets her grin with one of his own in a disgustingly couple-y way. "I'm also creating the framework for a brand new charity, and if that's not enough, I'm also learning to parent. It's kind of a hands on crash course." She shakes her head.

"I know a dozen wedding planners," I say. "I'd be happy to recommend several of the best to you."

The waitress shows up then, handing me my pancakes, and passing a plate of eggs and chive and onion biscuits covered with cheese to Paisley. She takes Mary and Luke's order and leaves again.

"Oh, those pancakes look amazing." Mary glances surreptitiously at Paisley's plate but clearly can't think of anything to say about her bizarre pile of food. I know the feeling. "It's obvious to me already that Paisley was right, but I understand that you never do weddings. I really do."

She says she understands, but she looks like she means the opposite. Her eyes are full of eager, irritating hope.

Luke clears his throat. "I'll pay you whatever you want if you can pull this wedding off by Easter in a way that keeps Mary happy and calm." He places his hand over Mary's and squeezes, and my heart contracts. I may not date, but I miss that, the knowledge that someone cares. I long for the days when I had someone else to look after me, and pick up the things I dropped.

A knot forms in my stomach. I cannot plan this wedding for this couple. I can't meet with them and watch all this disgusting happiness every single day. It will kill me.

I glance at Luke's work boots, calloused hands, and his tanned face and an idea occurs to me. I'll price them out and then I don't need to be the monster who won't help them with their princess-flower-garden-unicorn wedding.

"What parameters are we talking about here? What events, size, and locations?" I ask.

"We'd want help planning the bachelor and bachelorette parties," Mary says, "and we haven't quite decided on the wedding location, but as a fallback, it could be in my brother-in-law's back yard in Marietta."

"That's practically next door to you," Paisley says, one eyebrow raised. "How convenient."

I step on her sneaker under the table, but she doesn't even squeak. I should've stomped harder.

"We'd love it if you could help her sister plan the bridal shower," Luke says. "I'll pay for all of it, I really don't mind."

I glance at Paisley. She's going to get an earful later. "My friend Kevin is an amazing wedding planner. He is wonderful with people, and he pays attention to every detail."

Mary nods. "Does that mean you won't consider doing it yourself?"

"Honestly, I doubt you'd want to pay for me. I've been focusing exclusively on large corporate events for the past few years. I'm pretty expensive for a backyard wedding. Most people don't realize how expensive a wedding can really be, and the idea of adding a full time employee on top of the ordinary expenses of food, invitations, photography, decor, drinks, venue, and favors, let alone the dress and cake, well, it adds up."

Luke leans forward. "What would you charge?"

I tap my lip. "How many guests are you planning to invite?"

Mary grimaces. "That's part of the issue. I'd love to keep it small, intimate. A hundred people or less."

Luke shakes his head. "Most of my extended family has relocated to the States from Australia. I have work contacts

I have to invite. I doubt we can get away with less than three hundred." He grins at Mary and I sense an old argument. "Five hundred would be easier."

"Wow," I say, "with that many people, and a backyard venue, and a shower and two pre-parties..." I exhale slowly. What's a ridiculous sum for something like this? What fee would scare them off? I think about exactly how much money I need. I cannot do a wedding. But if by some bizarre twist of fate, these people are hugely loaded, I can't turn something like this away. Not if they're willing to pay me what I need. "I completely understand this is probably far too much, but a hundred thousand would be my absolute minimum."

I expect them to whistle. Maybe groan. Lean back on the bench. Look at one another awkwardly and ask for Kevin's information. Kevin could do a wedding for three hundred guests for ten to fifteen grand for sure. Toss on another few grand for the smaller events, and a few vendor kickbacks, and that would be a tidy sum for something like this.

Mary's eyebrows draw together and her lips compress. Luke kisses her forehead. "What if we pay you a hundred up front and twenty thousand on the back end, with a possibility of a thirty thousand dollar bonus if my Mary's over the moon?"

I turn to Paisley. "Is he serious?"

She's uncharacteristically quiet in her tiny corner of the booth. "I told you Mary's my *boss*."

"What do you do again?" I ask Mary. "I thought Paisley said you were an accountant."

Mary frowns. "Luke gets carried away sometimes. That's one of the reasons I need someone to help us. He overbids on things when he's unfamiliar with them. I'm an accountant, yes, although technically, I'm the President of the Atlanta branch of a big accounting firm. Partners do pretty well. But not that well."

Paisley smirks. "Luke's loaded. He invented the light bulb."

My eyebrows rise.

Luke chuckles. "Not the light bulb, no."

"Right," I say. "Duh. That was Edison, right?"

Luke glances at the ceiling. "Swan, Volta, a lot of others contributed, but Edison developed the filament that made the first light bulb cost efficient. I'm sort of the Edison for LEDs. I developed some LED affiliated technology that took another great stride forward in cost effective light sources."

I swear under my breath.

"I felt the same way," Mary says. "But the thing is, he has like a list of a thousand people his brother thinks we need to invite. And I want things as small as possible. I'd rather not spend our wedding day greeting a bunch of people I don't know. So we need to narrow the list, and I need you to be the bad guy with Paul."

"Also, we can't seem to pick a location," Luke says. "Mary likes the idea of my brother's back yard, but the only way to narrow the list may be a location wedding. I'm voting for Vail, personally. The glistening snow, the mountain peaks." He turns toward Mary and kisses her softly. My heart wrenches.

The only thing worse than planning this nightmare would be knowing I could have earned the money for Mom, but I was too afraid to do it.

"Not that we'd expect you to pay for your expenses in checking these places out," Mary says. "We'd obviously fly you to the locations we're considering to scout them out and look into logistics."

When I realize my mouth is hanging open, I snap it shut.

"So?" Paisley asks. "They've met your terms. Are you going to do it? Because I'm working like twenty hours a week of overtime right now, and things are still not getting done. I'll throw my plea as your best friend in there too. Please, please take over for me?"

A hundred and fifty thousand dollars. For one main event and three smaller ones. I'd be a moron to turn this down. A selfish, ungrateful jerk. I exhale heavily.

"What other locations are you considering?" I ask begrudgingly.

Paisley claps and hugs me. "Oh my gosh this is going to be so much fun!"

I hope she's right, but somehow I doubt it.

2

TRIG

I haven't seen Luke in months, so I figured my old college pal would be happy to see me. I certainly waited in the lobby for him long enough to deserve an effusive greeting.

"Trig! You made it." He smiles, but then his eyes lift upward, focusing above my face. He bobs his head toward the top of mine. "I know you're a little more couth than I am, being a trust baby and all, but there's this thing I'm going to tell you about that will revolutionize your life. It's called a comb. You can pick one up at most any pharmacy or grocery store."

He waves me into the conference room. He looks impeccable as always, in a hardworking electrician kind of way. Actually, now that I'm thinking about it, he might look better than usual. He's sporting a nice button down shirt instead of his typical t-shirt, and his shoes are shiny leather instead of scuffed work boots.

I try to run my fingers through my hair, but it's too tangled for me to succeed. "Early morning skydive, but I still look better than you do, old man."

I punch him on the arm, pulling back a little so it won't bruise. Luke used to block against that stuff when we were sparring partners, but he doesn't even flex this time. "You're slowing down grandpa. You been slacking?"

Luke shakes his head. "Haven't had time for Krav Maga in years. Just wait until you have munchkins of your own. You'll get old and flabby, too."

Luke may be a few years older than me, but he's definitely not flabby. "I think I could pull off a gut." I stick out my stomach.

"Even if you don't get a pot belly, maybe once you have kids you'll stop doing idiotic things so often."

"I like trying new things," I say. "And I don't plan to stop. But I don't think you can blame your kids for being boring. You've been like this for more than a decade."

Luke frowns. "But you haven't. You never hurled yourself from planes or base jumped in college. Come to think of it, you didn't do it when we worked on our start up either. When did all this start? Are you having an early mid-life crisis? Should I be scheduling an intervention?"

"I like living life on the edge," I say. "What do you care?"

"Duh, I'm worried about you," Luke says. "In case you hadn't noticed, it's freezing outside. I have no idea why you'd want to go a mile up to begin with, much less fling yourself into the arctic air. You're certifiable."

"This feels cold to you, but Atlanta's way warmer than Colorado right now."

"Level with me. What's the underlying compulsion?" Luke looks genuinely curious.

"As you already pointed out, I don't have kids to worry about."

"My kids don't factor into this." Luke sits down next to

me. "Even before I had the rugrats, I never would have voluntarily jumped out of a plane."

"Have you seen my jet?" I ask. "I doubt it's been inspected since the Clinton administration. By the time we reach altitude, I feel safer with that parachute on my back than hanging on for dear life in that airborne clunker."

Luke snorts. "When I saw him last, your dad was bragging about buying you a new Cessna for your birthday."

My dad only gives absurdly lavish gifts. If it's not something he can brag about, he won't buy it. "He says he got them 'buy two, get one free.'"

"He's practically a bargain shopper," Luke says.

"Right? But having a new jet ruins my joke. Actually, speaking of jokes, I heard a rumor I need to confirm. James told me something the other day. Something hilarious."

"What's that?" Luke asks. "I always appreciate a good laugh."

"I heard you joined that new timeshare for jets. JumpJet or some dumb thing. Say it isn't so."

Luke nods slowly. "It's worse than that. I'm living in a trailer, actually. It's parked in an honest-to-goodness RV park."

My jaw drops and I sink onto a boardroom chair. "Seriously?"

He drops into the chair next to me and leans on the table. "Times are tight, and as you know, if a few things go wrong, the money disappears. Quickly."

"Geez, is that why you asked me to come out?" I lean toward him. "Because Nometry's doing great. Let's talk. I can get you and Paul back on your feet. I could even give you both jobs if you need them. You'd be great at scouting for promising electrical and mechanical startups. Or if you'd rather not work for me, tell me what you're working on. Maybe there's something we can finance to keep you afloat through this rough patch."

Luke covers his mouth with one hand, and my heart goes out to him. How bad are things? His office looks fine, at least from the outside. A terrible thought occurs to me and I drop my voice. "Can you make payroll next month? Do you need a loan, like imminently?"

"What if I do?" Luke leans back in his chair. "Do you have enough liquidity to help me?"

"I just wrapped three projects." I run some numbers in my head. I could push a deal forward and I'd be fine. "What do you need? Two million? More?"

Luke stares at me blankly.

"Five million? I don't think I could go much higher than that in the next few days. How soon do you need it?"

Luke's face splits into a grin. "You're a better friend than I give you credit for Trig. Seriously, things are fine."

I cough out a laugh. "You're a punk, Luke. Always have been. I should've punched you harder."

"Maybe you should've." Luke pats the solid wood conference room table. "I do have some news though, and it's the good kind."

"Finally we get to the reason you wanted to meet." I exhale. "Oh, tell me it's a project. Is it a project? I've been wanting to work with you guys again for years. What have you got?"

"We do have something new, actually. If you can keep your big mouth shut, I'll tell you about it."

My eyes widen. "Yeah?"

"We're fine-tuning now, but we've finally perfected a car battery that's under five pounds. Four point three pounds to be precise. And it's got thirty percent more power than a typical battery, with a year longer life."

I swear under my breath. I cannot wait to get my hands on this. We've talked about it for years.

"But we aren't looking for capital." He tilts his head sideways sheepishly. "Paul would never agree to pay your cut again. Sorry."

That's just mean. He tells me about the idea of the year, and then yanks it away? I can't quite prevent my scowl. "Why am I here then?"

Luke sucks on his teeth and it reminds me of how nervous he looked pitching me that very first deal, almost fifteen years ago. I had been out of college for less than a year, and I needed to do something big or I'd never get out from under my mom's thumb. I was desperate enough to consider an idea from a tooth sucking electrician and his little brother. It helped that Luke had been my best friend and study partner for years, so I knew the electrician façade disguised a vast intellect.

Clearly the exterior and interior have remained the same. Which is one of the things I like best about Luke. Money didn't change him at all.

"I'm engaged," Luke says. "And I wanted to ask you to be my best man."

That explains the upgrade to the shirt and shoes. This girl must be special, because Beth never managed to change a single thing.

"Engaged?" I whistle. "I did not see that one coming."

Luke's smile this time is tinged with sadness. I know he still misses Beth, which must mean he found someone truly amazing. He'd settle for nothing less. Beth was the coolest girl I'd ever met, and she was a perfect fit for Luke. And now he's found someone? A twinge of jealousy shoots through me, but I stomp it down. He's asking me to be his best man. What kind of best man is jealous? A lousy one, that's who.

Besides. I don't even want a wife. I've seen where that goes for Thornton men, and I'm not interested.

"I could never have predicted Mary." Luke's eyes light up. "Amy absolutely adores her. Mary won't ever replace Beth, but she's gluing our family back together. I didn't even realize how many sharp places and cracks we were ignoring until Mary started fixing them without being asked. Amy took to her right away, maybe before I did, but Chase has been slower. A few days ago he started calling her 'Mom' too." Luke inhales deeply and I wonder whether he was tearing up.

"Congratulations," I say. "That's the best news ever. Seriously I am so happy for you. But won't Paul be upset if you make me your best man?"

Luke bobs his head. "He's my brother and he knows he's my top choice."

"That hurts a little," I say. "I'm not going to lie."

Luke rolls his eyes. "With this battery launching, Paul has even less time than me. We're pushing for an early May release, and Mary and I are shooting for a mid-April wedding."

"What's the rush?" I ask.

"She runs a tax office, for one, so they all get a week off after tax season, which makes it an ideal time to honeymoon."

"She's still working?"

"Uh, yes, Trig, it's not 1953."

"But it's not like you need the money."

"She loves her job."

"She loves taxes?" I raise my eyebrows because it makes no sense.

Luke shrugs. "But also, we don't want to wait. We can't cohabitate." Luke's eyebrows lift. "Kids."

A huge belly laugh escapes before I can stop it. "Got it."

"Plus, life is short. You wait too long for something and you're likely to miss out. If Beth taught me anything, it's to be grateful for every single second I have. I'd love to call Mary my wife tomorrow. But she wants a ceremony with friends and family, and I can't fault her for that. She deserves the big white dress, the flowers, the oohing and aahing from friends. She deserves all of it, and I'm going to make sure she gets it. But since Paul's stuck handling the lion's share of the details on our new launch, he has zero time to plan a bachelor party and whatnot."

"So you're using me . . . for my planning skills?"

Luke sighs. "For a guy, you can be a real diva. We've hired an amazing wedding planner, and she's on tap to set up the entire Bachelor party. You can do as much or as little as you want, but if you have time to meet her for lunch today, you can point her in the right direction. I told her you'd be in town and she carved out some time. You can tell her what you have in mind and she'll make it happen so you don't need to feel used."

"She'll make it happen? You have a lot of confidence in this woman."

"Mary adores her already and she's only been working for us a week. Anyone who lightens Mary's load and makes her smile gets rave reviews from me." Luke stands up. "You want to come see the operation?"

"Uh, heck yes." I follow Luke from the office complex to the R&D labs. Paul's hunched over a table examining something under a microscope.

"Hey nerd," I say. "I hear you've been busy."

Paul turns around to face me, and I'm a little annoyed to see that he's still as much of a pretty boy as ever. Age never seems to touch him much. He's even sporting the trendy beard everyone has right now and somehow making it work. All through college, girls flocked to Paul, and I'm sure they still do. He was too focused on school to really appreciate how little he had to work. What I could have done with his face, though. I swear.

"Bernie, good to see you."

I cringe when he calls me that. "You do not give up."

Paul crosses the room to give me a side hug. "Your name's Bernard, dude. You can thank your parents for that. If you've convinced everyone to call you Trig, well, I never bought into the rebranding."

I slap his back. Hard. "I hear you've followed your brother's lead to another huge success."

Paul backs up a step and his nostrils flare like they always do. "We can't all be innovators, you know. Some of us have to simply take the ideas from others and implement them well."

"I'm kidding, Paul. Luke wouldn't ever have made his lightbulbs work without you. Plenty of people have ideas. You make them reality."

"Well, this battery probably won't hit as big as your last venture. I mean, we can't all make the newest sugar substitute that also blocks the reuptake of fat cells, but we're happy with it."

"I didn't create anything. I just bankrolled it," I say. "And Brekka found that one, not me."

"You've always owed your success to her," Luke says. "How's she doing?"

"My sister never stops swinging," I say. "She's the strongest person I know, and probably the smartest."

"Tell her I said hello," Paul says. "I need to get out to Colorado soon. Maybe I can take her to dinner when I do, but it probably won't be until June."

"Launching in May, Luke tells me. I hope it goes smoothly for you."

Paul shakes his head. "Never goes smoothly, but I've

gotten pretty good at flattening out issues over the years. Mostly because I have a good legal team, strong contract negotiators, and a marketing budget that would make you cry."

"Good call," I say.

Luke glances at his watch. "I've got a few minutes to show you the prototypes, but if you want to meet our planner for lunch, you'll need to leave pretty soon. She said noon, and she's never late."

"I think she can wait for me a few minutes if she has to," I say. "She does work for you, and I assume you're paying her top dollar."

Luke nods his head slowly. "Sure, if you want to keep her waiting, that's your call. But you are going, then?"

"I don't plan to buy the cups and napkins for your party myself," I say. "So yeah, I think a lunch to point her in the right direction sounds like a good idea."

"Nothing crazy, okay?" Luke says.

"Could you clarify? Do you mean no strippers on poles? Or, like no trips to Paris? And does it make a difference if we use my jet? Because I am not taking your timeshare air bus anywhere. I might actually *need* to parachute out and that takes the fun out of it."

Luke shakes his head. "I have kids, Trig. I didn't think I'd need to tell you no strippers."

"Ease up," I say. "It's like literally the bachelor party joke. But I do want some parameters as to what crazy means. No skydiving, I assume?"

Luke smiles. "Absolutely no skydiving."

"How do you feel about cliff jumping?"

Luke groans. "No cliff jumping, or base jumping, no extreme skiing, and no paragliding."

"Parasailing?" I ask, just to annoy him.

Paul clears his throat. "Don't make me step in and take over as best man. Because I will totally do it if I have to."

"I'm kidding, geez. I'll come up with something decent that takes no more than two days and isn't too terrifying for the little old grannies I'm friends with."

"Have fun at your brunch." Paul smirks.

"It's a lunch," I protest.

Luke and Paul exchange a smile I don't understand before I follow Luke down to the applied science and testing unit on the ground floor. "What was that weird grin thing about?"

"What are you talking about?" Luke lifts one eyebrow like I'm crazy.

"Oh come on, I saw you and Paul share some kind of look. What's going on?"

Luke narrows his eyes at me. "Let's just say that Mary likes to play matchmaker. It's become a kind of weird hobby for her since we got engaged."

"How much matchmaking could she have done in the last twenty-six minutes?"

"I proposed at Christmas, thank you very much."

"Of course you did," I say. "Because you're completely unswayed by the emotions of the season." The elevator bings and we step out on the first floor, heading out of the office complex and over toward applied science.

"It wasn't an emotional decision," Luke says.

I choke back a laugh.

"It was, but I mean, I never regretted it. I didn't do it because of Christmas."

"Right, because everyone falls in love in a few weeks and proposes at Christmas."

He scowls. "The point is, Mary has a sister and—"

"Wait, tell me this wedding planner isn't Mary's ugly little sister."

Luke frowns. "Trudy's not ugly, and no, Geo's not Mary's younger sister. And it's Paul who Mary's eyeing for her sister, not you. He's been evading Mary's multitudinous attempts at introducing them like a stray avoids the dogcatcher. It's gotten almost ridiculous."

"She's that bad, huh?"

"Trudy's very attractive, just like Mary. Paul's just a little leery of trusting anyone right now." We've reached the large warehouse building by the Lit Up Applied Science office park. Luke opens the door and gestures me inside. "Mary did note that Geo's single and that if my best man was single, it might be nice if you met."

I pull up short. I'm sick of being set up with women who can't wait to meet the most eligible billionaire under forty. I liked it in college. Not so much now.

"Relax. This girl has some kind of rule. She doesn't date at all, from what I've heard, so she's definitely not going to be chasing you."

"So she's gay?"

"Something like that," Luke says.

We spend so long looking at the functionality and ease of the new battery that it's already noon when Luke walks me to my car.

"Where exactly am I going for this lunch?" I ask Luke.

"I'll text you the address."

"And how will I know who I'm meeting?" I ask. "What does she look like? 'Cute' isn't very helpful."

"Let's just say she's not your type, and she will be sitting alone, probably looking annoyed. If that doesn't help, I'm sure the hostess can help you find her. Her name is Geo Polson."

I eye Luke pointedly. "Should I be making up an excuse right now and doing this over the phone?"

Luke shakes his head. "Go, tell the kid what you want,

and let her plan it for you. Mary means well, and Geo knows nothing about Mary's hopes and dreams of all her friends getting married and being as happy as we are. It's not a sticky rat trap, I promise."

I click my key and slide into the seat of my black Aston Martin Vantage. I do enough business in Atlanta to keep a car here, thankfully. I cry a little inside when I have to drive a crappy rental car. They always smell like Cheetos. GPS routes me to midtown, some place called the Local Pizzaioli. Looks pretty decent. I wonder whether she picked it, or whether Luke did. It looks just like his kind of place.

I ease my car into a spot and give her a pat on the hood as I walk toward the entrance. Not my type, Luke said? What does that even mean? She's old? She's taller than me? Her teeth are wonky? When I open the door, a perky hostess with a pressed white shirt and black slacks greets me with a forced smile.

"Welcome to the Local Pizzaioli!" She pulls out a menu with a little too much enthusiasm and sends one flying toward my head.

I stumble backward, but I catch it without losing an eye. "Thanks. I'm supposed to be meeting—"

My eyes scan the room while I'm talking, but I don't see anyone sitting alone. I assume this Geo person must have already left. Unsurprising, since I am more than half an hour late. Then I see a woman tapping her black booted foot in the back corner. As if she senses my gaze, her face turns toward me and suddenly, I can't form any coherent words.

Her eyes are bluer than the ocean in Bora Bora, startling even from here. Her hair falls straight down from her face in a shimmering black sheet far past her shoulders.

Her cheekbones slant down toward a sharp chin, and if this is Geo, Luke is a moron.

She's exactly my type.

He could have told me she had a body that would make any Hollywood starlet jealous, or a face to launch a thousand ships. Instead he let me practically stand her up, probably laughing inside the whole time. I wipe my mouth to make sure I'm not drooling.

I shake my head. That must not be her. Luke's got an odd sense of humor, but he's not delusional. Plus there's no way this girl doesn't date. Maybe since this Geo has bailed, I could introduce myself to Miss America instead. Then at least it wasn't a wasted trip.

"Excuse me sir, you sort of trailed off there. Who are you meeting?"

Right. I clear my throat and swallow. "Um, her name is Geo something."

"Oh, yes, she's waiting right this way."

Right what way? Is it her? Please, please, let the breathtaking woman be Geo. The hostess takes three steps in the right direction and then pulls up short. She giggles like a five year old girl. "I should verify you're the right person."

"You need to verify who I am?" I lift one eyebrow. "Why?"

She giggles again and I suppress a scowl. "Let's just say a few guys have claimed they were meeting her here that weren't."

Let's say what? "Huh?"

"What's your name?" she asks.

"Trig," I say.

She smirks. "So I guess you're one of those creepy guys."

She was leading me to Geo, and then she stopped. I gave her my name, and now she thinks I'm a creeper?

Wait, maybe she's saying this woman is so breathtaking that men are lying and saying they're meeting her here. If it's Geo though, she really is supposed to be meeting me.

Then it hits me. I could kick Luke for his stupid sense of humor. I never, ever use my real name for anything, as he well knows. I grit my teeth and force the words out. "My full name is Bernard Thornton the third."

"Oh, it is you, wonderful. Right this way, then."

And we're walking toward her. The girl who's probably every breathing man's type.

I realize about halfway across the dining room that I have absolutely no idea what to say to her. Sorry I'm late? I'm not usually so inconsiderate? Isn't that what an inconsiderate guy would say?

I wrack my brain for some smart way to apologize that would make me sound charming, but every single line I've ever used withers and dies. I glance toward Geo, now only a dozen steps away, and I can barely remember my own name, much less come up with anything witty. Is Luke blind? He could have prepared me that she could be a print model if her career as an event planner doesn't pan out.

I'm five steps from the table, walking alongside the hostess, when a thirty-something man in a suit approaches the table before we can.

"Pardon me ma'am," he says, his voice unsure. "Are you here alone?"

Geo looks up, and even though she's not looking at me, the weight of her gaze makes me swallow again.

"Yes," she says, her voice low and sultry. "Can I help you with something? I know the area pretty well. I grew up around the corner."

The man gulps and I want to throat punch him. Buzz off idiot, I have an appointment. I'm stupidly late, but he doesn't know that. "I was wondering whether you'd like to join me and my buddy." He waves back at a table a few over from hers. "I travel a lot, so I know it sucks to eat alone."

What a tremendously sloppy line. I almost feel bad for the guy.

"It's terrible when people don't respect other people's time." Her eyes dart my way. "But I'm meeting someone, and I think he's finally here."

"Oh." The man blinks a few times. "Well, I could give you my phone number. If that doesn't work out, I mean. I'm very punctual."

I'm very punctual? Seriously? Just what every girl dreams of. A punctual boyfriend. I suppress the urge to laugh.

I clear my throat instead. "I'm finally here sweetheart." I step around the hostess and tap the table. "So sorry to keep you waiting." I turn toward the awkward guy and bob my head. "I'm Trig Thornton, but it looks like you've already met my girlfriend, Geo."

"I guess you don't want my phone number then?" he asks Geo.

"Scram, dude." I can't quite keep the irritation out of my tone.

He scurries back to his table, and at least he has the decency to look down self-consciously when he does.

"I imagine that happens to you a lot," I say.

The hostess catches my eye and wisely hands me a menu and heads back to the front of the restaurant.

"What? People pretending to be my boyfriend?" She arches one pristine eyebrow.

Heat rushes into my face. "Uh, no. I meant guys hitting on you."

When she simply stares at me reproachfully, I continue. "I'm sorry I kept you waiting. Luke didn't tell me about this lunch until it was almost time to be here."

"That doesn't sound much like Luke, but then I haven't known him long. From what I hear, you've known him for quite some time, which is why you're the best man." She stands up to shake my hand. "Geo Polson."

I sit down across from her. "Nice to meet you Geo. It really is past time we met, seeing as you're my girlfriend and all."

She frowns.

"What? Too early to joke?"

Finally a tiny smile. "I've found Luke to be pretty organized and punctual."

"We tech nerds lose track sometimes when we're focused on work things."

She nods at me. "Well, I'm glad you finally made it. I'd love to get some of the details hammered out for the bachelor weekend right away. With the wedding looming in the next three months, we don't have much time."

"Do you have a list of the groomsmen?" I ask.

She reaches into a black portfolio and pulls out a sheet of paper. "You, of course, although I do admit I had your name listed as something other than Trig? Is that what you said?"

"My given name is Bernard, it's true," I say. "But in college, I was so good at math that I got a nickname after I got a perfect score on every math test in class. First time a student had ever done it. Everyone calls me Trig now, for trigonometry."

Her eyes widen slightly, and she meets my gaze. When she does, I stare at her like a dope. I really, really wish I hadn't been late.

"I can barely do sums on paper." She grins ruefully. "But for the wedding party, I have you listed, Paul who I presume you know since he's Luke's brother, someone named James—"

"James Fullton."

"Right. And someone named Bradley Millhouse."

I don't like Bradley Millhouse, but it's complicated and I don't want to get into it. "I don't know him very well. He was a good friend of Luke's first wife."

Geo's eyes widen and she makes a note on the paper. "Thanks. That kind of information is invaluable."

"Need to make sure he doesn't blow up the wedding?" I ask.

"Something like that."

"Have you ever had anything truly crazy happen?" I ask. "I bet you have some great stories."

She nods. "I've had my share of odd occurrences for sure. But fair disclosure, I don't normally plan weddings. In fact, I usually avoid them at all costs."

"Why is this an exception?"

She sighs. "My best friend Paisley begged me, and her boss, Mary, is a hard lady to turn down."

I want to meet Mary now more than ever, after this description. "Well, with a deceased first wife and two kids, not to mention money thrown into the mix, and business contacts from each of them, I imagine you'll have your hands full navigating it all."

"The bride wants a guest list of one hundred, and the groom wants five hundred." She flips her menu open and focuses on it. "This is kind of my area of expertise though. I'll make sure this is a happy and respectful celebration of Luke and Mary's love, as it should be. Any information you can share or tips you may have for managing the groom's guests are greatly appreciated."

I want to say something that makes her happy. Badly. I can tell she's effective at her job. Not to mention, I imagine every guy she meets wants to tell her whatever she wants to know. "If I think of something I'll share, but I think everyone will be happy for Luke. He's had a rough couple of years. Beth died when Chase was born, in case you hadn't heard."

"Paisley mentioned that, and it's a heartbreaking story for sure. I'm glad Luke gets a second happy ending though. And with enough preparation, we can foresee and prevent any negative outcomes for this wedding."

I frown. "You don't really think that. No matter how much you plan, you can't anticipate everything."

She shakes her head. "I disagree. All outcomes in life can be prepared for. If you take the care and effort necessary, you can avoid 99.9% of undesirable events, especially for big parties like a wedding. You can prepare contingencies for the rest."

"Like a hurricane?"

"I always have a fall back venue in case of inclement weather or other emergency. Sometimes I even have a fall back date."

My jaw drops. "Are you telling me that you sit around and think about every doom and gloom thing that might occur?"

She snaps her menu closed. "It's my job, Trig. I imagine other people might find your number calculations boring. But I provide a service that helps people to enjoy their important days without dealing with any undesirable hiccups and with a minimum of interruptions. Can you say the same?"

She's so gorgeous with her eyes sparking and her lips compressed that I want to yank her across the table and kiss her senseless, but since she'd slap me and walk out, I pull out my menu instead. "Having now thoroughly perused the options, what do you recommend, Miss Contingency Planner?"

The waiter walks up as though on cue, a smile plastered on his face.

"I always order from the core at every restaurant. Which means here, the pizza's safe," she says.

"I'll have the fettuccine Bolognese," I say, one eyebrow cocked. "I never play it safe."

3

GEO

I like Luke so much that I'm surprised by how much I dislike his best friend. I knew he was younger than Luke—Mary said Luke started college pretty late in life, after he'd already been an electrician for a while. Trig's handsome enough, with shaggy, slightly curly dark hair, and eyes such a light shade of brown that they're nearly gold. And he's tall too, much taller than me, which is rare. But when he opens his mouth, I have to work overtime not to roll my eyes so far up into my head that they'll get stuck there.

"If you really wanted to live life dangerously," I say. "You'd order the fish."

"I didn't say I was a moron," Trig says. "I never eat fish that wasn't caught the same day as I'm ordering it."

Spoken like someone worth a gazillion dollars. Mary mentioned he was even richer than her fiancé, the dramatic over spender. It's bizarre talking to someone who could literally purchase the restaurant where we're eating. He actually seems way more normal than I expected in his dark green sweater and faded jeans.

"Your privilege is showing," I say. "I had fish sticks for dinner last night. Frozen, from a bag."

His nose scrunches up. "Please be kidding right now."

"I ate at Mary's house with Amy and Chase, and no, I'm not joking. You might be surprised how delicious fish sticks and oven French fries can be. Especially if you combine a little mayo and ketchup to dip them in." I kiss my fingers. "Mmmm."

He makes a strangled noise and sips his water. "I doubt that's true."

Needling him is actually pretty fun. "I'll be sure to put that on the menu for the bachelor party, then?"

"What did you have in mind for that?" he asks. "Other than loads and loads of fish sticks and pink sauce, obviously."

"Mary's an accountant, so she's pretty slammed supervising whatever those people do during tax season. She wants to make sure she doesn't let the parties happen too close to April fifteenth. The weekend Luke and Mary have requested that also fits with Paul's schedule is February 12 and 13." I pick up my glass to take a drink. My mouth feels dry for some reason, and my hands are a little shaky. Odd.

"Valentine's Day weekend?" he asks. "Seriously?"

I lie. "I didn't think about that."

"A female event planner who doesn't think about Valentine's Day?" he asks. "I thought all women had their wish lists on file at Tiffany's months in advance."

What kind of girl does he date? "I've never set foot in a Tiffany's in my life. Also, I hate Valentine's Day and everything about it. I try to pretend it doesn't exist each year. I mostly succeed, since I never date."

He tsks and shakes his head slowly. "That's a real shame. My sister doesn't date either, but she absolutely loves February fourteenth. She wears all pink, makes fancy frosted cookies, decorates the house, and invites her friends and family over for a strawberry tea service. I may or may not get stuck going every year. It's actually kind of fun."

He obviously needs some redirecting. "Will that weekend work for you? Or have you already RSVP'd to a Strawberry Shortcake party? Or maybe you have a big date planned." What's wrong with me? Why did I even say that?

Trig's mouth twists into a half smile. "Brekka's party will be on Valentine's Day morning, but no, I'm not seeing anyone currently. Which means I have no other plans."

"Perfect." Not that I care whether he's seeing someone. I'm really making a mess of this. "For the bachelor party, I mean. With the date blocking out of the way, let's talk options. Luke wants to keep this low key and appropriate. Most grooms are moving away from big, rowdy shows of excess testosterone these days, thankfully."

"He mentioned that he'd prefer we not feature strippers."

I glare at him. "Right. No strippers, obviously. I hope that wasn't something you had in mind."

Trig glares right back at me. "I think we may have gotten off on the wrong foot. Let's restart. I'm Trig, and I never go to strip clubs, but I do sometimes make poorly considered jokes. The person I care about most in this world is my sister, a female, and I'd never objectify women that way." He holds out his hand again. "Nice to meet you. And you are?"

I smile in spite of myself and reach up to shake, which is a mistake. His hand is warm and strong and when it wraps around mine, my heart flip flops in a way it hasn't in years. I yank my fingers back like his touch burns. I almost wish it had, because it would serve as a reminder to keep my distance. My rules exist for a reason. Like not scratching ant bites, or staying put when you get lost. Even if I was interested in breaking my own rule, Mary's fiancé's entitled best friend would definitely be at the bottom of any list I made. Even before Luke mentioned he goes skydiving for fun. I shudder at the thought.

I need to hammer out the details of this bachelor weekend so I can actively avoid him until he's a guest at the wedding. I pull out my lists, brandishing them like the shields they are.

"I made a list of optional weekend activities. I'm not sure if you guys would prefer a weekend at the beach relaxing or surfing to a weekend of ATVs in the mountains. Or if that all sounds too outdoorsy, I could plan some nice dinners and a pub crawl or something."

"I think a bunch of guys laying around at the beach sipping drinks sounds a little ...girly," he says. "No offense. Did Luke say what he wanted to do? I'm not much of a drinker, and I don't think Luke or Paul are either, so I'd rather more action than pubs."

Surprise, surprise. "He told me you'd come up with some great ideas and that you planned almost everything fun they did in college and for years afterward. Did you have any other suggestions?"

He leans back in his chair and looks up at the ceiling. "What about a weekend of driving stock cars? I don't know what weekends the track is free off the top of my head, and I think there's some kind of NASCAR cup qualifying day in February, but I'm not sure when. It should be free other than that, especially if we do it on a Thursday or Friday. I know the owner, and he owes me a favor. Or ten."

The owner of the Atlanta Motor Speedway owes him a favor? Of course he does. The waiter arrives with our food, my Margherita pizza and Trig's fettuccine, just in time to allow me to recover from my idiotic fangirl moment.

He thanks the waiter for the food, and takes a bite. I rest a little easier when he seems to like it, chewing slowly with his eyes closed. I study his face while he's not looking at me, my gaze lingering a little longer than it should. My fingers itch to touch the five o'clock shadow on his jawline. He swallows and licks his lips.

"You've noticed how good my fettuccine is, right? Sometimes taking risks pays off."

I was definitely staring at the noodles, that's it. "It can pay off, occasionally. But other times the pasta's too hot and you burn your mouth. Or the sauce stains your shirt." I point at the orange blotch on his collar.

"Umm, hadn't you heard? Stained is the new black."

I can't suppress my laugh, and I see a little more why Luke likes him. "I guess I'm a little behind on my fashion primer for the season. Maybe I better pick up a few magazines and study up this weekend."

"Speaking of, are you free this Friday? Since you don't date, I figure you're usually free."

"I have client events most weekends," I say.

"Including this one?"

He's persistent. I'll give him that.

"I'm only asking because I'd be willing to stick around a little longer so we can go together. To talk to Nick about using his track for a few days, I mean. Would you be up for that?"

"Oh, you don't need to stay for me," I say quickly, my breathing accelerating at the idea of spending all weekend with Trig. "You can write down Nick's information and I'll follow up. I'm pretty good with people. I bet I can convince your friend to make his track available, possibly without using up one of your favors. All I really need is an introduction."

"I'll bet you can," he says, eyebrows bobbing. "But maybe I don't want you to convince him."

"What does that even mean?" I ask.

The smirk slips from his face. "Nothing, I'm just saying that to be successful in your job, I'm sure you must be quite good with people. But Nick can be a pain, and sort of inappropriate sometimes, too. Besides, it's no bother for me to introduce you in person since I'm already here. Details may be your thing, but convincing people to do what I want is my job."

"Is that so?" I set my napkin on the table. "You're like a car salesman, then?"

He shrugs. "Sure, in that I convince people to trust me so I can help them. Then I actually make all their dreams come true."

"So you're basically a saint."

He nods. "Exactly. And I'm happy to help you, out of the goodness of my saintly heart."

No matter how tempting it might be to spend more time with Luke's terminally cocky friend, I shake my head. "I can't meet anyone this weekend. I'm checking out venues for the wedding, and we're running very short on time. I'm booking a flight to Colorado for first thing tomorrow."

A smile spreads slowly across his face. "Colorado, huh? You don't say."

"I do say."

"Now that my services have been turned down flat, I happen to be flying to Colorado tomorrow myself."

I snort. "Sure you are."

"I am. Because I happen to live there. I'd be happy to give you a ride."

In his private jet. Because of course he has a private jet.

There's absolutely no way I'm about to join the scads of

girls who have flown a mile high with him in that thing. Luckily, I can use his lack of knowledge about the real world against him. "I appreciate the offer, I really do, but oddly enough, it costs more to fly one way than it does round trip. I'd hate to submit a bigger expense form to Luke and Mary. I'm sure you understand."

He lifts one eyebrow like he's not sure that's right, but he doesn't challenge me, thankfully. "Well, even if you're choosing to fly commercial, which I do not understand, I'd be happy to show you around. Are they thinking Vail or Aspen?"

They hadn't said. Which would he less likely to be familiar with? On my internet research last night, Aspen looked more exclusive. "I think they said Vail, but I'm not sure. I know the season closes around the same time as tax season, and Easter's late this year. They want the wedding on Easter weekend if possible so most people will have Friday off from work. I hear the ski resorts will be closed by then, but there will be snow for the photos. Does that sound about right?"

He nods. "It should be. Warm enough for a dress and a cape, but still a breathtaking white backdrop. The guests won't be able to ski, though. If you want them to be able to ski, sometimes Aspen stays open through late April. Or at least Aspen mountain does."

I pull out my phone and text Luke and Mary. IF WE CHOSE COLORADO, WOULD YOU WANT GUESTS TO SKI? OR DO YOU JUST WANT THE MOUNTAINS FOR PHOTOS AND AMBIENCE?

As I set my phone on the table, I notice my fingernail polish is chipped. Time for a manicure. I've barely had time to sleep since I started managing this wedding on top of my other events.

"I prefer Vail," he says. "I spent every day there as a kid, but Aspen's definitely snootier if that's what they're going for."

In spite of having spent very limited time with Mary, I'm fairly certain she's not aiming for snooty. "Do Luke and Mary strike you as fancy people?"

"I've never even met Mary," he says. "Maybe you can tell me about her. I doubt I can trust Luke's descriptions. He's a little smitten."

"With good cause. Mary's smart, no-nonsense, and organized. At least, until you plonk a kid down next to her she is. Then she kind of melts and turns all gooey. She seems like the kind of person who was born to be a mom, and those kids adore her. On top of all that, she's also beautiful. My best friend from college works for her, and from some things Paisley's said, I'm guessing she's kind of a hard friend to have."

Trig tilts his head. "How so?"

"You know, lots of girls don't like her because being around someone that amazing sort of makes you feel bad about yourself. Not that Mary makes people feel bad, but it's sort of a byproduct of being fabulous. She's prettier than you, smarter than you, more advanced in her career, generous to a fault, and more organized."

Trig bites his lip.

"What?" I ask. "You obviously have something to say."

"You appear pretty *organized* yourself."

"That's literally my job description. But it's an aspect of her personality from what I can tell. And she's wicked smart and runs an entire office of people who somehow also adore her. It'll make more sense when you see her. You'd expect her to look like Janet Reno, but she looks like... like a young Meg Ryan, maybe."

"If this Paisley person is your best friend, I imagine

she's comfortable surrounding herself with beautiful women."

Blood rushes to my cheeks and I frown at my reaction. I'm sure he's used to every woman he meets falling at his feet, so flirting probably comes second nature to him. It doesn't mean anything. Still, better to be clear from the outset. "Flattery will get you nowhere with me, Mr. Thornton. I don't date at all, but I certainly never date clients or their friends."

"I get it."

"You do?" Some of the men I meet, especially the good looking or wealthy ones, can be pretty persistent. After the past few years, I practically have a PhD in turning men down. Ironically, the more I turn some of them down, the harder they try. It can get exhausting. I wish there was a way around that. A fake boyfriend, maybe.

"You clearly command the interest of every man you meet, but I'm different."

Because of his boyish charm and all American looks? Because of his private jet? Because he's respectful and smart, even though he's inherited gobs of money? Because he's a whiz at math?

"Do tell me, how are you different?"

"For one, I'm not a client."

"You're client adjacent. My client's best man," I say flatly.

"A job I'd gladly step down from for the slightest inducement. James would probably do a better job anyway."

My face heats again. "Look, I don't know how I could be clearer. I'm not interested, and in fact, I don't date anyone, clients or otherwise."

My phone buzzes, which thankfully saves me from this awkward conversation. It's Luke.

WE'D LIKE GUESTS TO BE ABLE TO SKI IF

THEY COULD, BUT NOT ALL OF OUR GUESTS HAVE PRIVATE PLANES. VAIL'S AIRPORT HAS COMMERCIAL FLIGHTS.

"They'd prefer Vail," I say. "So that Mary's friends can fly in easier. Apparently Aspen accepts private flights only."

"Good thing for you, or you'd have to beg me for a ride. Which might be embarrassing after you turned me down so resoundingly."

I roll my eyes. "I think I'll manage just fine. You may not realize this, but the vast majority of people on Earth survive, and some even thrive, without ever flying on a private jet. At all."

"Fine, spurn my wings. But I went to high school with the director of the resort. You sure you don't want any help from me at all? You could even ski for free with me along. I've skied free ever since my buddy took over management there. Perk of being an alumni of Kent Denver High School."

"The only perk of my high school days is free snow cones from the only guy on the cheer squad with me." I shrug. "Maybe I went to the wrong high school, but I'd be happy to take you for a free one sometime. He makes a mean crème de menthe." I gulp. That sounded an awful lot like flirting, or even a borderline date offer. "Not that anyone wants a snow cone in January."

"If you leverage my connections this weekend, I promise to come back in July and take you up on your offer."

He'll fly out in July on his private jet... for a free snow cone? This whole interaction is getting far too flirty. I ought to turn him down on principle, but I am on a tight timeline to book a decent venue. If he could grease the skids on securing the date we want, or maybe even secure a discount for Luke and Mary, I'd be a horrible person to turn him down. "I suppose if you're not busy, I'd appreciate an introduction, but I don't ski."

Trig beams. "I'm happy to meet you there, and I can totally teach you to ski. Saturday morning at ten a.m.?"

How could I be clearer? "I didn't say I don't know how. I said I won't be skiing. Let me just clear this timing." My fingers fly over my phone keys, texting Mary and Luke.

TRIG OFFERED TO INTRODUCE ME TO THE DIRECTOR OF VAIL'S RESORT. SATURDAY MORNING FINE? I'LL PROBABLY BE OUT OF POCKET FOR A FEW DAYS, DEPENDING ON FLIGHTS.

Luke texts back immediately. DEPENDING ON FLIGHTS? TELL THAT LOSER TO GIVE YOU A RIDE IN HIS FREAKING CESSNA.

I take that as consent to the timing. "They said it's fine. Should I call and set up the appointment? What's your friend's name? Is he the Charles Corning listed on the website?"

Trig shakes his head and when he smiles this time, I can't seem to look away from the impish curve of his mouth. Or his straight, shiny white teeth. I shouldn't be admiring anything about him, and certainly not those. After all, every shark has shiny white chompers. "I'll handle that part."

"I hope you're not trying to steal my job." Again with the involuntary flirting. Get a grip, Geo.

"I do steal things sometimes, but your job won't be one of them," he says. "I promise."

"What exactly do you steal?" I clutch my purse against my chest melodramatically, apparently unable to help myself.

"Like I'd ever admit what I really steal."

"I think I can guess," I say. "Girlfriends. Companies. Maybe stock options? Hopefully not pensions."

He chuckles. "I'd never touch pensions, but I can neither confirm nor deny any of the other allegations."

The waiter shows up again. "Was everything okay?" He glances at my plate where more than half of my pizza's still uneaten.

I look up at him sheepishly. "I ate about a dozen breadsticks while I waited for this guy." I point at Trig. "The pizza was great. I just can't eat another bite or I'll have to undo the top button on my pants."

I set my purse on the table and reach my hand out for the check, but Trig's faster. He hands a black card to the guy, who totally takes it, the sexist.

"This is a work meal," I say. "I insist on paying."

"That's cute." He turns to the waiter. "Can you believe how far this woman will go to make sure everyone knows we aren't on a date? Turning down a free meal and insisting on paying at the top of her lungs. How ugly am I?"

My cheeks heat up again. "You can pay, but it's certainly not a date. And not because I think you're unattractive, but because it would be unprofessional."

"So you do find me handsome. I knew it."

I roll my eyes.

"You have to know that Mary meant to set us up," Trig says.

The waiter takes the check and looks back and forth from me to Trig before turning tail and running. Chicken.

"No way," I say. "She actually asked me whether I was single, and I told her I'm not dating anyone, not now, and not at any point in the future."

"Did she ask why?" Trig asks.

"She did." I purse my lips. He's good. "And I didn't tell her either, because it's no one else's business."

"That was a major shut down," Trig says. "Duly noted."

I stand up and slide my arms into my leather jacket one at a time. "Thank you for lunch. I'll see you Saturday morning at the main business office lobby of the Vail Mountain Resort?"

Trig nods. "You might need my number. Just in case something comes up."

Not a bad idea actually. I whip out my phone. "Go ahead."

"It's 720- Trig-Rox, with an 'x'."

"You're kidding." I grin. I can't help it. "I'm so sorry I let you pay. I had no idea you were fifteen years old."

"I was a teenager when I got my first cell phone and that number was available. I thought it would be easy for girls to remember. Plus, I'd just gotten that nickname and I was kind of proud of it."

"You realize you don't have to tell people your number like that anymore," I say. "You could just list the numbers. I'd never have noticed."

He smirks. "I might still think it's kind of cool."

"You'd be wrong." My smile softens my words. I still don't like him, but he's almost endearingly goofy, like a puppy fumbling around on oversized paws. "And since you're paying, I don't have to hang around, so thanks. I've got a meeting in twenty minutes."

"Who knew that paying for your lunch would cut our date short?" Trig says.

"You'd have had an extra forty minutes if you'd been punctual."

He feigns an injury to his heart. What a cornball.

"Thanks for lunch. I hope your fettuccine was good."

"The pizza looked better," he admits. "I was just being contrary, and then I doubled down by lying and saying it was amazing."

"The pizza was excellent in truth. You're welcome to my leftovers."

He reaches over and takes a slice. "I think technically they're my leftovers."

"See you Saturday." I step toward the door, but a hand on my shoulder spins me around.

"You might want this." Trig slides the strap to my purse over my shoulder. "Even if men offer to pay for you everywhere you go, you'll need your ID for that commercial flight you insist on taking."

"But if I flew with you to Colorado, flying coach on the way home would be too depressing. You might ruin me for all future flights." I'm going to have to duct tape my mouth shut. The flirting keeps spewing out unchecked.

He's standing so close I can almost feel his basil scented breath on my face. "If you asked nicely, I'm sure I could fly you back home, too."

"I'll see you Saturday," I repeat and practically sprint to the door. Bad Geo. No flirting with anyone, especially not spoiled billionaires.

❧ 4 ❧

TRIG

I think about Geo the entire flight home. And when I doze off, I dream about her.

It's not PG rated.

When I reach the family cabin in Vail and breeze through the door, I'm surprised to discover it's already occupied.

"Brekka," I say. "I had no idea you were here."

My little sister's face used to be sun kissed year round. Now it's pale against her dark hair, almost ghostly really. "I cleaned up the fallout from the Feather Lite deal early. Mom said you were headed this way, so here I am."

I lean over and press a kiss to her cheek. "Thanks for dealing with that."

"What did Luke want?" she asks.

I plop down on the tan microfiber couch. "He's engaged."

Brekka's face is always beautiful. Delicate features, dark brown eyes like velvety butterfly wings, and a fringe of hair that's always falling in her eyes, but when she smiles, she's truly breathtaking. She doesn't smile much anymore, so I treasure each one.

Brekka beams when she hears Luke's news. "I'm so happy for him. I hope I'll be invited."

I nod. "I'm sure of it. He asked me to be his best man."

She exhales. "Uh oh. What about Paul?"

My sister has crushed on my best friend's pretty-boy little brother for fifteen years. "He's too busy with some new project. Apparently I'm his top fall back." I grin so she knows I'm not upset, and neither is precious Paul.

"He asked about you, you know."

Brekka's cheeks flush and the color looks good on her. "You should go outside more often," I say.

"It's freezing, and I can't take my wheelchair outside when it's snowy, which you know."

"I could take you for a piggy back jog."

She slaps my arm. "I'm not a kid, B."

"I know that, but you weigh about the same as one."

"Oh shut up. So why are we up here?" she asks. "I expected you back in Denver. In fact, when Mom said you were routing to Vail, I assembled a pile of files. We've got a lot of good ones to choose from, now that we've closed out three of our biggest ventures."

Brekka's the brains of our entire operation. I run the numbers and handle client interface and negotiations, but she has an uncanny knack for finding projects that will succeed, which is the only thing a venture capital firm really needs to get right. I got lucky with Paul and Luke way back when, but she can spot which ventures will yield a thousand percent return almost every single time.

The same talent that helps her spot the baloney with business presentations makes it hard to lie to her. She spots every evasion and omission, even small ones. It started with her knowing every time I took a piece of her Halloween candy, and it's grown from there.

"I wanted some mountain air."

She doesn't reply, just says, "Mhmm."

"I haven't been out here in weeks. I wanted to ski."

"Trig."

I roll my eyes. "Fine, okay? I'm doing Luke a favor."

"Why didn't you just say that? Because there's more to it, that's why. Spill."

I swear. "Fine, maybe Luke didn't ask for the favor, but it is for him. His wedding planner is checking out Vail as a wedding venue."

"And you're introducing him to Charles?" Brekka lifts one eyebrow.

"Charlie, yes. I've got to call him, actually. Thanks for the reminder."

Charlie agrees to meet me Saturday at ten, happy to help me out. He really does owe me a favor. "And one more thing," I say into the receiver, lowering my voice. I notice Brekka's face is angled my direction and drop my voice a little more. "The girl I'm bringing? I want to take her skiing. She's never been."

"Of course, man. You don't even have to ask, obviously."

"I know. The skiing isn't the favor. She doesn't want to ski, so I'm going to need help convincing her. If you could have an emergency half an hour or so into our meeting and ask us to ski for a while until you're free again. . ."

"You sly dog. How hot is she?"

I clear my throat. "Just have an emergency, and keep your paws off, okay?"

"I'm offended you think I'd try to poach your girlfriend. I actually do well on my own, thank you very much."

"That's what I'm afraid of. And when you see her, trust me. You'll want to poach."

When I hang up and turn around, I nearly trip over a very smug Brekka.

"You like this very female wedding planner."

I collapse onto the dining room chair, defeated. "What if I do?"

"Why didn't you give her a ride here? Why are you meeting her there?"

I shrug.

"Oh come on B, just tell me."

"Fine, okay, I offered her a ride. Twice. And she turned me down flat both times."

"Whoa, you like someone who didn't immediately fall at your feet? I like her already."

"She likes me too, I can tell. But she's too polite. She didn't want to cost Luke and Mary extra money, since one way tickets cost more than round trip."

Brekka's laugh sounds like the tinker of bells. "Oh, B. You've taken a liking to a fiery one. You're too entitled to know this, but that's a lie." Her fingers fly over the buttons on her phone and she turns the screen toward me. "Round trip. Seven hundred." Her fingers fly again and she spins her phone again. "One way, five hundred."

My jaw drops. She actually doesn't like me?

"I think I misspoke before. I love her already." Brekka's still smiling.

She's a traitor.

"So what am I doing wrong? I told her she was beautiful."

"Is she?" Brekka asks. "Beautiful, I mean? Because if she's really, truly stunning, she's sick of hearing that particular compliment. Or she won't believe it no matter what you say, depending."

"What does that mean?"

Brekka shrugs. "Most women like being told they're

attractive. After all, who doesn't like a compliment? We all want to think people like to look at us. But breathtaking women often fall into one of two types. The first never quite believed people and worked hard instead of coasting on their looks. They shaped something from the raw material of who they are. If she's type one, she's going to ignore people who compliment her, because she will believe they only see her outside and not what she's chiseled herself into. Any compliment will feel like an objectification. Like you're shoving her into a box, and she'll fight it."

I narrow my eyes. My sister can be annoyingly perceptive, but in this case, I'm grateful for the knowledge. "And the other option?"

"Most models fall into this category. When they spend a lot of time thinking about their looks, they put all their value in them. No compliment, no matter how genuine or effusive, will ever be enough. And they'll live in constant fear that if their looks slide, they'll be worthless. One carefully placed insult can shatter them. It's a dangerous place to live, and too many men will have taken advantage of their utter vulnerability. So while they'll know they're better looking than almost everyone they meet, they'll never feel safe in that. They'll never be confident, not like an average woman who has based her self-esteem on something that grows instead of shrinking with time. Because no matter how stunning she is, there's always someone else who's prettier, and even if there isn't now, one day there will be. I call them evil queens. You know, from *Snow White*. Mirror mirror."

I shake my head. "She's definitely not an evil queen. She didn't even want to hear me compliment her. She brushed me off like I was irritating her, or worse, insulting her."

"Plus she's a wedding planner. That hints strongly at

version one, because most of the evil queens I've met are in professions that directly relate to their appearance."

"She could definitely have been a professional model," I say.

"I like her more and more. Doing something harder with your life, something that will grow and not fade, it takes gumption. It's the hard path, even if it's the more fruitful one. Not that I think modeling is easy, it's not, but I think you get what I mean."

I nod. "Well, I like her too."

Brekka's sly smile sets me on edge. "Don't get excited. I don't like her, like I want to get married and have two point four kids."

She quirks one eyebrow. "Three point six kids?"

I chuckle. "No. I'm still not interested in getting married and having a family. I don't want anyone waiting at home while I skydive and ski and surf, tapping her foot and telling me little Johnny needs his dad. I've got too much living to do. But if I could loosen her up some, I might have fun doing that public service."

"Not every wife in America is like Mom."

I exhale heavily. "But enough of them are. The odds of me finding a wonderful woman who will support me and lift me up aren't great. And our wealth kind of dooms us both. Don't pretend you don't know it."

Brekka doesn't argue, because she knows I'm right. We were raised in the same house.

The next morning, I'm wearing my favorite pair of black ski pants when I walk into Charlie's office. I'll never admit to anyone how many times I changed my sweater. Except Brekka of course, since she was right there telling me which one looked better.

Charlie's wearing a suit, but even so, I can tell he's lost

some weight. Gone is the chubby guy from last ski season. I wonder what prompted this.

"Looking good," I say. "Impressive. How much weight have you lost?"

Charlie stands up, his desk chair rolling backward. "Bern. Good to see you."

"It's Trig," I mutter.

"Whatever you say," Charlie says. "And it was because of a girl. Breakups look good on me, I guess."

I whistle. "I'm sorry to hear it. Maybe she'll come to her senses."

"Probably not, but I'm better without her, am I right? Two single guys. We should go out sometime."

I nod. "We should, actually. I'll text you."

Charlie's secretary buzzes his office. "Mr. Corning, I have a Miss Polson asking about you. She claims she has an appointment. I told her you're with an old friend, but she insisted I let you know she's waiting."

"Send her in," Charlie says. "We're expecting her."

"Oh," his secretary's voice sounds surprised. "Yes sir. Right away."

When Geo walks through the door, Charlie's face goes blank and I'm pretty sure he looks just like I did at that pizza place. I pat his back and walk toward where she's standing in the doorway in a form-fitted grey suit with a knee length skirt and stiletto heels. "Geo, you made it. Welcome to Vail. This is my old high school chum Charlie Cornish."

She really meant it when she said she had no intention of skiing judging by her outfit. Good thing Vail boasts a killer ski shop.

"How was your flight?" Charlie asks. "I hear the weather is stirring up out there. We monitor things pretty closely, and it looks like the storm expected to swing north didn't get the memo."

"My flight was wonderful, thanks." She smiles at him and I feel the same slack-jawed look sneaking up on me again, too.

My recollection of Brekka's words snaps me out of it. I can't have Geo thinking I only like her because she's breathtakingly beautiful. "I told Charlie about the dates we're looking at. He's got another event that weekend, but he can make it work. How many guests are you planning to have?"

Geo navigates the business end of things with Charlie effectively, quoting numbers and asking about Vail policies.

"What kind of friends and family discount do you offer to friends of old high school friends?" she asks with a sparkle in her eye. "I already noticed you have an off-season booking discount, as well as an eco fee for green weddings. We'd qualify for both."

Charlie turns toward me and gulps. "You didn't tell me your girlfriend studied negotiations at the Grand Bazaar in Istanbul."

I shrug. "I didn't know, probably because she's not my girlfriend. I just met her a few days ago."

But I realize that I wish she was, which sort of makes my shoulder blades feel too tight for my sweater.

Geo and Charlie talk about numbers for another moment, including the deposit amount, and then Charlie rubs his hands together. "How about I show you our banquet hall and one of our meeting rooms that could be used for the rehearsal dinner?"

She nods graciously. "I'd be pleased to see those. And some rooms too, of course, including a honeymoon suite. And the groom has young children, so we'd want rooms that could accommodate them with their grandparents."

He nods.

I follow them, content to watch Geo do her job. When Charlie pulls out his phone in the banquet hall and groans in dismay, I almost forget his crisis is fake.

"Uh oh," he says, "I've got a little problem to attend to. Do you mind?"

"Not at all," Geo says. "You've been so accommodating to meet with me on such short notice. Please, do what you need to do."

"I may be a little while. After I resolve this issue, I have a lunch appointment. Can we resume around two p.m.? You could ski or relax in the spa—"

Charlie cuts off when he sees me shaking my head vehemently. "Err, actually, I heard this morning that they're booked up right now. But you could hang out in the bar or ski, for sure."

I nod.

"And of course, anything you order or need is comped. We really value this chance to earn your business."

I follow Charlie out the door and whisper, "Thanks."

"I hope you know what you're doing," he says in a low voice.

"What does that mean?" I ask.

He shakes his head. "That's not some empty-headed model. She's beautiful, but man, she's sharp too. Don't screw up or I will poach her."

"Some friend," I say.

"All's fair," Charlie says. "But I'm giving you first shot."

"How kind of you." I scowl at him and walk back inside.

"So, any interest in skiing? Because I hear the barstools here suck."

She smirks. "I'm hardly dressed for skiing, Mr. Thornton."

"Please," I say. "Call me Trig, seriously."

"Trig, I obviously can't ski in this."

"It would be my pleasure to buy you some ski gear."

"I couldn't possibly accept that," she says.

"Fine, then let Charlie comp it. Business deduction, you know. Plus, having you wearing their clothing is like an advertisement." I regret the words the second they leave my mouth.

She closes up like a flower at sunset. "I think I'll wait in the lobby. I have some work I can do on my laptop."

I grab her hand, and she turns toward me. "Seriously Trig, I have a lot of work to finish. And I should take some photos and send them to Luke and Mary."

"Luke and Mary wouldn't mind you taking an hour or two to do something fun," I say, my voice soft. I might be imagining it, but it seems like she's inching toward me slightly. Her eyes certainly relax.

"I would look idiotic on the slopes," she whispers. "I've never even been sledding."

A smile grows on my face. "I'll be there. You'll be fine, I promise. Trust me. I could teach Sponge Bob to ski."

She rolls her eyes and I know I have her. Geo is going to love skiing.

5

GEO

I detest skiing.

Trig very sweetly bought me the cutest ski outfit I'd ever seen, a fitted, navy blue, retro 70s suit with adorable red and blue chevrons at the sleeves, shoulders and hem on the pants, but it was all downhill from there, and not in a good way.

"Don't take this wrong, but I kind of hate you," I tell him. "I look idiotic on this toddler slope, where all the kids are doing fine and I'm completely panicking."

"You don't look idiotic. You look—"

"Don't you dare say I look cute or adorable or anything you could use to describe a child under the age of sixteen."

He snaps his mouth shut.

"My neck hurts, and my back hurts, and I'm sick of doing this. Can you toss me over your shoulder and ski me down to the bottom?" He's kind enough to point out that it's not actually very far away. Which just reminds me how good he is, and how much I suck. "What am I saying? You can do that with your eyes closed, I'm sure."

He laughs. "Your neck and back only hurt because

you're doing it all wrong." He points down the slope. "This hill is almost flat. You don't need to cut back and forth like you were. It looks like you're trying to decorate a cake. You can actually point your skis downhill and..." He gestures with his hand. "Slide. The sliding, or skiing as some people call it, is kind of the goal."

I glance at the allegedly flat hill he's taken me to the top of. It's not flat at all. In fact, it looks so steep that if I point downward in the slightest, I'm sure I'll plummet to my death.

"I don't kind of hate you. That was a lie to spare your feelings. I straight up want to shoot you between the eyes. The only reasons I haven't are that I don't have a gun, and I need someone to drag my body back down the hill to my mom."

He laughs. "Trust me, Geo. Try pointing downward and letting go."

"I don't let go."

"I'm gathering that. But just this once, try it."

I grit my teeth and try taking his advice before I have time to overthink it. My poles fly backward and my hair flattens to my face, some strands sticking in my mouth and eyes, but the feeling, oh the feeling!

It's unlike anything else I've ever experienced. I love it. I zoom past a little kid clinging to his mother's leg. I squeal as I pass a teenager poking buttons on her phone, and I coast to a stop near the base of the ski lift where the snow turns dirty and clumpy.

When I turn back, Trig's smiling down at me, only a foot away from where I stopped. He, of course, skis like a professional, but for a moment, for one shining moment, I don't even begrudge him all that natural skill and coordination.

"Again," I say.

He doesn't gloat. In fact, he doesn't say anything at all. He merely takes my poles and helps me shuffle over to the lift and take my seat as it flings around on its trajectory back up the slope.

The second time I ski down the bunny hill is the most fun I've ever had in my entire life. When we reach the bottom and Trig looks down at me, my heart lifts and I do something stupid. I lean toward him.

His head curves over me and his eyes lock on mine. His face moves closer and closer, slowly so I could totally pull away. I should pull away, because I don't date. I don't even want to date, and you definitely don't do this when you aren't dating. I never date, which means I really never ever ever kiss anyone.

But I want Trig to kiss me, so I don't move.

His golden eyes shine brightly in the cold air, and his lips part, steam puffing out from them. My eyes follow the movement until I'm staring at his mouth.

He murmurs, "You did it."

I nod dumbly. "I did."

"You delight me, you know." Then his mouth closes the inches between us and his lips cover mine.

I was wrong before. This is the most fun I've ever had. Trig's mouth over mine sets off a chemical reaction in my body, or maybe an emergency evacuation of all my senses and willpower. I drop my ski poles and wrap my arms around his neck, and his hands circle my waist. I've never worn more clothing, but I've also never been more aware of where a man's hands were. Likewise, I've never been in a colder place in my life, and yet the heat from his mouth where it's locked on mine leaves me warm from the top of my head to the tips of my toes.

He murmurs against my mouth, "I'm glad you relented."

I'm not sure whether he means about skiing in the first

place, actually zooming down the slope, or about dating someone. I don't really care. "Me too."

Someone behind me giggles and my eyes open and track toward the sound. A very annoyed mother scowls at me. "You're blocking the lift."

"Oh," I say. "We didn't mean to."

"Terribly sorry." Trig lifts me, dragging me and my skis around in a circle, and setting me down again. "Please proceed." Once the woman and her child have moved past us, he mutters. "I certainly intend to."

He kisses me even slower this time, and I hear the little girl giggling as she floats away on the lift. The teenager who still lives deep inside me wants to giggle with her. When Trig finally pulls back, the girl in the purple ski suit is gone, presumably whisked up the hill, but I'm still giddy.

I brush away the hair that's fallen forward into Trig's face, tucking it under his cap with one gloved hand. "Should we go again?"

He nods and helps me on the lift. We ski the bunny hill three more times before he convinces me to try a blue slope that's only one extra ride up.

We're halfway up that lift when my ski pops off without warning and drops into a snow drift below us. I lurch forward, alarmed, and Trig's hand shoots out and pulls me back. "Don't worry, we'll get it. It's fine."

"How?" I ask. "How will we get it?"

He shrugs. "I can ski down and grab it for you. It'll just take a minute, but don't lean forward like that. You gave me a heart attack."

I gave the insane skydiver a heart attack. Whoops. "Fine."

I don't say anything on the way to the top, too nervous thinking about how I'm on my first blue slope with just the one ski. As the end of the lift approaches and I think about the mechanics of getting off with only one ski, my stomach ties in a hard little knot. "I can't do it."

Trig takes my hand and squeezes. Then he wraps one arm around my waist and carries me off the lift. I fumble and bobble, doing my best to topple over and take him with me, but it's like trying to flip a buoy. He's unshakable. He tugs me gently over to a huge pole holding up the lift above us, and pats the snow. "Wait here, and I'll be back with your ski in a few minutes."

"I feel like an even bigger idiot than before right now."

He shakes his head and cups my face gently. "No, don't. This had nothing to do with you. It has happened to most all of us, at some point or another."

I swallow. "Okay."

He leans over and kisses me gently. "I really will be right back. Don't fret."

I nod this time and wave him off. Then I sit at the top alone while he flies down the hill and practically leaps to grab my ski from a huge snowdrift. I half expect him to ski back toward me uphill, but of course he just turns to wave and continues down the hill toward the lift.

While I'm waiting for him to come back, I notice a little girl skiing on only one leg. Her other leg is tied behind her back. No lie. She's coming from above me, clearly headed home after a long day up on the black diamonds. I hate feeling pathetically inadequate, but she's an adorable little girl. She smiles at me and waves, her pigtails bobbing.

"Great job, sweetheart," I force myself to say.

She beams as she zooms past.

By the time Trig circles the corner on the lift and slides easily over to where I am, I'm relieved to click my awkward boot back into the stupid ski. "Thanks," I say.

I wish I sounded more grateful. Trig has been trying

ridiculously hard to make sure I have fun. I'm sure he's not having a very good time on these stupidly simple runs.

As if to punctuate that thought, a beautiful blonde, her golden hair streaming behind her pale pink ski suit, flies past us, her cheeks rosy, barely glancing at the course. She's clearly an accomplished skier. A far cry from me, clutching at Trig's sleeve like a drowning woman.

I refuse to be a pathetic, clinging barnacle.

I turn my newly attached skis downward and shoot down the hill, clearing the blue with only a few heart stopping moments, and hurtling down to the bottom of the bunny slope easily.

"Ready for a break?" Trig asks.

I notice the blonde in the pink suit blowing on a hot chocolate at the bar. I want a hot chocolate so badly it almost hurts, but I want Trig to be proud of me too. Inexplicably. Skiing might have knocked a screw loose in my brain.

I shake my head. "Let's try the next slope up."

"It's a black," Trig says.

"I thought you loved those."

He frowns. "I want you to like skiing Geo, not hate it."

"I am having fun," I say. "At least let's try the blue again."

He grins, "Who knew you were such an adrenaline junkie? Okay, let's go."

This time I slide over next to him on the lift and he puts his arm around my shoulders. I notice the blonde girl staring at us as we float up and I can't help smiling. I haven't had another woman glare at me with jealousy in years. It feels good. This is feeling decidedly like a date, but of course, it's just a break in one work meeting. And in a few hours, I'll fly home and I won't see Trig until the wedding.

It's fine.

"Thanks," I say. "I'm glad you twisted my arm."

Trig's whole face is transformed when he smiles, like sunrise over the ocean. His smile exposes depths of emotion I didn't expect to see.

On the second lift, after he puts his arm around me, he leans over and kisses me gently. "You're not at all what I thought I'd find when Luke told me Mary wanted to set me up with her wedding planner."

"I don't dislike you nearly as much as I did."

He laughs. "What a ringing recommendation." He brushes his lips over mine again and then turns and looks at the slope. "I've been skiing this slope with my sister since we were in preschool, but it's like I'm seeing it anew with you here."

"I can't even imagine sending a preschool child to ski."

"You don't even get poles at that age. Mom and Dad didn't want to be bothered with us too much when we were growing up," he says. "Or maybe Dad did, I'm not sure. But Mom was far too busy."

"With what?" I ask.

He shakes his head. "She was working. I should be grateful she's so adept with business matters, I know that. Dad had a sizable trust fund when they got married, but Mom, well I didn't get my business sense from my Dad, that's for sure. Mom seized control of my dad's family money and instead of spending every dime she could like all the other spouses, she tripled it. Quadrupled it maybe, within five years. I have no idea how many times she's doubled it since, but she manages the corpus for the entire Thornton clan at this point."

I want to ask how much money they have, how much money he has, purely out of curiosity. But that seems hugely tacky so I don't say anything. And then we're exiting the lift. I point toward the next lift. "Come on, let's go up one more."

Trig takes my hands in his, my poles dangling by my wristbands. "One of the most important things you have to learn when you're risking something new is to never exceed your limits. You're a brand new skier. There's no rush. That black will be waiting for you. We can try it tomorrow if you want, but let's not ruin today."

His eyes are so warm, so full of contentment, that I should be enjoying this, but something he said set off warning bells.

Tomorrow.

I can't ski with him tomorrow. I need to be on the next flight out. Even one more day and it would be like we were dating. And I may have slipped a little, but this isn't strictly a date. My rules have worked for four years, and I'm not going to start changing things willy nilly now, because I like hot cocoa and the little shiver that kissing him sends up my spine.

"You're right," I say. "I know my limits, and I should stick with what's safe. The blue is fine, plenty for me."

We've barely pointed our skis downward when the pink clad blonde flies off the lift behind us. "Bernie, is that you?"

Bernie? Trig flinches when she calls him that. She must've known him longer than, when did he say he got the nickname Trig? College? And I've seen her several times, so I'm sure Trig has too. It's almost like she waited for him to notice her, and once it became clear he wasn't going to, she pretended to see him for the first time.

Trig turns toward her. "Nat. What a surprise to see you here." His tone is flat, like it's not surprising at all.

She cocks her head coyly. "I can't believe my luck—at being here the same day as you. It's been way too long since we got together last. Actually, I've been wondering whether you sold your gorgeous cabin."

He shakes his head. "Nope, I'm staying there now."

"I should come by later. I'm just around the corner, and I look for any excuse to take the snowmobile out."

He frowns. "I've got a huge pile of work to do. Brekka would kill me if I push it back."

"Don't tell me she's in town too?" Nat frowns. "I just want to cry every time I think about—"

"We better get going," Trig says. "I'm here with someone and I wouldn't want to be rude."

Natalie's perfectly defined eyelashes fly wide, her eyes full of faux innocence. "I am so sorry, I hadn't even noticed her. Who is this?" Her smile would make a mannequin jealous, as plastic as I've ever seen. "I'm Natalie Morgan, one of Bernard's oldest friends."

"Geode Polson," I say. "Nice to meet you. I'm impressed you can ski so well, since you're as old as Trig here."

Natalie scowls at me, but recovers quickly.

"So you live here then?" I ask.

She laughs and the sound grates on my nerves. "Of course not, silly. There's nothing here but piles of snow. I live in New York City. I'm a publicist. I just vacation here, but you better believe I keep my eyes peeled for this one whenever I come into town." She paws at his chest, and Trig takes a small step away from her and closer to me.

"Geo and I are just heading down our last run of the day. We've got a meeting with Charlie later."

"Oh Charlie, can you believe it?" She winks at Trig. "He looks amazing, doesn't he? He had turned into such a butterball for a while."

"Charlie's in great shape," I say. "I doubt he'd love being called a butterball."

"Oh, he doesn't mind." Natalie looks down her nose at me. "We've all known each other practically since diapers."

I compress my lips.

"If your friend has a meeting, why don't you come down a few runs with me for old time's sake," Natalie purrs at Trig. "Drew here won't mind, will you?"

"It's Geode," I say, "like the rocks that look dingy on the outside, but sparkle on the inside."

"Uh huh," she says. "Well, you don't mind, right? You can meet with good old Charlie for a minute without my Bernie. I haven't seen him in ages."

I shrug. "I can certainly handle the meeting myself."

"Which isn't the point," Trig says. "I came with Geo and I'm leaving with her. Because while I haven't seen you in a while, I didn't miss you Nat, as you surely recall. Enjoy your vacation."

Trig takes my hand and slides toward the slope.

I'm sure my smile is so smug it's practically insufferable, which is probably why I don't notice the ice patch. My skis skitter across it, sending me off the course and down the side of a mountain. I promptly crumple into a ball and tumble head over heels into a tree.

Pain shoots down from my knee toward my foot, and when I shift to try and scramble upright, slushy snow slides down into my collar. I want to wad up my fists and bawl like a newborn, but I can't. Not without looking even more ridiculous.

Trig appears at my side seconds later, his strong arms lifting me out of the snowdrift I plowed into. "Are you alright? I'm so sorry about that."

I don't know whether he's apologizing for darling Nat, or the subsequent crash. Maybe both, but I perversely blame him for all of it.

"I didn't even want to ski in the first place."

He sighs. "I know, and I'm almost sorry I made you do it. I'm definitely sorry you smashed into that tree. "

"Yeah, what did that poor tree ever do to me?" I try to smile, but I also put weight on my foot for the first time. I cry out when pain spears from my knee down toward my ankle.

"Looks like someone's headed for Vail Health ER," Nat says over my shoulder.

I wish I felt steady enough on my feet to punch her in the face. I eye one discarded pole and wonder whether I could reach her with it.

"Thanks for that assessment," I bark. "Dr. Natalie."

"I think we've got it from here," Trig says.

"I was only trying to help, sheesh. You've turned into a real drag." Natalie turns with a huff and skis downhill.

Good riddance.

Trig wraps one hand around my waist, and I sling an arm over his shoulder, poles all but forgotten. "Let's go get you checked out," he says. "Maybe they can do a memory wipe so you forget Natalie and the fall. Buy one get one free."

I shake my head. "Let's just erase the whole day and start over."

Trig's eyes widen. I don't want to hurt him, but the pain in my knee reminded me of how stupid I was to bend my rules. There's a reason I set them up to begin with, and those reasons haven't changed.

"You don't get injured unless you do something stupid that exposes you in the first place." I won't be making that mistake again.

6

TRIG

"Sometimes you're driving along, minding your own business," I say. "In life I mean, and someone just crashes into you. Not every bad outcome can be predicted or avoided."

"If I hadn't let you talk me into skiing, I wouldn't have a torn ACL right now," Geo snaps. "So don't pretend like this was an act of God or something."

"Note to self," I say. "Geo gets crabby when injured."

She scowls at me, and I don't tell her she's even cuter when she's angry. I want to pull her against me and kiss that frown away, but I doubt she'd appreciate my attempt. Instead, I use my pole to poke the release on her skis and lift her out of them.

"What are you doing?" she practically snarls.

I smile back at her. "The strain of skis pulling on your boots won't help that knee. In fact, the only thing that will is getting you to a doctor, Miss Growly. Then we can see if there's really any long term damage."

I wave at one of the kids snowboarding past us and

hand him our poles and Geo's skis. "Can you take these down to the main office? My friend's injured and I'm going to take her downhill."

"Sure," the kid says. "You know if you were snowboarding, you wouldn't need to worry about poles."

"But you'd still need to carry her board," I say.

"One thing instead of four," he says.

"Scram, kid," I say, but I grin at the little punk.

"Whatever you say, grandpa." He shrugs and takes off, and even weighed down with all our gear, he gets some decent air off a snowdrift, spraying me in the process. At least he took Charlie's stuff back down the hill.

Geo's flexing her leg like it might miraculously improve. "It might be best not to try and use it at all," I say.

"You're a doctor now too?"

Her snappishness ought to be annoying me, but she reminds me too much of an injured badger. I want to pat her on the head and give her a snack. "Look Geo, I'm as sorry as you are—"

"Somehow I doubt that. You'll just ski on to your next adventure. I'm the one who can't walk."

I sigh and scoop her up, silencing her with a little forward motion. Even in ski gear with boots, Geo's light for such a tall girl. We clear the blue run and the bunny hill in twenty seconds and coast into the rental shop.

I set Geo down on a bench and her eyes flash, but she says nothing. I pop my skis off and carefully unbuckle her ski boots. She winces when I tug the right boot off and I feel a pang of guilt. She really wouldn't be injured if it wasn't for me.

I don't have the best track record for keeping the women around me safe.

I breathe in through my mouth and out through my

nose. It's backward, but it works for me. "Look, Vail has an amazing ER that sort of specializes in skiing trauma, as you might imagine."

"Uh oh," the perky girl behind the counter says. She has her hair in two fuzzy French braids, making her seem about twelve until I look more closely. I'm guessing she's early twenties. "Did you get hurt up there?"

Geo nods. "I managed to gracefully plow right into a tree." She scrunches up her nose. "First time skier."

"Well don't give up yet," the girl says. "You may be fine, and it's not the tree's fault it's so hard to pick it up as an adult. Even so, some of the best skiers out there learned later in life."

"Really?" Geo asks.

I take the chance, while braids is chatting Geo up, to pull my heavy street boots out of my locker and change into them. I hand my ski boots to the girl.

Braids nods. "Yep, in fact my dad skied for the first time two years ago. Now he can keep up with me at the top of the slopes."

"You're kidding." Geo fishes her key out of her pocket. "Do you mind grabbing my backpack for me?"

Braids shakes her head. "Not at all." She walks around to grab the key, and snags Geo's large black backpack. She wisely passes it to me and then turns to Geo. "I'm serious about my dad, though. He blows me away."

"I live in Atlanta, so I doubt I'll be carving up the mountain again. At least, not any time soon."

Braids shrugs. "You never know."

Their conversation transformed Geo's scowl into contemplative reflection. I certainly approve of the upgrade. I lean toward Geo slowly, checking for her permission before scooping her up again. "Ready to head for the ER?"

She purses her lips. "What about Charlie?"

I shake my head. "You can't really be thinking of hobbling in to finish the meeting?"

"I need to get the final numbers he said he'd work up and try to haggle him down before I send them on to Luke and Mary. They need to make their decision quickly."

I laugh. "I'll lean on Charlie, okay? And if the number isn't rock bottom, I think Luke will survive." I think about the joke he played on me and mentally want to add a zero or two to Charlie's quote. "In any case, they can't possibly expect you to negotiate injured."

"They expect me to do my job, and so do I. My poorly considered recreational activities should never work a disservice on my client." Her brow is furrowed and I lean over and kiss it without thinking about it.

She pulls back like I mauled her and glances at Braids sideways like she might be a card carrying member of the paparazzi.

"Let's just go to the ER," she says.

I slide my arms gently under her knees and around behind her back and underneath her arms to lift her up. Braids throws me two thumbs up on our way out the door. She's more optimistic than I am about my chances just now.

When I slide Geo into the passenger side of my Land Rover, she takes my hand. "I'm sorry I was so rude in there."

I meet her eyes. "It's normal to be upset when you get injured. Believe me, I know."

"Have you ever torn your ACL?"

I laugh. "You're pretty literal. I haven't had that exact injury, but I've had my share of broken bones and believe me, I always feel a mixture of embarrassment for some reason, and anger. It's completely normal, and you don't know me that well yet. Which only makes it even harder to be calm."

Her hand touches my cheek. "Thanks for being so forgiving. It was embarrassing. Especially when your friend Natalie skied by so adeptly. I'm obviously not the type of girl you usually spend time with."

I snort. "Neither is Natalie. She told you she's a publicist? As far as I can tell all she publicizes is how much of her parents' money she can spend. She has an apartment in New York she never stays at. She flies from one of her daddy's cabins to the other. Non-stop. You could probably take a girls' volleyball team to nationals with her frequent flier miles each year."

Geo's gorgeous blue eyes narrow at me. "How do you know so much about her travel habits?"

Is she jealous? Usually I hate possessive women, but this time I find myself hoping she is. I toss Geo's backpack in the rear seat of the SUV. "She's a shameless self-promoter on social media. Half of America knows her whereabouts. I wouldn't be surprised if she took out ads."

Geo laughs. "Fine."

I slide the buckle toward her and she takes it from me, our hands brushing in the process. I want to kiss her, but I imagine her shutting down again if I do. Reluctantly, I cross to my side of the car and climb in, bound for the ER.

The Vail ER shows us into a room almost immediately. After an x-ray, a tall, fit bald doctor comes in to talk to us. "Mrs. Polson, Mr. Polson, I have good news."

"We aren't married," Geo says. "He's not even my boyfriend. We're working together and he brought me in today when I was injured."

"Ah, okay. Sorry about that." He redirects all his attention toward Geo. "Well then Miss Polson, the good news is that you likely only have a level one or two sprain. That means one of your ligaments is injured, and as far as injuries go, it's pretty much the least severe. There's nothing on the x-ray, but there's no way to know for sure how badly the ligaments were injured or whether they'll recover on their own. Judging from your current mobility, I'd say you'll be fine in two or three days. We won't know for sure until we've waited a bit. Have you heard of RICE?"

This one I know, and I might be feeling a little left out, so I butt in. "Rest the joint, ice the area, compress, and elevate," I say.

The doc nods at me approvingly.

I shrug. "I've skied for a long time."

He chuckles. "That would do it."

"I'm on the last flight out tonight," Geo protests. "Will I be fine to make that? I can call the airline and arrange for a wheelchair, maybe?" She wrings her hands.

The doc glances down at an iPad. "Are you sure about that?"

"What do you mean?" Geo asks, her brows drawn together like a quotation mark.

"Last I heard, they were grounding all flights for the storm."

"Grounding flights?" She closes her eyes. "This can't be happening."

"There's a huge snowstorm hitting tonight," he says. "I seriously doubt you're going anywhere."

She groans. "I have an important meeting Monday that I can't miss."

He shrugs. "Maybe it'll clear up fast. Colorado's pretty effective at clearing runways of ice and snow, as long as the blizzard's done dumping precipitation. I'd be more worried right now about finding a place to stay. The nearby hotels are all full, from what I'm hearing. We've got patients requesting transfer to Denver and I'm not sure if we can arrange it before the storm hits. If your flight leaves from there, I'd head over immediately to try and stay ahead of it."

Geo's jaw drops. "I was just outside. It looked fine."

The doctor shrugs. "Storm shifted about an hour ago. It's barreling straight toward us."

Geo swears. The doctor leaves and she taps on her phone screen, her face falling. "My flight has been cancelled." She swears again, and taps more on her phone.

"Hello," she says into the receiver. "This is Geode Polson. I was supposed to be meeting with Mr. Corning right now, but I'm afraid I've injured my knee." She pauses. "Yes, I can hold, but more pressing is that I don't have anywhere to stay. I was hoping you could—"

She gulps.

"No, I completely understand," she says, and hangs up.

She turns toward me slowly. "I hate to ask this, but any chance you can pull some strings with Charlie?"

I grin at her. "I can call Charlie for sure, but with that knee, you're going to struggle at the resort."

She frowns. "What are you suggesting?"

I shake my head. "I'm offering, not suggesting. I'm happy to call Charlie and I'm sure he can find you a place, so there's no pressure from me. But I have a cabin a few miles away. It's where I'm staying tonight."

She opens her mouth and then closes it again. It looks like interest warring with fear.

She's afraid I'll seduce her. I can't quite help the grin that sneaks onto my face. "My sister's staying there with me if that helps, and there are seven bedrooms. I promise to be on my best behavior." I cross my heart, and the next words just pop out of my mouth. "I won't even try to kiss you."

I have no idea where that came from. Gentlemanly isn't usually a word people would use to describe me, but there I am, Trig Thornton, white knight. Now that I've promised not to, the only thing I can think about is kissing her.

The doctor clears his throat. "Far be it for me to interfere, but if you have a cozy cabin like this, and there's food and a generator for when the grid goes down?" He lifts his eyebrows and I nod. "I'd take him up on it before he changes his mind."

Geo nods. "Thank you, Trig. I'd really appreciate it."

"No problem. I should let my sister know and make sure I don't need to pick anything up."

I text Brekka right away. I'M BRINGING GEO FOR DINNER. NEED ANYTHING?

ROSA JUST BROUGHT SUPPLIES. SHE'S STILL HERE ACTUALLY.

DID YOU OFFER TO LET HER STAY? I text.

OF COURSE, BUT SHE LIVES A MILE AWAY. SHE'LL HEAD HOME ONCE I HAVE DINNER READY.

PERFECT. I glance up at Geo, who looks at me nervously. "She says it's fine."

Brekka always has a lot to say, so of course she keeps texting. WITH A STORM BARRELING THIS WAY. I'M GIDDY TO HAVE COMPANY. WHAT SHOULD I MAKE? CHICKEN PARM? FILETS? OR SOMETHING SIMPLE LIKE CHICKEN SOUP?

I text her back. SHE'S SPRAINED HER KNEE SO SHE WON'T BE VERY SPRY.

Brekka sends me a heart eyes emoji. JUST MY SPEED.

OH PLEASE, I text back. YOU WHEEL CIRCLES AROUND ME.

YOU GOT THAT RIGHT. CAN'T WAIT TO MEET HER.

I grin. I MAY NEED YOUR HELP. SHE'S PRETTY UNDECIDED ABOUT ME.

Little dots. I glance up and notice Geo's ready to go. Brekka's text comes through just in time to read before I need to carry Geo out. I'M UNDECIDED ABOUT YOU TOO. I'M NOT SURE I CAN HELP YOU MUCH.

OH SHUT UP, I text back. YOU LOVE EVERYTHING ABOUT ME.

LOVE AND LIKE AREN'T THE SAME, B.

I roll my eyes and pocket my phone. I swing Geo up into my arms again, and my heart swells alarmingly. I'm just supposed to be teaching her how to loosen up. I'm not ready to get attached. I like my life too much to contemplate adding a wife.

Don't I?

I think about my mom and dad, and I cringe. I won't ever subject myself to that kind of misery. No, I'll figure out why Geo doesn't date, loosen her up a little and pass her along to someone else. Maybe Paul. I bet once he's met Geo he'll make time for her, new product launch or not.

Thinking about Paul meeting Geo makes me want to slam my fist into the wall. I stomp down the hall and load Geo into the Land Rover. It's already snowing as I navigate the familiar streets toward my family cabin.

"On no." I slam my palm into the steering wheel. "I forgot to grab your luggage. Is it at the resort?"

She shakes her head. "That backpack's all I brought."

"Your suit is stuffed in there?"

She shrugs. "They're doing amazing things with synthetic blend fabrics these days. Although, I don't have any shoes other than those heels." She shakes her head. "Maybe I can buy a pair of sneakers at the airport or something. I doubt I can even hobble in those right now."

"They're made more with looks in mind than practicality, that's for sure. I'm sure you can have a pair of Brekka's." She doesn't really use them anymore, but I don't mention that. I always let Brekka handle that part. She's particular about it. "You look about the same size."

"Brekka's your sister?"

I nod. "My little sister. My best friend. And a pain in the neck, too. You'll see soon enough. She's making dinner now."

"She didn't need to do that," Geo says. "I feel bad. I really appreciate you putting me up, especially since I'm gimpy."

I wince. "You're injured, but you're not gimpy."

"You know what I mean."

"It's no problem, really," I say. "Brekka's been excited to meet you ever since I told her how you declined my offer of a ride here from Atlanta."

"Oh yeah?" Geo asks.

"Yep." I smile. "She thinks you lied to me, actually."

"Excuse me?" she asks.

"Apparently round trip flights *do* cost more than one way trips."

"Oh." Geo blushes. "I might have exaggerated that a little. But you were coming on a little strong."

"And you don't date."

She nods. "Right."

"So what exactly were we doing earlier, if that wasn't a date?"

"Skiing you mean?"

I grunt. "Skiing. And I seem to recall some memorable kissing."

Her face turns even redder. It's unbelievably cute. "I think we agreed that was a mistake."

"Excuse me?" I brake for the turn onto Booth Creek Drive. "I never implied, much less said, any such thing."

She scowls at me. "Well, it's not going to happen again. You said as much in front of the doctor."

"I said I wouldn't try to kiss you," I say. "I didn't say you wouldn't throw your gorgeous self at me. And when you do, I make no promises."

She rolls her eyes. "That happens to you a lot, does it?"

"I've had my share of interest from the ladies."

"I bet," she says.

"What does that mean?"

I pull into the driveway slowly, unsure how ice-free it is.

"Holy wow, this is your 'cabin'?" Geo's eyes dart back and forth, taking in the wood beams and glass joined with copious amounts of stone. My mom may be crazy squared, but she and my dad got this right. Our Vail cabin has always been my favorite.

"Expecting something different?" I ask.

"Smaller, and maybe with logs?"

"Logs are made of wood, and there's lots of wood."

She shakes her head. "How big is this, exactly?"

"I warned you it had seven bedrooms. You were expecting a Lincoln Log home?" I smirk and hit the clicker for the garage. The pine trees covering the mountain behind our house are snow covered now, and a decent dusting already covers the flagstone driveway. The wooden garage door shoves powdery snow out of the way as it lifts, and I pull into the clean garage space with relief. I like snow, but I hate being out and about during storms. I try to ignore the warm feeling in my chest at the thought of having Geo here with me, snowed in, at my favorite family cabin.

"Not Lincoln Logs, no." She sighs. "This is just a whole other level."

"It's pretty basic for a Vail cabin in this area. A few living areas, a pool, a hot tub, another hot tub upstairs. I'd offer you the room that connects to that one, but I don't think you're supposed to heat that knee for at least twenty-four hours."

She looks a little shell shocked.

I sling her backpack over my shoulders and open her door. I pull her out of the seat and carry her inside. Brekka's sitting on the sofa, but she turns and waves. "Hey B, welcome home. This must be Geo?"

I carry Geo into the family room and set her on the sofa. "Geo got in a fight with that knotty pine at the corner of the downturn by lift two."

Brekka shakes her head. "I hate that pine. It's taken me out a few times. Hit the ice patch?"

"You ski, I take it?" Geo asks.

Brekka grins. "I spent every day of my childhood skiing that slope. The stupid light from that nearby light pole melts the snow and it re-forms as ice every night. Got me every time I wasn't paying attention. Sorry that happened. How's your knee?"

She leans forward and pokes Geo's snow pants delicately.

"It's throbbing, but I think if I get some ice on it soon, it'll be okay. Doc thinks it's just a sprain, thankfully."

"You sound like you know a little about injuries," Brekka says.

Geo bites her lip. "I cheered in high school. I tore my left knee and needed surgery. It was a bear to recover from. I'm just relieved this seems minor."

Brekka raises her eyebrows. "I bet." I'm not even surprised that Brekka's already getting more information out of Geo than I have. She hates being forced to interact with people, but when she does, she's naturally adept. Introverts.

And now thanks to her, I can't get the image of Geo in a cheer uniform out of my head. Which only makes me want to kiss her even more. Thanks for that, Brekka.

7
GEO

The 'cabin' Trig brought us to more closely resembles a palace, or a mansion at the very least. The lines are gorgeous, light streaming from oversized picture windows on every wall, with stone and rough hewn wood accents. A thirty foot tall marble fireplace stands at the center of enormous windows rising on either side and on the far wall. The trim is all shiny mahogany. The surfaces are painted in that greige that's so popular everywhere right now. Pine trees spread their needles outside the family room as though they were designed to frame these windows. For all I know, they were.

The furniture's a complimentary mix of fabric, fur, and leather that looks expensive without being too heavy.

"You need to change out of that ski suit." Brekka's such a tiny little person nestled in the corner of the large sofa. "I'm sure the pressure from it isn't helping matters. Plus, there's no way ice will permeate the fabric, which is kind of the point."

Trig's sister reminds me of a china doll, resting on a throne. Perfect, dainty features. Dark, liquid eyes, and highlighted russet hair that falls forward to frame her face. She's small too. It's hard to tell with her sitting, but I'd guess she's several inches shorter than me at least. Trig's truly clueless if he thinks we'd wear the same size. Maybe in shoes. I glance down at her feet and he might be right. She could be a size eight, or close. I hope so.

"I only have a pair of pajamas in case I got stuck, and my suit," I say. "I was supposed to fly back to Atlanta later today."

Brekka tsks, a sound just like her brother makes. "That won't do. You can wear your pajamas tonight if you'd like, but you're welcome to anything in my closet. In fact, I insist on it. We'll go shopping in my closet right now if you want." She lowers her voice. "Are your pajamas decent?"

I giggle. "Yes, they're flannel, plaid flannel actually. I knew I was flying to Colorado in the winter."

She leans back, clearly relieved for me. "Oh good. Well, tonight Trig and I can wear pjs too, as a show of solidarity. But tomorrow you'll get a tour of Brekka's closet."

She talks about herself in the third person. I like her already.

"Thanks," I say. "Trig said you were great, and it sure seems like he was right."

She glances at Trig and rolls her eyes. "He's prone to exaggeration in most areas, but he's spot on about that one thing. I am fabulous." She pats my good knee. "Trig can carry you upstairs to one of the guest rooms and you can get changed." She freezes then, like a deer that's just seen a human. "Unless you'd rather have my help instead?"

I shake my head. "I wouldn't want to impose. Trig says you're making dinner."

"Oh, it's done, but if you're okay with his help, that's probably easier."

I nod. "Thank you again. I'm sure it's weird having a stranger invade your home."

Brekka glances slyly at Trig. "I was shocked when my brother suggested it. He never brings anyone here. I think he's afraid of what I might say to them. I don't filter what I'm thinking." Her eyes widen purposefully.

Trig leans over and scoops me up again carefully, like I'm the china doll lookalike instead of his sister. "Let's get you changed."

"Don't change her too much," Brekka says. "I like her the way she is."

"Very funny," Trig says. "Always with a little quip."

"I like her," I whisper in his ear as he carries me up a stunning, curved, floating staircase that wraps around a piece of blown glass installation art that must have been custom made for this space. "And this cabin, I don't even have words." I'm not exaggerating in the slightest. The blend of modern and rustic in the home is staggeringly well done.

"You study design?" Trig's eyebrows raise.

I duck my head against his collarbone. "Not really. I love watching home makeover shows and look at a lot of magazines. I might even spend an unhealthy amount of time on Zillow, peeking into other people's houses."

His chest shakes as he laughs. "Well, my mom and dad have made some ghastly purchases in other locations, but they listened to me and Brekka on this one. We helped design it a decade ago. It's one of my favorites."

His words sunk in. One of his favorites. "How many cabins do you have?"

"Cabins?" He looks upward as though he's counting in his head. "If you mean cabins, just four. But if you meant all vacation homes, sixteen."

"All your parents?" I ask.

He shakes his head. "I have two, Brekka has two, and we own one together. The others are Mom and Dad's. But we sort of all use them interchangeably. That and the house in Denver. I have my own place downtown, but I still kind of think of Ivy Court as home."

I have no idea how to respond to that, so I don't. He bumps a door open with his foot and pushes through. He sets me gently on a thickly cushioned mattress with a bright ivory duvet. The room could have been featured in a Pottery Barn catalog on a page titled Neutrals that Shine.

"I could put you down the hall in a nicer room, but this one's a lot smaller, which means the bed's closer to the bathroom."

"This is perfect," I say. "Thank you."

He sets my backpack down next to me and straightens up. "You think you can manage from here?"

I shake my head and stare at him for a moment before saying, "I was hoping you'd strip my ski suit off. It might be awkward. I'm only wearing underwear beneath it."

His jaw drops satisfyingly.

I can't help the laughter that bubbles out of my chest then. "I'm kidding, Trig. I'll manage."

He gulps and nods quickly. "Right." He backs up toward the door. "If you shout for me when you're changed, I can come get you and take you down for dinner."

I smile at him. He may be a spoiled rich trust fund baby, but I get why Luke likes him. He really does resemble an exuberant puppy dog at his core. I shouldn't have teased him like that. It was beneath me.

"I really appreciate your help today. You may have bullied me into skiing, but you've certainly taken care of me in the aftermath."

"Math always has been my strong suit." He closes the door behind him.

I sink back against the fluffy linens. They smell like cotton and lilacs. I close my eyes, relieved for a moment that my knee isn't throbbing, I'm warm, and I'm safe.

But eventually I have to move. I strip my ski suit off, and I wasn't lying. I peel it off slowly, shifting as minimally as I can manage to avoid jarring my knee. Eventually I'm sitting in my underwear, staring at the black backpack. I lean forward and pull out my pajamas, which are perfectly respectable. Purple plaid button down top, and plaid pants with a drawstring and pockets.

I really wish I'd brought something nicer. Silk, or maybe even a cute girl cut t-shirt and yoga pants. Anything that didn't remind me of something my mother would wear. Oh well, nothing I can do about it now. I tug the pants on first, slowly, only banging my bad knee once. The shirt buttons on easily.

Only then do I drag myself into the bathroom, hopping inelegantly on my good leg. I brush my teeth too, for good measure. Not because I plan to kiss Trig again. Because that's not going to happen. I check my phone to see if I have reception, which of course I don't. Brekka must have a different service provider than I do.

I hope Paisley's not worried. It's not like my mom would worry about me. She doesn't worry about anything.

I yell. "I'm ready Trig."

I hear footsteps in the hall, and then the door opens. Trig was almost disgustingly handsome the first time I saw him. Mussed hair, a roguish smile, impeccably dressed, and devil-may-care glint in his eyes. But tonight, in plaid pajama pants and a black t-shirt, I could eat him with a spoon. Like one of those huge serving spoons. I think about putting a dollop of canned whipped cream on top, and then my thoughts really go downhill.

"You okay?" Trig asks. "You're kind of staring."

I clear my throat. "You got here really fast is all."

"I took the room next door to you so I'd be close if you need anything later."

It's thoughtful, but a tiny shiver runs up my spine, knowing he'll be sleeping a few feet away from me. I squish that idea fast. Loving someone just gives you another way to hurt. I terminated that line of thinking years ago.

"I'm sorry to be such a bother. Seriously, you were right, this is embarrassing."

He turns around slowly. "How about a piggyback ride, then. We can make it a game."

He can't see my smile when I lean toward him. He's careful with my right knee, his hand wrapping under my thigh carefully. My chest tingles where it presses against his back and I'm glad I brushed my teeth, since my breath puffs out right next to his cheek.

This might have been a mistake. It feels much more intimate than having him carry me in his arms.

Before I can protest, he leaps to his feet and shoots through the door, tearing down the hall like a very spry father, bouncing me along like a little kid. He spins around the corner and flies down the stairs, my heart in my throat.

"Slow down," I say. "I don't want to break my neck!"

He slams on the brakes and takes the last ten stairs so slowly that I finally thump him on the shoulder. "Idiot man. I didn't mean you should crawl down."

He shakes his head and I can tell he's grinning when he looks back at me. "You just can't make some women happy, no matter what you do."

I squeeze his back and can't help noticing the lean muscle in his shoulders and arms. He may not feel like a Marine, but he's bulkier than a runner, with defined muscle. I like that he feels solid enough I know he's not going to break, without looking like an underwear model.

I enjoy the feel of his back under my fingers enough that I'm reluctant to let go when we reach the kitchen, but when I take a good look around, I'm amazed. I've never seen a kitchen like this outside of a magazine. The cabinets look like one huge slab of wood that's been expertly sliced into individual compartments. The counters are a smooth grey marble that is six inches thick, everywhere but on the island. The huge central island counter only has a two-inch thick marble slab, and it sits almost a foot lower than the rest of the kitchen. I haven't seen rooms with such differing counter heights in any magazines, but the color of the lower marble contrasts well with the high counter and bar across from it.

The cabinets on the back wall of the kitchen are formed the same, seemingly from one slab of wood, but it's a much darker wood. The dark outer ring and lighter, lower inner ring were clearly expertly designed. And the cabinetry is so fine that the refrigerator and freezer almost disappear into the wall. The entire home is a study in color —a careful mixture of deep browns, warm golden tones, slate greys and frosty whites that should clash, but thanks to the colors in the stone accent walls, blend seamlessly. Watching such striking styles mix elegantly is freeing, somehow.

The dining table's actually one huge granite slab that's raw around the edges. Brekka's already seated in one of the tall leather dining chairs. I'm still clinging to Trig's broad shoulders, almost dreamily, like none of this is real and I'm in a storybook.

Brekka's knowing smile when she glances at us brings me back to reality.

This isn't a fairy tale, even though Trig really is probably the closest thing to a prince that exists in America.

I will never marry this prince. Happily Ever After has

never been my destination, at least not since my huge detour years ago.

"Dinner looks amazing," I say.

Trig sets me in a chair, arranging my injured knee so it's up on the chair next to me.

The food really does look phenomenal. Chicken parmesan with fresh marinara sauce if I'm not mistaken, sautéed green beans, spaghetti noodles twisted into a knot and topped with more marinara and parmesan.

"You don't have any allergies, do you?" Brekka asks from her seat at the head of the table, twisting her napkin between her hands frenetically. "I'm a little late asking that. Sorry."

I bite my lip. "Actually, I'm gluten free, vegan and I prefer low sodium."

Brekka's face falls and I can't suppress my smile any longer. Not that I should, with as little as I know her.

"I'm kidding," I say. "No allergies and I love gluten. You?"

She shakes her head. "Trig and I can eat anything. And Trig frequently eats everything."

"Hey, now. I have standards."

"No fish sticks," I say. "I know that one already."

Brekka glances from Trig to me and back again. "Fish sticks?"

"Never mind," I say. "Just a dumb joke."

"You two already have inside jokes?" Brekka picks up her fork. "That's promising."

I shake my head. "No, it's not like that. Really. Trig and I just had a business lunch the other day and I mentioned that I love fish sticks."

Which I actually don't, but that's not the point.

"I might have to give them a try then." Trig takes the seat between Brekka and me. "But I promise you, no matter how delicious they are, they can't top Brekka's chicken parm. It's to die for. I can't even order this at restaurants anymore, because it's never as good as hers."

I pick up my knife and fork with relish and slice off the edge of my chicken. Trig's assessment is spot on. The chicken's warm, crunchy on the edges, and tender simultaneously somehow. Not at all chewy. It falls apart in my mouth, and there's just the right amount of salt in the sauce. No acidic after taste.

"Oh man, you're right. Although, I'm not sure whether to say thanks or be annoyed."

"Annoyed?" Brekka asks. "Why?"

I shake my head slowly, solemnly. "What am I going to order at Olive Garden now?"

"Stick with me kid," Trig says, "and your Olive Garden days may be numbered."

My heart stutters in my chest. Danger Will Robinson. Danger. I shake my head. "But I love Olive Garden. I don't want those days to be numbered. And this chicken endangers my future satisfaction. That makes it a liability."

"Are we still talking about chicken here?" Brekka arches one eyebrow.

"Of course we are." I gobble the rest of it down.

"Tell me about Luke's new bride," Brekka says. "I can't wait to meet her. I absolutely adore Luke. No one deserves happiness more than he does. And those kids get cuter every time I see them."

I slurp down a mouthful of noodles. "Mary is. . ." I pause. What can I say? I've only been around her four or five times. Which I suppose is four or five more times than these people, and they clearly care about Luke. "Mary's defining trait is that she cares about her people deeply. She takes care of everyone in her life. When we met, one of the times was on her lunch break, and she had a meeting directly after ours with the head of her new charity."

"She runs a charity?" Brekka groans. "Don't tell me she's one of those people."

Brekka hates people who are charitable? I think for a moment. She's mega rich. Maybe she's opposed to generosity, but I doubt that. Perhaps she hates the Natalies of the world, people who use charity as part of their act to show how great they are. "Do you mean one of the people who pretends to care so everyone thinks she's amazing?"

Brekka smirks. "I guess that's what I mean. I didn't realize quite how cynical I've become."

I shake my head. "Mary's not a do-gooder for show. She runs a charity for kids at Christmas, kids who have nothing. She substitutes for Santa Claus for them and she's run something like it since college. She loves everything about her program and pores over the details, if the few moments I saw are any indication."

Brekka bobs her head back and forth. "That's admirable, I guess."

"Luke mentioned she was a recipient of that charity when she was young," Trig says.

Brekka leans back in her chair. "So she's a self-made woman, just like Luke."

"Something like that," I say, "although not quite on the same magnitude. But she takes care of the people in her life pretty carefully, monetarily and emotionally. Like her little sister. And my best friend Paisley. Mary's always putting other people first. And if that doesn't make her sound odd enough. . .she loves doing taxes."

The horror and disbelief on their faces matches my own.

"Why would anyone...what could she... I don't even know what to say to that," Brekka mutters.

"To clarify," I say, "I don't think she likes paying them. She likes getting the liability for her clients as low as possible."

"Still," Trig says.

I nod. "I know, right?"

"Not to be shallow, but what does she look like?" Brekka asks in a small voice.

"She's adorable in a 'girl next door' kind of way. She has a lovely smile that fills her whole face. And she smiles a lot."

"What does Paul think about her?" Brekka asks.

"You've met Paul?" I ask. "I hear he's great. I haven't even seen him yet. I'm supposed to meet him for lunch next week to go over some details for the wedding. I guess I'll be working with him a lot in the next few months if Vail doesn't work out. His back yard is our fallback for the reception."

"That's a terrible idea," Trig says.

"His back yard?" I ask. "Why? Is it swampy?"

He clears his throat. "I just meant that Paul is super busy right now. He and Luke are launching a huge new tech project—"

"They are?" Brekka asks. "What is it?"

Trig sighs. "It's confidential, obviously. But if you guys won't say anything." He glances at each of us, and I nod right along with Brekka.

Who would I even tell?

"It's a five pound car battery," he says. "It will be small and manageable, which means this will be huge."

Brekka slaps the table and I jump, bumping my knee on the tabletop. "That's amazing. Paul has talked about that for years. How'd they finally work that out?"

I check out for a minute while the two of them geek out in nerd speak. I poke at my tender knee and shudder.

Trig slaps his forehead. "I forgot to get you ice. I'm such a dunce." He hops up and jogs from the dining room into the kitchen, opening drawers and banging around until he comes up with a Ziploc bag for me full of little frozen blocks. "Sorry I spaced it."

I reach up and tug on the bag. "No big deal, really."

He doesn't release it. "It is a big deal. It's the second letter in RICE."

"Ah, good old RICE," Brekka says. "My old friend. I had to rest, ice, compress and elevate almost twice a year for a decade or more."

"Well, here's to hoping the ice part helps," I say. "Because I need to fly home tomorrow."

"Right, you have that big meeting Monday," Trig says. "Is that with Paul?"

And we're back to Paul. "No, that's not until late in the week, and his secretary hasn't confirmed. She's moved it twice already."

"Then what's Monday?" Trig asks.

"A recurring thing. I have the same meeting every Monday with a long term event planning client. My bread and butter."

"That's right," Trig says. "I heard you don't normally do weddings."

"Is that because brides are just awful?" Brekka asks. "Because I secretly love that show, *Bridezilla*. Probably because I'll never. . . Well, anyway. I can imagine it would be horrible dealing with overwrought women who are entirely focused on one day going perfectly." Her eyes are round and her lips slightly parted.

"Emotions do seem to run high around weddings," I say, "but that can be true of lots of events, especially family gatherings like reunions. I still plan those." Why did I say that? I'm opening myself up here like an amateur. I should have agreed, regaled them with a few of my friends' more absurd bride stories and moved on.

"Then why don't you plan them?" Trig asks, his eyes curious. "Are you opposed to marriage as an institution? Because that I can understand."

"Not everyone's parents are like ours," Brekka says, a note of reproof in her tone.

"I'm surrounded with successful marriages actually," I say. "My Aunt and Uncle are going strong after twenty-three years together, and both sets of grandparents. Or well, one set. The other stayed married until death did them part. And my parents were happily married for thirty-two years."

"Were?" Trig asks. "But not now?"

"My dad passed two Christmases back now. Esophageal cancer."

"Yikes, I'm sorry to hear that," Brekka says. "I wish we could just cure cancer already. But if your parents were so happy, you'd think you'd love watching others who have found the same."

"I'm not opposed to marriage or weddings, okay?" I push my remaining noodles around. "In fact, I planned two or three weddings when I was starting out, but I decided to focus in another direction."

Brekka's scrunches her nose. "But aren't weddings kind of where the money is for event planning?"

I sigh. I've been backed into this corner before, and I can see they aren't going to let go. I try one last time to change the subject before going nuclear. "Not everything is about money."

"I beg to differ," Trig says. "Maybe everything isn't about dollars and cents, but it certainly moves things along. After all, money is our simplest calculation of leverage. If you're in a business where the money is in weddings, and you're competent at your job, why choose to take the lower paying work unless there's a compelling reason to do that?"

"There's a story, okay?" I look down at my lap where my napkin's now wadded into a ball. "The last wedding I planned was my own. When my fiancé's unit was hit with an IED unexpectedly, he died in Libya three weeks before our wedding. I got the news three days later. On Valentine's Day. I quit planning weddings after that."

I wipe a tear away and meet Brekka's gaze defiantly. "Is that a good enough story for you?"

Trig and Brekka's mouths fall open at the same time. Even if I'd never met them before, I'd know they were siblings.

"That's why you hate Valentine's Day," Trig says.

"It didn't help," I admit. "And I think I'd like to go back up to my room now."

Trig stands up and wipes his hands on his jeans. "I'm really sorry we pushed."

"You're not sorry about that," I say. "You're just sorry the conversation turned awkward so fast. But I get it, it's human nature to poke and prod at injured creatures."

Trig reaches for me, and I push his hands away. I don't want to ride upstairs piggy back, or breathe on his ear, or flirt. I know where all that leads in the end, and it's never anywhere good, not for me. Because the more you love someone, the more it hurts when they die. Or leave. Or forget all about you. Or get blown up.

"I think I can hop upstairs myself, if Brekka can help me."

"Oh," Brekka says. "I'd love to, but I'm sorry." She shakes her head and looks up at me with wide, doe-like eyes. "I can't."

I stiffen. "That's fine. I can probably get up alone." I set the melty ice bag on the table top. "My knee actually feels a lot better already."

She shakes her head and reaches one hand out toward me. "I'm not trying to be rude, I'm really not." She pivots in her chair so her legs swing toward me and I notice she doesn't move them. Like almost at all. It's more like she drags them actually. "While we're ripping off Band-Aids to bare painful wounds, I may as well tear mine off too. I was in a car accident a few years ago, and I came away with an injury to T10. I'm mostly paralyzed from the hips down. I would love to help you, but I actually need a wheelchair myself. Trig would have given you the only downstairs bedroom, but I selfishly hog that one for myself."

My world spins a little, and then a lot. I think about the limited interactions I've had with her.

Brekka was sitting when I came inside, and already seated at the kitchen table when Trig brought me down. She never stood up. Why didn't I notice that? The lower island in the kitchen makes sense now, so she can reach things to cook from her wheelchair. I think about how Trig flinched earlier when I called myself gimpy. I could have said something insensitive like that to Brekka.

"Where's your wheelchair now?" I glance around the room. "And why didn't Trig mention it earlier? You'd think it might have come up."

Trig clears his throat. "Brekka likes it when people can get to know her first, before they find out."

"Otherwise I'm just the wheelchair girl, the disabled girl, the girl who can't walk, and as long as they know me, that's my defining attribute. I'm sorry," she says in a small voice. "I wasn't trying to trick you. I prefer people to know me a little bit before they find out, whenever possible."

I bob my head because more than most people would, I understand. It's the same reason I don't talk about Mark if

I can help it. I hate being the poor, sad girl who was left at the altar by a dead Marine. I guess I should be grateful my wound is a little less visible than hers.

"I guess you can help me up," I say to Trig.

He picks me up without a word, carrying me with his arms under my knees and behind my back again, just like before.

Except even if that's the same, everything else has shifted. He looks at me with the same sad eyes I now turn on Brekka. Everyone always does once they know.

8

TRIG

I wake up to the sight of three feet of snow blanketing the world outside my window. My parents included enormous, panel free, floor-to-ceiling windows in every room of this house, all of them lead reinforced and over an inch and a half thick. Even insulated, the glass can't be good for the heating bill, but you can't beat the views, summer or winter. The entire world outside looks clean, pristine, and perfect.

I wish the past could be whitewashed as effectively.

She found out her fiancé died on Valentine's Day. And I blathered on and on like she was unfeeling for blocking that day out of her consideration. She probably knew exactly what weekend the Bachelor party was falling on, but if she tries her hardest to make it a day like any other, she wouldn't have allowed that to impact her decision making.

I treated her the same way all those calloused jerks treat Brekka. Maybe worse. She can hide her injury, but I didn't let her. I picked at it, forcing her to tell me before she was ready. I shake my head and push the covers down when I sit up in bed. My bedside clock says it's ten a.m. Poor Geo's probably still sitting in her room, twiddling her thumbs.

I knock on the wall. "You alive in there?"

She bumps back. "I was starting to worry about you. I've already put together three different options for the wedding program and assembled fifteen different menus. I should take connectivity breaks more often when I've got planning to finish. As long as I have my legwork done in advance, it gives me a great chance to pull things together without interruptions."

I chuckle to myself. She's definitely the first type of gorgeous person my sister mentioned. A knockout who works even harder than everyone else to make sure no one thinks she got where she did because of her appearance.

"Hungry?" I ask.

"I am. Think we could make breakfast for Brekka, since she made us dinner?"

I don't even have to hide the grin that conquers my face when she says 'we' and 'us' since she can't see me. But it gives me pause. Why would I want there to be an us? What's wrong with me?

"Brekka got up at least three hours ago," I say. "She's like clockwork. She'll probably have raspberry rolls ready for us downstairs. That's her specialty, and I noticed berries in the fridge last night."

"You ready to go?"

"I need to shower first. How about you? I could offer my services."

"Hilarious," she says. "But I already took a bath. The good news is that my knee feels much better already. I wrapped it with the bandage the ER doc gave us and it felt good enough that I almost hobbled downstairs myself."

"What stopped you?" I kind of love talking to her

without looking at her. Her exquisite face is almost too distracting.

"Maybe I like piggy back rides."

I lean closer, my heart racing. "Do you?"

"I said maybe."

I place my hand against the wall, wondering whether she's touching it, too.

I finally drag my hand away and shower as fast as I can. Water from my hair drips onto my shoulders as I tap on her door. I almost trip on the box sitting outside her room even though I'm the one who put it there the night before.

"Come in," she says.

I pick up the box and turn the knob. "Brekka gathered some things she thought you might like last night." I hold out the box like a shield to deflect the brilliance of seeing her for the first time today, but her eyes nearly stop my heart anyway. They're like deep blue sapphires in the morning light, and I completely understand why her parents named her Geode. I almost wish I could wrap her up so the entire world couldn't see how brightly she sparkles. Although that would be a disservice to, well, to everyone.

She's still in her pajamas and almost snatches the box from my hand. She rifles through the contents, settling on a cotton blouse with some kind of bunchy fabric around the waist, and tight black pants. Bless Brekka for including those.

"What about shoes?" she asks.

"Uh, I don't know," I say. "But I assume we can work that out downstairs."

"Duh," she says. "Thanks. I'm going to hobble over and try these on." I reach over to help her stand, but she doesn't need me, and I have to ignore the sad twinge her returning independence causes. She hops over to the bathroom and closes the door behind her.

When she emerges, she looks nothing like my sister and I'm relieved.

When I spin around for a piggy back ride this time, it's different somehow. I feel the touch of her fingers on my collarbones, the pressure of her legs against my flank, the crush of her ample chest against my back. My heart races and for the first time in my life, I wonder if I'm old enough to suffer a catastrophic heart attack.

Don't fail me legs, not now. As I shove up to standing, her minty, just-brushed breath blows into my nose. I don't bounce her on the way down the stairs this time, focusing on not tripping over my own suddenly clumsy feet. The rapport we had when a wall separated us evaporated somehow now that we're touching and it's almost like there's a buzzing underneath my skin.

I set her down on the same seat as the evening before and Brekka wheels easily over to the table, placing a plate of raspberry rolls on top of the granite, just as I predicted.

"Morning!" Brekka brightens every room, always. But even her smile seems a little damp for such a gorgeous, frosty morning.

The next twenty minutes feels so forced that when the cabin land line rings, I leap up to grab it.

It's Charlie. "That gorgeous lady staying with you?"

"Uh, yep," I say, hoping Geo can't hear his side of the conversation. I take a few steps into the family room to be safe.

"And? How'd it go last night?"

"She hurt her knee skiing yesterday," I say.

Geo's face turns toward me when she realizes I'm talking about her.

"It's Charlie," I tell her.

She sighs. "I wish we could meet today. If only to go over the numbers . Has he worked them out?"

I convey her wishes to Charlie, who offers to chat with her instead. "I can email her the details, but I could answer most of her other questions on the line right now."

"So you're calling me to talk to her now?"

Charlie snorts. "Dude, this is a favor for you. We don't really have room for this party at all."

"I know," I say. "I do appreciate it."

"But. If you struck out, I have a green light, right?" Charlie asks. "Because I have a snow mobile. I could come pick her up right now."

I don't snarl into the phone. I'm sort of proud of that. "I don't think so. Try anything and there'll be a repeat of sophomore year's Homecoming. I'm sure you remember how that went down."

Charlie chokes on the phone in a satisfying way before I pass it off to Geo. Their call lasts a while, but eventually I get my phone back.

And somehow, even though I don't know what to say to Geo today, Brekka navigates toward some kind of bizarre equilibrium with her. A balance that my presence throws off for some reason. Every time I walk past the family room, they're giggling or one is talking while the other one's mouth gapes open.

I'm not sure how inviting Geo accomplished this, but I'm suddenly unwelcome in my own home.

I stomp up the stairs, and neither of them even notices. I bang through the door to the upstairs hot tub and scrape off the snow. Once it's heated, I put on my swimsuit and march across the second floor catwalk hoping they'll look up and notice me. If Geo's knee feels better, which it certainly seems to, you'd think she might want to join me.

She doesn't.

When Chad comes by to plow our driveway around four p.m., I check my phone. Cell towers are back up. I call my pilot. He says we're clear to fly after six p.m.

"Hey Geo?" I call down from the catwalk, my towel wrapped around my waist. "I just got confirmation the airport's opening again at six."

She leaps up from the couch and only grunts a little when she puts pressure on her knee. "Then I need to call the airline right away."

She practically jogs over to the stairs, but stops at the bottom eyeing them with a determined look.

"Don't overdo it or you might reinjure it," I say. "I'll go grab your phone."

I snag her phone out of her cute red purse and run it down to her, noticing that she's got three missed calls from Paisley, and five from someone named Rob.

Who the hell is Rob?

I bite my tongue so I don't blurt out my question the second I hand the phone over. I completely forget I'm still wearing my swimsuit. Geo's eyes on my chest remind me.

"Uh, sorry. I was in the hot tub."

"I can see that," she says, her eyes burning a path from my chest downward, and then zooming back up to my eyes. I can't quite keep the corner of my mouth from turning up.

"You've got a few missed calls."

"Thanks," she says.

She doesn't offer anything else, like an explanation that she has a half-brother she's embarrassed of, who happens to be named Robert. Or a stalker-adjacent client. Or maybe a pest control guy who's worried about a rat infestation at her place. It can't be a boyfriend, because she doesn't date. Right?

Or does she not date because she's already committed?

I want to swear, but then they'd want to know why I'm

mad and I have no reasonable reason. Nothing I can disclose anyway. It's not like I can say, "When I was snooping on your phone, I saw a guy's name. He called over and over. Who is this guy? If you don't date?"

Geo spends the next thirty minutes on the phone with the airline. I shower and change back into clothes. It didn't look like Geo was about to join me in the hot tub anyway.

She throws her phone at the pillows on the sofa as I walk back into the family room.

"Not good news?" I ask.

She shakes her head. "Flights will be taking off at six, but since I'm a nobody who rarely flies, I get last priority. The soonest I can fly out is six p.m."

I don't understand. "It doesn't open until six. We'd barely have time to get there in time for you to leave by then anyway," I say.

Her scowl could skewer a wild boar. "Six *tomorrow*."

"Is that a problem?" Brekka asks. Bless her for prying when I can't. "It's not like we're torturing you, right? And we've got Monopoly in the game cabinet. Although on second thought, playing that with Trig is sort of like playing scrabble with Stephen King."

Geo snorts. "So he'd scare me into quitting?"

I flop down on the sofa. "I'd do no such thing."

"Fine, maybe not Stephen King. Nicholas Sparks," Brekka says with a smirk.

I throw a pillow at her head. "I'm definitely not Nicholas Sparks."

"Trig: the Nicholas Sparks of the business world," Brekka says. "I like that. I'll need to remember it for later. That will kill at the next board meeting."

I sigh dramatically. "Has it occurred to anyone here that I have a private jet? I could probably give you a ride."

Geo sits up straight and stares intently at my face.

"Would you really? Do you need to go to Atlanta? Or maybe you could just loan me your plane?" Her expression is so earnest. I want to yank her up against me for a kiss that would send Brekka wheeling out of the room. A kiss that would make her forget this Rob and make her long for Valentine's Day again.

I don't of course, not with Brekka already scowling at me from two feet away. Geo needs my help, not a good solid snogging.

Why does she need to race back to Atlanta? Brekka was teasing, but it stings a little, snowed in with me and my delightful sister, and she's so desperate to claw her way back home any way she can.

"What's the rush?" I ask. "I mean, jet fuel isn't cheap."

She swallows and tucks her hair behind her ear. "No, I know it's not. I'm sorry I asked."

"Trig's just being annoying," Brekka says. "His feelings are just hurt you want to leave, and he doesn't know how to process that you won't reschedule your meeting."

I scowl at Brekka. "I'm not hurt," I say. "More like curious."

Geo tilts her head. "Oh?"

"I'll take you," I say. "But you have to pay for it."

Geo's mouth drops open. "Uh, what does that cost—"

"Not the fuel. You have to pay with information. Why is this meeting so important?"

Brekka claps. "Yes, I want to know too, now."

Geo sighs melodramatically. "It's really no big deal."

So why hasn't she already told us?

"I have dinner every Monday with a friend of mine. It's a tradition."

"What's his name?" I ask.

Don't say Rob, don't say Rob.

"How do you know it's a guy?" Brekka asks.

I shrug. “I guess I don’t. Is it?”

“It’s my oldest friend. I’ve known him since I was five years old. His name is Robert Graham. But seriously, it’s not that big of a deal. I can skip it. I’ll just head back tomorrow.”

I want to strangle Rob freaking Graham. Because Geo just threw the closest thing I’ve seen from her to a temper tantrum at the thought of missing their date. Oldest friend? I don’t think so. And now I’m on the hook to hand deliver her to him in time for their weekly whatever it is. Or isn’t. Hopefully isn’t.

I don’t swear, and I don’t stomp. I calmly call my pilot and let him know I’ll be headed back to Atlanta within the hour. Then I walk upstairs as slowly as I can to throw some clothes in a bag. I’m proud of myself, because I don’t even hit or smash anything.

9

GEO

Brekka insists I keep her clothes and a pair of boots that were way too big for her when they arrived, but fit me perfectly.

"You could return them for a refund, surely," I say.

She shakes her head. "But I won't. I never mess with that stuff."

The label inside says Prada.

"I can't keep these," I say. "They cost more than two months' rent."

Brekka laughs and the sound lightens my heart. I wish I could bottle it up for the hard days.

"You're delightful," she says. "And now there's no way you aren't keeping those boots." She drops her voice until it's barely more than a whisper. "I never had many friends you know, not girl friends, and not even that many boys."

I frown. "I don't believe you."

She shakes her head. "I didn't. And now." She gestures at her wheelchair. "It's harder than ever to make friends. I hope I've made one this weekend."

"I am your friend Brekka, even without boots so beautiful I want to run back up to my room and look at them until it's time for bed."

"But this way, even when my brother turns out to be more obnoxious than you can handle, I hope you'll stay in touch with me." She looks down at her lap. "Was that too 'high school yearbook' to say out loud? See? I don't do great with new people."

I lean over and pull her tightly against me into a hug and I'm surprised when my eyes water a little bit. "I don't make friends easily either. For some reason, girls almost never like me."

Brekka lifts one eyebrow and looks me up and down purposefully. "You don't say. I have no idea why that might be the case."

I shake my head. "I honestly have no clue. I've tried everything I can think of, but I'm not someone most girls feel they can trust."

When Brekka's laugh rings out, even louder this time, I want to hug her again. But that would be weird, so I don't.

"I'll keep in touch," I promise her. "I'm pretty good with texts. And if you ever get boots that are too big again, I'll gladly send you a prepaid shipping label." I wink.

She crosses her heart with her finger. "It's a deal."

Trig grabs my backpack before I can and swings it up and onto his shoulder. "Ready?"

I nod and follow him outside, only hobbling a little. My knee already feels worlds better. Which is good, since I'd really prefer Trig not need to carry me onto his jet. Talk about embarrassing. Not to mention, he can't carry me home, obviously.

I don't know what to say on the drive, and he doesn't offer anything either. When his phone rings, it's almost a relief. Now I can stare at the mounds of glistening white snow, piled up like unbelievable caches of diamonds on the side of the road, without having to cast about for something clever to say. Why should I care whether he thinks I'm witty in any case?

It's better not to pull on some loose threads.

"Hello?" He's quiet for a moment. "Uh huh. Oh, that's great news. Don't tell her though. I'll do it." He pauses again. "No, because it took me years to get her to even submit to that test and you idiots talk to her like she's broken, that's why. And no, I don't care about HIPAA." He shakes his head. "I said it's good news, didn't I?" Pause. "No, it is great news, I agree. But the reason I gave you my number instead of hers is that she won't necessarily see it that way unless it's presented properly." Another pause. "I know you're the experts. I don't mean presented in a medically accurate way." He huffs. "I didn't bankroll your entire study so that you could bungle this. Just wait for me to contact you."

He hangs up.

I don't ask who called, no matter how much I want to know.

His hands tighten and then relax on the steering wheel. He exhales heavily. "That was Brekka's neurosurgeon."

"You seemed annoyed with him."

"How the man graduated first in his class from Harvard Medical School is beyond me. He doesn't understand the tiniest thing about Brekka's feelings."

I can't quite keep myself from asking. "Was the news really good?"

He nods. "She's a candidate for a new surgical procedure, one that could, possibly restore complete use of her legs."

I gasp. "That's not good news, that's practically miraculous news. I heard that if a patient doesn't regain function in the first two weeks or so, they probably never will."

He cocks one eyebrow. "It's more like six months, but that's true. You know a surprising amount about spinal injury."

I shrug. "Fiancé was a Marine, remember? They're injured a lot."

"It's a little experimental." His lips compress into a flat line.

"A little?"

"Okay, a lot experimental."

"How long has it been since Brekka's injury?"

"Four and a half years," he says. "Which means it's way too long for anything that isn't experimental. The docs keep telling her she's lucky. Some people don't keep bowel control. Some people have zero mobility. She can't walk more than a few steps, and she needs either arm braces or hand holds, but even without equipped bathrooms, she can maneuver from the chair to the toilet alone."

"It doesn't feel lucky."

He shakes his head. "No. Being able to wiggle your toes and do very limited exercises with her legs doesn't feel lucky at all. Brekka was six months from winning a gold medal before her accident. There was no question, Geo. She would have won at least one of her events, and she excelled at all of them. Such different sports, slalom and downhill, and she mastered both. She was the best skier I'd ever seen, and at the top of her game too."

I think about Natalie sliding down the slopes like a seal and wonder what tiny little Brekka, delicate, fragile Brekka looked like carving up the snow.

"I know she's small, but my sister was extraordinary." He gulps. "She still is extraordinary of course, but I meant physically speaking, she had control of her body in a way most people will never understand. She knew exactly what each muscle twitch would do. She was graceful and always in complete control."

I think about how she told me she'd crashed into the same tree as me. "She never ran into my tree, did she?"

He laughs. "No, that was a blatant lie. But the rest of us did at one time or another. She's not kidding about that icy spot being irritating. She wasn't laughing at you, I swear."

I knew she wasn't. It wasn't something Brekka would do.

"So will she do the surgery?" I ask, already imagining Brekka walking around, dancing from one room to the next. My heart lightens at the thought. I'd love to see her in Prada boots just like these, scuffing the soles on cobblestones.

He shakes his head in frustration. "I doubt it."

My jaw drops. "Why not?"

"Because you're right. All the research says if she hasn't regained function within a few weeks, odds are low. Or non-existent. Once you reach a year, most surgeons won't even discuss surgical options without there being a change in status. Once the spinal cord is damaged, there's not much they can do. But Geo, she can move her feet. Not much, and not for long, but there's some function. It gave me hope. Enough hope that I can't give up."

Can't give up? Or won't accept who Brekka is now?

"I've found dozens of surgical options over the years. She always declines emphatically, insisting they're more science fiction than reality. She claims the risks outweigh the benefits. She's fine, she tells me. She doesn't miss skiing. She likes her life."

I think about it. I consider the little bit I know about his sister. "Maybe she does."

I knew Trig wouldn't want to hear it, and I'm right.

His head whips toward me. "Are you kidding me right now?"

"Experimental surgery sounds risky. How would you feel if she never woke up?" My voice drops to a whisper. "If she not only didn't walk again, but if she didn't breathe again? If you never heard her laugh again? Could you live with yourself, knowing you pushed her?"

He swallows slowly, eyes trained on the road. "I don't know. I like to think that God wouldn't do that to me, to us. Not now, not after all we've been through."

"I don't think God works like that. Ever read the book of Job?" I ask. "That poor guy. Things just got worse and worse."

"I'm not talking about the Bible, or like the Christian God or whatever. I'm just saying, if there's anyone, or anything out there watching over us, and I like to think there is, I can't imagine that he or she would let Brekka not wake up. Not after what she's already overcome." His voice drops to a rough whisper. "I have to fix it, Geo, because it's all my fault."

I reach across the console and place my hand on his. His knuckles relax slightly.

"I was driving that night. I'm the reason she's paralyzed."

"Were you drunk?" I ask. "Or impaired in any way?"

He shakes his head. "Of course not."

"Were you being reckless?"

He denies that too. "No, heck no."

"Well then, it's not your fault. When Mark was deployed, he had a chance to come home two weeks early if he took an especially dangerous mission. He called me and asked my opinion. Every single day he faced danger you and I don't even understand. Libya's still a mess, but it was beyond unstable then. He thought it was worth the risk to be home with me two weeks before the wedding. I told him he could do it."

I stare out the window at the piles of clean snow. "That ate me up for years," I whispered. "But you can't let it. Brekka doesn't blame you, and I finally decided that Mark wouldn't want me to blame myself. We shouldn't have taken that risk, but I can't change a decision we made now that I'm faced with the consequences. All I can do is make better decisions in the future, safer ones, more informed ones. And Brekka has to make her own decisions too. She can't live her life to help you feel better about yours."

When I look back toward him, he's scowling at the road.

"You have to let her decide, Trig. If she's happy with her life, celebrate that and let go of your desire to fix things."

"You can't let one bad thing that happens scare you into quitting," he says. "You and Brekka are both hiding."

"You don't even know me," I say quietly.

He doesn't argue, because it's true. After that, we don't talk the rest of the way to the airport.

I'm able to walk up to his shiny white jet on my own, but I don't decline Trig's hand when he extends it to help me up the stairs. His plane looks every bit as posh as I imagined it would inside. Huge tan leather chairs with little tables in between. Two sofas that look like they'd convert to beds near the back. A stewardess with an ear-to-ear grin who offers us drinks when we board.

I shake my head.

"No thanks Ivy, I'm good," Trig says.

She disappears into the cockpit, maybe to keep the pilot company.

"Sometimes I forget you're totally Richie Rich for like a second," I say. "And then I look around at the lavish, private jet I'm sitting in and I'm like, whoa."

Before he can reply, my phone rings. It's Rob and I know he's worried since I still haven't even taken the time to text him back. I hit the green button. "Rob, I'm fine."

"Thank goodness," he says. "What's going on? I saw that a blizzard hit Colorado and then I didn't hear from you. I was about two hours from taking the next plane out there to assemble a search and rescue team. You know, with one of those fluffy St. Bernard dogs that carries hot chocolate in a little cask under its neck."

With anyone else, I'd assume they were kidding. Rob probably had his bag packed and a friend or two on call.

"I'm sitting on a plane now," I say.

"The lady I talked to said the first flights don't leave for twenty minutes yet."

"That's right," I tell him. "But I'm on one of the first ones out."

"How'd you manage that?" he asks. "I figured peons like you and me would be the last ones to get through. Your new clients pull some strings for you?"

I glance over at Trig, who's smiling at me. "Something like that."

"We still on for tomorrow, then?"

I bob my head before I realize he can't see me. "No, yeah, we are. I'll be there. Same bat time, same bat station."

"Great. See you then. I've missed your voice."

"Me too," I say, and it's true.

Rob shores me up at my foundation. He always has, ever since we played that first game of kickball on Racine Street. He body checked a kid who slammed me in the face with a ball, and then helped me stand up. He's been doing the metaphorical equivalent ever since. When I fell in love with his best friend Mark, he cheered us on. And when Mark died, well. Rob kept my head up until I could tread water myself again, all while dealing with his own grief and his recovery. I missed Rob anytime I went without talking to him for more than a day or two.

"Was that Rob?" Trig asks.

I giggle. "Why do you care?"

"I don't," he says. "Just curious."

I lean back in my chair and close my eyes.

"It's going to be a pretty long flight," Trig says. "You going to take a nap?"

I crack one eye open. "Should I not?"

He taps his fingers on his armrest. "You can, absolutely. But then you might have trouble sleeping at home tonight."

I sit up. "True. What did you have in mind instead? I figured you'd be counting your money, or painting something in quick drying molten gold."

"Quick drying gold?" he asks. "Actually, I should look into that. I bet Natalie could promote it for me. The newest line of designer nail polish. Only $5,000 per ounce."

I roll my eyes. "We all know she would welcome your call."

"Which is one of the many reasons she'll never hear from me," he says.

"What were you planning, then?"

"How about a game to pass the time?"

"Please tell me you aren't thinking truth or dare," I say.

"I wasn't, but now that you mention it." He shifts closer. "Which would you pick?"

"I don't play that kind of game."

"What kind do you play?" he asks.

"Do you like chess?"

His eyes light up. "I do, even more than Monopoly, in fact. I actually have a chess set on the plane."

Why am I not surprised the math whiz likes chess? He stands up and walks across to a cabinet. He comes back with a wood carved chess board. When he sets it in front of me, I see it's actually quite cleverly made, with carved pegs in the bottom of each piece that fit into spaces on the board so they won't fall over or slide in turbulence.

He sets the board up on the table in between our seats. "White or black?" he asks, his eyes gleaming.

I don't mention that I won the Kids Chess Federation National tournament three years in a row. It doesn't seem relevant. But when he suggests we make the game more interesting, I don't turn him down, either.

"What did you have in mind?" I ask.

He shrugs. "I don't know. Winner gets a boon?"

"A boon?" I ask. "Did we get sucked into a medieval portal? Do you mean a favor?"

He grins at me. "Yes, a small favor from the loser. Anything within the power of that person to grant."

"Done," I say. "I wonder what I'll ask for. Maybe a new car. Or I know, a month at your chateau outside of Paris."

He smirks. "I don't have a chateau anywhere. That's like a castle owned by nobility, which I know because I've met some of those snobs."

"Cottage, log cabin, apartment, I'm not picky. I just want to eat my weight in crepes."

"Well, unfortunately I don't have a chalet or a cottage or anything of the kind near Paris. The people are too rude, and I get sick of food made with too much butter after a few days. But I do have an amazing villa in Florence. I'm not sure one chess game merits a month, but a long weekend, sure. And if you win and you get lonely over there, I can eat my weight in gelato, for the record."

I roll my eyes. "I bet you can."

I make the opening move, relishing the thought of making him squirm. Time slows as we both focus on the board, one move at a time, our brains whizzing many more ahead.

By the time I figure out his plan, it's too late. I'm glad I didn't mention my past success when he beats me.

"You're kidding me," I grumble. "I'm clearly rusty."

He stretches, his hands clasped and reaching far out in front of him. The way his lean frame arches up and out sends a little zing down my spine. I want to reach out and run one hand from his shoulder down to his forearm and interlace our fingers.

I sit back abruptly.

"I guess that weekend in Italy is out," he says. "And now the question is, what does Trig want from Geo?"

His eyes meet mine and shift downward, slightly, until he's staring at my mouth. I lick my lips compulsively, remembering the slopes in Vail.

"What do you want?" I ask, my mouth suddenly dry. "What could the man who already has everything possibly want from a poor little event planner?" I bat my eyes at him. "Isn't my pride enough?"

He leans back in his chair. "Not hardly. That was one of my hardest fought wins in years. I deserve something for it, and I want to know who this Rob guy is. And why you really wanted to get back to see him so badly."

His request startles me and I almost blurt out the first thing that comes into my head, the absolute truth. Luckily I catch myself in time. The last thing Trig needs to hear is my full sob story. The part about Mark is pathetic enough. "Rob's my best friend."

"I thought Paisley was your best friend," he counters.

"You've been paying attention," I say.

"Always," he says, his eyes intent on mine. "Occupational hazard, really. Details matter and my brain kind of tucks them away."

Mark couldn't even remember my favorite flavor of tea, much less the names of my friends from school. That thought feels disloyal somehow, and heat rises to my cheeks. "Well, Paisley's my best college friend and we've stayed in touch ever since. She's hilarious and I love her, but Rob's more like family I guess. My dad died and my mom, well, she's not very reliable. But Rob is. He's like the tides."

"Cold and full of crabs?" Trig asks.

I bark out a laugh. "No, and he's allergic to shellfish, actually. He's just rock solid and steady, and he's always there for me, no matter what I need."

"So he's like a dog, then? I'm guessing this guy delivers pizza or something, some job he can drop whenever something comes up and you crook your little finger."

I shake my head. "Actually he's a former Marine, but he was honorably discharged after an injury in the same operation where Mark, well. He came home and took over the family business."

"A mobster?" Trig's boyish smile is contagious.

"No," I say. "His family owns a couple of car dealerships in Atlanta."

Trig frowns.

"What's that look for? Not everyone can be worth three point six billion," I say.

"Barely over two billion, actually," he says. "And that's only if you include my trust fund."

"If you count the trust fund." I roll my eyes. "You do not live in the real world, Trig. And here in the real world, people need old friends. Which is what Rob is. Our weekly dinner isn't a date. It's at Macaroni Grill, for heaven's sake."

"Macaroni Grill?" Trig's eyebrows climb. "Seriously?"

"What's wrong with that?" I ask. "I love their bread and I love sun-dried tomatoes and Farfalle pasta."

"Is that why Rob goes?" Trig leans toward me, his

elbows falling to his knees, his head dropping down near mine. "He has a thing for sun dried tomatoes?"

"He loves their bread." I shrug. "Have you had it? I mean, really, who doesn't love their bread? Plus, you can color on the table."

Trig shakes his head slowly. "That's not what I'm asking. You know that and you owe me a real answer."

"Then yes, that's why Rob goes, to be my friend and to eat some comfort food. He's not interested in me romantically, like not at all, if that's what you're implying."

Trig snorts then, and when his eyes find mine, they're incredulous. "I very much doubt if you're on the same page in that regard."

"What does that mean?" I ask.

"Maybe he's just waiting for Cupid to fire a little arrow. I bet if you reached over and held his hand or blew him a kiss, you'd find out just how uninterested he is."

I scowl. "Rob doesn't want to kiss me. I promise you that."

"On the contrary, I think he does." Trig's eyes burn into mine. "I feel another bet coming on."

"You've never even met him, so your opinion is worth exactly zero cents. Probably the only thing of yours that's worthless."

"But I've met *you*," he says. "And you're the funniest, the most particular, the most demanding, and the most breathtakingly gorgeous woman I've ever met. Plus, you have this energy about you that I can't even begin to explain. I only know it draws me in like a magnetic field."

"I've known Rob for twenty years, and he's never complimented my looks. Not one single time."

"Then he's a moron, and probably even more smitten than I thought. But I find I don't want to talk about Rob anymore." Trig slides forward in his seat until only inches separate us.

"Is your seatbelt fastened?" My hands are suddenly both jittery and inexplicably clammy.

He grins. "Is yours?"

"Of course."

"Then it's good that mine isn't, or I couldn't do this." Trig closes the inches between us before I have time to think about it. His lips cover mine smoothly, his hands settling on top of my thighs and I lean into him, limited only by the seatbelt keeping me safely in place.

When my hand slides up to his jaw, pulling his face tighter against mine, he groans and whispers against my mouth. "Skip your dinner tomorrow and go out with me instead."

I want to unbuckle my seatbelt and crawl onto Trig's lap. I want to slide my hand between the buttons on his shirt. I want to devour him from the inside out and then lick my lips.

But that's stupid, and I've obviously forgotten everything I ever learned. It takes every ounce of control I have to pull back and away.

"I can't do that. And I don't think I should see you again at all, honestly."

Emotions flash across his face so quickly I can't pinpoint any single one. "If that's really what you want."

"It is," I say, before I can change my mind.

But if it's true, then why does the next forty-five minutes stretch so painfully against my skin, as though I'm sinking into the sands of the Sahara?

Because I've let myself get in too far already, that's why. The only solution for that is to cut Trig off entirely. Once I get off this plane, I'll come up with excuses not to see him.

I absolutely must not, under any circumstance, see him again before the wedding.

Of course, that doesn't stop me from googling Bernard Thornton the Third as soon as I reach my home Wi-Fi network. The first fifty hits are about his many many many deals, and Nometry, the name of his venture capital firm, is mentioned repeatedly in each article. Brekka's beside him in most of those photos, the images of the last three years carefully cropped so you can't tell she's in a wheelchair.

Guilt pricks at my conscience when I think about my plan to cut Trig off. That means I'll never see Brekka again either. I glance at my new Prada boots, staring at me accusingly from the floor near my closet.

Although, it's not like I need to be dating Trig to stay friends with Brekka. Sweet, wickedly smart, fragile Brekka, who needs friends as badly as I do. Friends I need. Trig, whatever he wants, I don't need. Which makes me wonder what I'd find under that name. If anything.

I type 'Trig Thornton' into the search engine and a completely different type of photos appear.

Over and over and over.

So many photos I find myself clicking through them at an alarming rate. I've never understood why my friends spent so much time poring over tabloids, but maybe I get it a little bit now. I can't seem to stop looking at the photos of Trig.

He's doing something insane in every single one.

Skydiving.

Extreme skiing after a helicopter drop.

Surfing dangerously tall waves in the open ocean.

Executing insane skateboard aerials with a bunch of teenagers on a random Saturday night.

Swimming with sharks.

On safari in Africa.

Motocross.

NASCAR.

He's done every single thing I've ever thought was moronic. And he's done them all a lot of times. Enough to be splashed across my screen in hundreds of photos. There's actually an entire website some idiotic twenty-year-old girl runs for Trig sightings. They vote each month on the hottest image of him.

I guess I should have expected something like this. He is a billionaire after all, and there aren't many single billionaires, much less ones under forty who look like he does.

I slam the laptop shut with disgust. How could I be so stupid, spending that much time with anyone, much less someone like him, practically dating him, letting him kiss me. I deserve the pain in my chest right now, every agonizing, stabbing second of it. I couldn't have picked a dumber person to develop a crush on. A billionaire with a wickedly handsome smile who does his best to kill himself every day, and twice on Sunday.

I brush my teeth and go to bed, determined not to dream about Trig or spend another minute thinking about how his hair curls around his temples, or how his lips feel pressed against my forehead or curled into a smile against my mouth.

Too bad we can't control our dreams.

10

TRIG

I should fly back to Colorado instead of laying around like a loser at the Hyatt in Atlanta. Brekka's got a huge list of possible deals I should be digging through.

I pull out my phone to text my pilot so I can tell him wheels up in an hour.

I find myself texting Brekka instead. SEND ME THE FILES VIA EMAIL. I'M GONNA BE IN ATLANTA A FEW MORE DAYS.

OF COURSE YOU ARE, she texts back.

IT'S NOT LIKE THAT. GEO DOESN'T WANT TO SEE ME ANY MORE. And I have a strange desire to order everything off the room service menu just so I can pick at it all.

WHAT DID YOU DO?

I almost drop my phone. What did I do? Whose side is she on? I DIDN'T DO ANYTHING.

MAYBE THAT'S THE PROBLEM. YOU JUST EXPECT HER TO FALL INTO YOUR LAP.

I wish Brekka was here so I could glare at her properly. Emojis aren't the same.

Although, the thought of Geo in my lap isn't a bad one. I shake my head. I DON'T EXPECT HER TO FALL IN MY LAP, BUT SHE DUMPED ME. BEFORE WE WERE EVEN TOGETHER. FOR NO REASON WHATSOEVER.

TRIG. ALMOST EVERYONE IN AMERICA GETS DUMPED "FOR NO REASON." IT MEANS THEY AREN'T TELLING YOU THE REASON.

WHY WOULDN'T SHE TELL ME THE REASON? I ask reasonably.

Eyes upward emoji. WELCOME TO THE NORMAL WORLD BROTHER. I GUESS WHEN A SPOILED BILLIONAIRE DATES A WICKED SMART SUPER-MODEL, THE TYPICALLY IMBALANCED PLAYING FIELD IS LEVELED. I WON'T LIE AND SAY I'M NOT ENJOYING THIS.

I want to throw my phone against the wall, but I'm not a toddler. I don't throw tantrums. My fingers fly furiously over the keys instead. WHY AM I IN SUCH A FUNK ABOUT IT? IT'S NOT LIKE I WANTED TO MARRY HER OR ANYTHING. I WAS JUST TRYING TO HELP HER OUT.

WHAT COULD SHE POSSIBLY NEED FROM YOU?

I roll my eyes. There should be a rolling eyes emoji. I wonder if there is. I search for one and the closest I can find is the eyes looking up one that Brekka way over uses. GEO COULDN'T BE MORE UPTIGHT IF SHE TRIED. SHE NEVER HAS ANY FUN. SHE NEVER DATES. CLEARLY SHE NEVER GOT OVER LOSING THAT GUY. I JUST FIGURED I'D HELP HER GET OUT THERE AGAIN.

Those stupid three dots appear and sit on my screen for what feels like forever before Brekka's reply finally pops up. She must have typed something and deleted it more than once, because her response is quite short. YOU'RE A MORON.

EXCUSE ME?

No reply.

THANKS FOR YOUR HELPFUL SISTERLY INSIGHT. SEND ME THE FILES.

The next few lines pop up so fast I know she's been working on them for a bit. THAT GIRL WAS INJURED, AND HER INJURY IS AS REAL AS MINE. IF SHE DOESN'T WANT TO PUT HERSELF OUT THERE WITH THE BUNCH OF MISCREANT LOSERS WHO ARE SINGLE AT THIRTY, WELL, SHE'S JUSTIFIED. BUT SHE LIKES YOU, B. AND IF YOU STRING HER ALONG AND DUMP HER, YOU BETTER NOT TELL YOURSELF IT'S A FAVOR FOR HER.

At least I always know what Brekka's thinking. She never pulls punches. UH, OKAY. GOT IT. DONT' STRING HER ALONG.

I MEAN IT. I LOVE YOU B, YOU KNOW I DO. PROBABLY MORE THAN ANYONE ELSE IN THE WORLD, BUT IF YOU HURT HER, I'M GONNA SLAP YOUR PRETTY FACE THE NEXT TIME I SEE YOU. IF YOU BLOW THIS, IT'S BECAUSE YOU'RE A COWARD. YOU'RE MANY THINGS, BUT I NEVER THOUGHT TO INCLUDE THAT BEFORE NOW.

Her words sting, and that pisses me off. HEARD FROM RUTLEDGE YESTERDAY. SHOULD I SET UP YOUR SURGERY FOR NEXT WEEK, WHILE WE'RE PLACING SO MUCH VALUE ON BRAVERY?

Her text back to me isn't lady-like at all. I toss my phone onto the bed in disgust.

Why didn't I just text my pilot? I hate fighting with Brekka. Other than the surgeries she keeps refusing, we almost never fight, and this one's on me. I picked that fight with her. She was just trying to help.

I reach for my phone again, determined to get out of here and shake off this ennui that's settled over me. I'm probably just struggling because I'm in between deals and bored. I really need to review those files.

Except once I have my hands on my phone again, I still don't text the pilot. My fingers, against my will, text Luke and Paul.

DINNER TONIGHT?

Luke replies within seconds. YOU'RE STILL HERE? MAYBE MARY'S SMARTER THAN YOU THOUGHT. Laughing emoji, dang the man.

Then Luke texts again. I'D LOVE TO, BUT I CAN'T. RECITAL FOR AMY. RAIN CHECK?

Paul texts a minute later. I CAN GO. FINISHED SOME THINGS UP EARLY. WHERE YOU THINKING?

I'VE BEEN CRAVING ITALIAN, I text.

PORTOFINO? BOCCALUPO? Paul asks.

ACTUALLY, I WAS KIND OF THINKING MACARONI GRILL. I hold my breath.

ARE YOU KIDDING ME?

I wish I was. SIX PM. ALPHARETTA.

NO WAY. IF I'M EATING FRANCHISE FOOD, YOU'RE COMING TO ME. MARIETTA. SEE YOU AT SIX, Paul texts back.

I check the map on my phone and swear. It didn't even occur to me there might be more than one Macaroni Grill in Atlanta, which is epically stupid. I don't know what time Geo's meal is, and now I have no idea whether I'll even be at the right location. This is looking like a complete waste of time. Although she was pretty clear about not seeing me again. So maybe striking out is better than actually finding her. Barging in on her non-date might be even more idiotic than moping around a hotel room in a city I should have left already. I wonder what Brekka would say about my stalker-adjacent plans, but I don't wonder enough to ask.

She might warn Geo.

The rest of the day crawls along, but luckily Brekka sends me the files. I dig into them, glad of something to distract me from thinking about sapphire eyes and shiny black hair. Two options are promising, one predictably in San Francisco, and the other in Hawaii. Not horrible places to travel at least.

I text Brekka and tell her to set up a meeting in both places later this week.

Without Brekka here to give me her opinion, I drag the housekeeping girls into my room and make them share their thoughts on my different button down shirt options.

"Yes, she'll like that one," one of them says about my blue shirt.

"No, no," the other says. "The green is better with his eyes."

The first girl shrugs. "If she doesn't like either one, you could always take me out."

She leaves her number on the Hyatt notepad on the desk before she leaves. I feel a little guilty tossing it in the trash, knowing she'll see it there. I fish it out and flush it down the toilet instead. Then I worry about what it might do to the plumbing.

I can't win lately.

I reach Macaroni Grill thirty minutes early, possibly because I'm a little nervous I'll miss her. If we're even in the right location. Why are there so many Macaroni Grills in Atlanta? I should have had my assistant look up her event planning business address to find out where her office is located. Odds are good she'd go to the closest one. Or maybe the one that's closest to Rob.

This is starting to feel a little creepy, even to me. I could have just texted her, I guess. Except if she shuts me down again, I don't know how I can work around that.

I'm on my second drink when Paul finally shows up, ten minutes late. He's got the top few buttons undone of his shirt like he thinks he's a young David Hasselhoff.

"Nice shirt," I say. "But you don't really get your money's worth out of it when you don't use all the buttons."

"Shut up," Paul says. "Since when do you like Macaroni Grill? You made fun of me incessantly in college for liking T.G.I. Fridays."

He's right, I did. I shrug. "I'm craving sun-dried tomatoes. So sue me."

He frowns. "Do they have some kind of monopoly on sun-dried tomatoes I didn't hear about?"

"Chill, dude. You'll survive one meal at a chain restaurant."

He orders a drink and turns around to face me. "So weren't you in Atlanta just last week? Why are you back already? Looking at a tech company here? And what does Mary have to do with it?"

I forgot how annoying Paul is. He doesn't do social niceties, like at all. "Good to see you too. How's the launch coming?"

"You don't want to talk about why you're here?" Paul's left eyebrow lifts.

"I want to talk about you," I say. "I saw Luke last week, but you were too busy. We haven't caught up in forever."

He stares at me like he's running a lie detector on my words. I hope that's not some kind of new tech he's testing. Surely I'd have heard of it.

"Your table is ready," the hostess tells us.

Thank goodness. We follow her to a table near the left side of the restaurant. It's not ideal. I can really only see about half of the room.

Although, as it turns out, I could have been sitting most anywhere. The waiter had just brought us our bowls of pasta when Geo walks in the door. Every guy in the room turns and drools when she walks in wearing an absurdly tight red dress and the black boots Brekka just gave her. She's standing next to a table in the middle of the restaurant, waiting for them to change the paper on her table, when the guy with her says something funny.

She laughs and touches his chest and I find myself half standing, ready to cross the room and tell him to back off.

"Uh, what's going on?" Paul follows my eyes across the room. "She's really hot. Do you know her?"

He turns back to me, and I try to play it casual, but I can't take my eyes off her.

"So that's why we're here? We're stalking some girl? That's not like you." Paul looks like a cat munching at long last on the family goldfish. "How the mighty have fallen."

That grabs my attention. "I'm not stalking her, okay? I heard she was meeting some guy here, and he sounded kind of, I don't know, suspect."

Paul turns back to the table. "You're worried about the huge, muscly Channing Tatum look-a-like guy she's with? What exactly are you going to do if he's suspect? Pay him to go away? Hire someone else to beat him up?"

"You think he looks like Channing Tatum?" I bite down on a mouthful of pasta and force myself to chew. "Some stuff Geo said about him made me think maybe he was dangerous."

Paul's eyebrows rise. "Wait, Geo? That name's weird and it sounds familiar."

I grit my teeth.

He snaps. "Geode Polson. That's Luke's irritatingly persistent wedding planner, right?"

I nod tightly.

Paul swears. "I've dodged about four calls from her. She wants to meet about the wedding. Guess I should call her back, huh? Since you've clearly already struck out."

He presses his lips together smugly and I want to throw my bowl of pasta at him. Paul has always been a little obnoxious, but usually his stupid comments roll off me. What's wrong with me tonight?

"Okay, fine. I'll ease up. But fill me in. You met Luke's freaking gorgeous wedding planner and you want to hook up, but she's playing hard to get. Is that it?"

I scowl at him. "No, I mean, she's friends with Brekka and so I'm looking out for her as a favor to my sister. That's all."

"Wait, how is she friends with Brekka?" Paul asks.

"She got snowed in while she was checking out Vail as a venue."

"And you have that cabin there. Brekka was there too?" He whistles low under his breath. "That must have been a little annoying. In terms of you putting the moves on her."

"Stop being gross. I don't even like her, not like that. I already said. I'm doing Brekka a favor."

Paul puts his fork down and crosses his arms. "You're telling me we came to a Macaroni Grill, the first chain restaurant I've ever seen you drive to voluntarily, and the chronically late Trig came early too, just so that we can make sure some guy doesn't punch her in a public place as a favor to your sister, who she just met. Is that right?"

Paul's words force me to examine my behavior. I'm acting kind of crazy. What am I really doing here?

"Fine. Let's say I buy that beach front property in

Nebraska. Explain why you've been staring at her nonstop since she walked inside if you don't like her."

I jerk my eyes back toward him. "I haven't been staring."

He rolls his eyes and jerks a thumb back toward Geo's table. "The guy she's with has a Semper Fi tattoo on his arm. I'm guessing that means he's a Marine. Tell me our plan here. Because I'm sure not going to throw down with that Marine, and I don't know whether I have enough cash on me to pay the restaurant when he breaks a table with your face, either."

"Fine," I say. "I have no real reason to suspect he's a jerk, okay? He's supposed to be her oldest friend, but I think he likes her. And maybe I think about her a little bit more than I should."

Paul's belly laugh annoys me.

"I'm glad someone's amused at how crazy I sound."

Paul nods. "Actually you sound human. For the first time since college, I might genuinely like you right now."

"That makes one of us," I mutter.

"Are you insulting me with that, or yourself?" Paul asks.

I hate how literal and annoying Paul always is, but I appreciate him pulling me out of my funk. "You're kind of a jerk, but I'm glad you're here tonight to tell me what a moron I'm being." I pull my phone out. "I'm texting my pilot right now to tell him I'm ready to head back home."

Paul slaps my hand. "Absolutely not. I've known you for fifteen years and I've never seen you do a single thing beyond a casual 'Wassup' to pursue any girl. There's no way I'm leaving this restaurant without meeting that woman."

"Absolutely not," I say. "If you think I'm acting crazy, Geo definitely will. I'm sitting right here until she leaves."

Paul laughs again. "Suit yourself."

When he stands up, I want to sink into the floor and

disappear. I hate Paul. My options are to follow him over and act like it's all a coincidence, or. . . Maybe I could hide in the bathroom. In which case I have no idea what Paul might say to Geo about me, or why we're here.

I'm definitely telling all my friends to boycott his stupid five pound car battery.

I leap from my seat and rush after Paul. When Geo looks up at me, her eyes widen and her lips compress. Not a great sign.

"Trig? What are you doing here?"

"I asked him to meet me over here on my side of town for dinner," Paul says.

That was pretty smooth. I almost forgive Paul for being an irritating idiot.

"But then he glances over here and sees you. He says he knows you," Paul says, "and I realize you've been calling me and I've been a flake. I insisted on coming over to introduce myself." He holds out his hand. "I'm Paul Manning, Luke's better and much younger brother. I hear you're Geode Polson, wedding planner extraordinaire."

Rob's sitting across from Geo, and at Paul's words, he grins at her. "Wait, you're planning a wedding? Why didn't you tell me?"

She blushes and I wonder why.

"I am," she says, "but only because Luke and Mary offered me enough to nearly pay for the Phineas Enrollment."

Phineas Enrollment? What's that? I make a mental note to look it up.

Rob's eyes widen and he reaches over to touch her. I want to grab a fork and jab it into his meaty hand. Judging from his tattoo, which does indeed say Semper Fi, and his muscles, and the small scar on his jaw, that would probably be the last thing I ever did.

"How much time do you have left?" Rob asks her. "Because I'll make up the difference if you need me to—"

Geo waves her hand at him and shakes her head in tandem, cutting him off before he can say anything more helpful. It has the look of a reaction to an old discussion, which piques my curiosity even more. She turns toward Paul, standing up and holding out her hand. She specifically doesn't meet my eyes, which leaves my stomach in knots. "It's so nice to finally meet you. I've heard so many good things about you from Luke."

Paul takes her hand and keeps it for a few seconds too long. "The pleasure's all mine. Normally I could simply pick a date and meet you for lunch, but with the launch and another side project, I've been running mad. I'm under strict orders not to plan anything without making sure it doesn't conflict with the rest. I'll have my secretary confirm which day next week will work and reach out to you for lunch. Please forgive me for being so rude, and I'm so sorry to interrupt your date tonight."

Rob stands up. "Oh don't worry. It's not a date, just a weekly dinner with a friend. I'm Robert Graham, Geo's oldest friend."

Paul's an evil genius. He smoothed things over and got Rob to admit this isn't a date, all while looking like a good guy.

"Oldest?" Paul asks. "You don't look much older than twenty."

Rob chuckles, a low sound in his chest. "Twenty-seven. One year older than Geo. Old enough to run four car dealerships. Which is probably nothing to the two of you, but it keeps me busy."

Paul points at the tattoo on his arm. "And a Marine to boot."

Rob nods in an irritatingly tough way. Like he eats rocks

for lunch. Or maybe walks to work across the snapping snouts of crocodiles. I hate him even more in person. "I was honorably discharged after half my task force died and I took shrapnel to my back."

My eyebrows rise. "You seem fine now, thankfully."

He shrugs. "Four surgeries later and untold hours of physical therapy and I get by. Docs say I'm lucky I was young and healthy when it happened. Still have some hardware in my back, but the bones fused again and the spinal cord was intact."

Geo takes his hand in hers. "Rob had those four surgeries over the course of three weeks. Every time I was a wreck, sitting at the hospital and praying. I almost never pray."

Rob laughs. "She was worse than my mom." He turns toward me. "I've met Paul, but I haven't met you yet. What's your name?"

"I'm Trig," I say, extending my hand in the hope that he'll drop Geo's.

He does, and I breathe a small sigh of relief.

"Trig you say? What a unique name. And I may be reading it wrong, but it seems like you know Geo."

"I gave her a ride back home so she could be here tonight," I say. "And she stayed at my cabin last weekend near Vail." I'm irritated he doesn't already know who I am. Why wouldn't Geo have mentioned me to her oldest friend?

Rob's eyes widen. "You don't say." He grins at Geo then. "You may have shared an edited version of events with me, G. I wonder why."

"I keep asking her out," I say. "But she insists she doesn't date. And even though you said it's not, this sure seems like a date to me."

"One time." Geo's eyes flash. "You asked me out one

time. And I told you I don't date a million times because it's true."

"Well, if you're not going out with Trig tomorrow night, I'd be happy to meet with you over dinner instead of lunch," Paul says. "I'm sure I can clear my schedule for that."

I'm going to punch him, I swear.

"That should work, actually," Geo says, smiling at me sideways.

"No, it won't." I have an epiphany. "Because you owe me a boon."

She shakes her head. "I paid up."

"Oh please," I say. "You answered one question. You were going to ask me for a weekend in Italy. I hardly think my little question and what you planned to request are comparable."

She purses her lips. "What do you want?"

"One date," I say. "Break your rule for one single date with me, and if you never want to go out again, we're even."

She puts one hand on her hip and looks me straight in the eyes.

"What are you afraid of?" I ask.

She scowls. "Nothing. Fine. One dinner."

"So you're dating again?" Rob asks. "This is big news, and also, it's about time."

What if she hasn't ever dated her oldest, muscliest, most masculine friend who owns lots of car dealerships because she doesn't date at all? If she goes out once, does that end her rule, so she can date Rob? Or maybe I just introduced her to Pretty Boy Paul and broke her hiatus so the two of them could hook up. They both live in Atlanta already.

My pasta isn't sitting very well.

I don't know why, because I don't care whether she

dates someone else. Or, actually I do. I'm obviously helping her get out there, which has always been my only goal. Brekka should be proud of me. Maybe it'll make up for the borderline stalking today.

As if he can read my thoughts, Rob clears his throat. "What a happy accident you two wound up at Macaroni Grill the same time as us."

Geo's eyebrows draw together.

Paul says, "Not so odd. I live like two miles away, and I love sun-dried tomatoes." He winks at me.

"I love them too," Geo says. "And I live less than two miles from here as well."

"Small world." Paul grins at me. "Also, how convenient. Even if you're busy tomorrow, don't be a stranger. We can get together anytime at all, really. You could bike over to my house. I live in Chattahoochee Plantation, right on the river."

"By the Atlanta Country Club Estates?" she asks.

Paul nods. "Exactly."

"I love that area," Geo says. "It's so gorgeous. I live in the Riverview Condos, right around the corner from you."

"You don't say," Paul says. "I jog in Chattahoochee park with my dog several times a week."

"I go jogging too! I bet I've passed you and never even noticed."

"I think I'd remember you," he says. "I jog in the morning."

She shakes her head. "I usually jog after work. Too many client and vendor meetings in the mornings."

"Maybe I'll aim for an evening jog now and then," he says. "Couldn't hurt."

"And you have a dog?" She grins. "I love dogs. Luke mentioned your backyard is the fallback reception spot.

Maybe I should come take a look at it, and I can meet him or her."

"Him," Paul says. "Sir Winston, but I call him Winny because he's so whiny. He whimpers a lot whenever he isn't in my lap. He's a golden lab, so he's way too big to be sitting on people. You're welcome to come check out my yard anytime, but I'd love it if you came while I was home so I could show you around and keep an eye on my overly exuberant fur ball."

Another five minutes and they'll be picking out china patterns. "We better let you two get back to your evening," I say. "I'll text you to work out details of our date tomorrow."

Geo nods her head. "Sure, text me."

"That reminds me," Paul says. "I don't have your cell number handy."

Geo raises one eyebrow. "I left it on your voicemail enough times."

"Duh," Paul says. "I'll grab it from there."

Seeing her treating Paul with the same critical skepticism she showed me the first time we met reminds me that I've moved past that. She knows me.

She's kissed me.

I take a big step toward Geo and pull her toward me for a quick hug. "Those boots look amazing," I whisper into her ear. "Glad they fit."

Her breathing hitches in a way I adore, and I let her go.

I pay the check and walk with Paul out to his car without picking a fight. I consider that a major accomplishment. But I can't quite help saying something when he climbs into his Lotus.

"I appreciate you taking the heat for being at Macaroni Grill tonight."

Paul smiles. "That conversation was possibly the most fun I've had in months."

"Glad you enjoyed yourself," I say, "but I like Geo. So back off, okay?"

Paul's smile doesn't waver. "She's not really my type, but I'll make an exception. You can't really want me to quit trying? It's no fun to win by default."

"Be serious."

"I am serious," Paul says. "That was fun back there. May the best man win."

He slams the door and I regret not punching him when I had a clear shot.

11

GEO

"It's about time you finally went on a date," Rob says. "Because no matter what Trig suspects, our weekly dinners here aren't dates. You haven't been on a date since Mark died, have you? Not one."

I shake my head. "This isn't a date either, not really. I'm just letting him take me to dinner because he beat me."

Rob raises one eyebrow. "You're going to have to explain that one for me."

"Fine, so we played chess." I let that sink in.

"Wait, he played you in chess?"

I nod.

"And he beat you?" Rob doesn't believe me.

"No one beats me, I know. But he did."

He swears. "So he's rich and he's smart."

I shrug. "I guess so. I mean, he was born rich, but I think he's actually done quite a lot himself. I don't think he just spends his trust fund."

"Like I said. I'm glad you're finally dating."

I shake my head. "It's not a date. I'd never have agreed to go out with him if I actually liked him."

"That may be the dumbest thing you've ever said," Rob says. "And I was around for your Pokémon years."

"Shut up," I say. "Pokémon is awesome."

"That's a controversial position," Rob says with a smile. "But I'll let it slide. The point is, in case you're feeling guilty at all, I'd be remiss if I didn't tell you that Mark would be proud of you." He pauses until I meet his eyes. "I'm proud of you."

I toss my napkin on the table. "You're supposed to be making me feel better today. That's the whole point of having these stupid Monday dinners instead of just going over the dealership stuff at your office."

"I'm not trying to pick a fight, G. Seriously, I'm not. But it is past time for you to be out there meeting people. Rich people, handsome people, funny people. You won't find someone you like if you never date at all. It's the only way to do what you need to do." He leans toward me and emphasizes each word. "Move on with your life."

"I'm not moving on," I say. "I'm never moving on. I can't. Mark didn't dump me." My voice cracks when I say, "He died."

"I was there," Rob says. "I'm aware."

"Then you should leave me alone about it. It's my life, not yours, and it's not like you've moved on. Name one date you've been on since you got back."

"I thought you'd remember this, but for the first year after my discharge, I did five hours of PT every morning and spent the next five hours curled into a fetal position. Every day." Rob scowls.

"Valid," I say. "And I do remember. I brought you food every single day. I know. But the next three years?"

"I'm not Croesus," he says. "But I run a huge business locally. And I have friends. I've taken a few girls out, but none have struck my fancy."

"I'm sorry, did you just say fancy?" I giggle.

"My point is that I have dated."

"You never mentioned that to me."

He shrugs. "I haven't really liked any of them. But I would move on if I could."

"I'm seeking joy too. Just in other areas."

He shakes his head. "No, that's not a valid argument. It's not zero sum. You should be seeking joy in all areas. It's been brutal, but I recovered from that accident and I'm living in the world every day. But you weren't even there and it's like you died with him, except you're still here. You need to crawl out of that hole and learn to live again."

I hold up my hand. "I'm rubber and you're glue. Everything you say to me bounces off of me and sticks to you."

But Rob doesn't laugh like he usually would. "It's not funny. You're hiding and it's killing me to watch it."

I fume. "Hello Pot. I'm kettle. You're black."

"Fine. I haven't been on just one date," Rob says. "I've been on hundreds."

I gasp. "When? You're always at home when I call, or hanging out with me."

He stares at me flatly. "Exactly."

"You just said these aren't dates."

"I said I would move on if I could, and I meant I've been wanting to move on with you. These dinners, or going to movies, or getting ice cream, they aren't dates for you, but they are for me."

I have no idea how to reply to that.

"I've loved you for years, G. I don't expect you to respond, because I realized something tonight. You don't love me like that, not even a little bit, and you never will."

My mouth drops open. I have no idea how to respond.

"You lit up when you saw that tall guy. In a way you've never, ever done when you saw me. I never even saw you look at Mark that way, if I'm being honest, which clearly I am tonight. That realization hurt, but thinking of you shutting down for the rest of your life hurts more. I love you too much to let that happen."

Rob stands up and tosses a hundred dollar bill on the table. "I'll always be here for you Geo, but I'm done pining. You should move on, too."

I'm not sure how long I sit at the table, staring at that hundred. When I finally stand up and walk out, I don't notice much about the people or cars around me.

How could I have been so blind? Rob, who's basically an older brother to me, who taught me to ride a bike, who I told about my first kiss with Mark, who held me while I cried on his shoulder in the hospital for months, who has taken me to dinner to sob about my mom for years, Rob loves me?

I only feel guilt that I never even noticed.

I am a horrible person.

When I get home, I try to finalize some suggestion pages for Mary, but I can't focus on them. I keep glancing at my closet, wondering what I should wear tomorrow. On my date with Trig.

Because Rob's right. I'm looking forward to it. But Rob's wrong that Mark would be pleased. I'm sure Mark's looking down at me right now in disgust. I know I would be.

And even knowing that, I still feel an embarrassing amount of excitement about seeing Trig tomorrow. I might have even checked my phone fifteen times to see whether he's texted me yet. I stand up and get a big glass of water. I clean up my family room. And my bedroom.

When my fingers get too itchy, to avoid texting Trig, I text his sister.

WORE THE BOOTS TONIGHT. LOVE THEM SO MUCH. I'M LUCKY TO BE YOUR CHARITY CASE.

Brekka texts back right away. TRIG TOLD ME HE RAN INTO YOU AND THE BOOTS LOOKED AMAZING. GLAD THEY'RE GETTING SOME USE.

So much for my thought that he hasn't texted me yet because he's driving. He's already texted Brekka. I want to ask her what else he said. I want to push for information, which is totally unlike me. I suppress the urge. Sort of.

SHOULD I SEND YOU THAT PREPAID POSTAGE NOW?

I had to text her back. It would be rude not to, and that's not about Trig. Although it is kind of beating the dead horse of what was only a mediocre joke to begin with. Actually mediocre was probably generous.

I hate this kind of social stuff.

BETTER YET, COME BACK OUT FOR A VISIT.

I grin. I'VE KIND OF GOT A WEDDING TO PLAN.

WEDDING, SCHMEDDING. COME SKI.

YOU CAN'T EVEN SKI. I text, and then I wish I hadn't hit send. Did I just offend her?

YOU CAN SKI FOR ME. I MAKE TRIG DO EVERYTHING I CAN'T. BUT THE THINGS HE CAN'T DO BECAUSE HE'S NOT A GIRL, MAYBE I'LL MAKE YOU DO THOSE.

LIKE WHAT? I ask.

LIKE GO ON A HOT DATE.

She knows. My fingers hover over the keys on my phone. I want to ask her what Trig said, but her loyalty is clearly to him. This is a really dangerous conversation. Brekka's really nice, but I need to keep in mind she's with the enemy.

I text back and hit send before I can change my mind. I HAVE ONE PLANNED FOR TOMORROW.

Two can play the vague game. Chew on that, Brekka.

I HOPE THE GUY IS GOOD ENOUGH FOR YOU.

ME TOO, I text back.

WHAT ARE YOU GOING TO WEAR?

I tap my lip. NO IDEA. NOT SURE WHERE WE'RE GOING YET.

WHAT KIND OF GUY HASN'T TOLD YOU? ROB? TEXT HIM RIGHT NOW AND TELL HIM THAT'S RUDE.

Is it possible Trig told her he saw me, but didn't tell her we had a date?

WHY DON'T YOU TELL HIM FOR ME.

WAIT, HOLD THE PHONE. IS TRIG TAKING YOU OUT? she asks.

When I don't reply, dots appear. I sip on my water.

BECAUSE HE SHOULD KNOW BETTER, she says. I HAVE FAILED YOU, BUT NEVER FEAR. I'LL FIX IT. ALSO. Love eyes emoji. THIS IS VERY EXCITING.

Twenty seconds later, my phone bings with a text from Trig. I laugh out loud. I might be a little in love with Brekka.

APPARENTLY YOU'VE BEEN TEXTING MY SISTER. I GUESS THAT MEANS YOUR DATE'S OVER?

IT WASN'T A DATE, I text.

I WAS TRYING TO GIVE YOU SOME TIME TO BE POLITE. BUT JUST SO YOU KNOW, THAT GUY LURVES YOU.

Trig might be more insightful than I give him credit for. In any case, I'm not discussing Rob with him.

I'M HOME.

WHAT ARE YOU WEARING? He sends me the same heart eyes emoji his sister just sent, which is frankly kind of odd.

GRANNY PANTIES AND A FOOTED SLEEPER.

MY FAVORITE, he texts back. SPEAKING OF CLOTHING, I FIGURED YOU MIGHT WANT TO KNOW WHAT TO WEAR TOMORROW.

MIGHT BE HELPFUL. I sip more water.

FOOTED SLEEPERS ARE ALWAYS A GOOD OPTION. BUT THAT MIGHT BE BULKY UNDER YOUR NEW BOOTS.

I snort the water out of my nose. MIGHT BE AT THAT.

The dots appear and I patiently wait. DINNER AND A MOVIE IS A LITTLE BORING FOR ME.

WHAT DID YOU HAVE IN MIND? I ask.

IF YOU'RE ABLE TO GET AWAY EARLY ENOUGH, WE COULD GO SKYDIVING. LAST TIME I ONLY SPRAINED YOUR KNEE. I FIGURE IF I'M LUCKY, I COULD AT LEAST BREAK YOUR ANKLE.

HARD PASS. In fact, I should be begging off from this date entirely. The fact that he thinks I might go skydiving...

I WAS KIDDING.

I sigh in relief.

HOW ABOUT A BRAZILIAN STEAKHOUSE? I HEAR CHAMA GAÚCHA IS DECENT.

SURE. I LOVE THE GUYS WITH SWORDS, I text.

PERFECT. SHOOT ME YOUR ADDRESS AND I'LL PICK YOU UP AT SIX.

After that, I brush my teeth and climb into bed. I'm drifting off when Mark's face floats to the surface. Rob might think Mark would want me to move on, but how could Mark want me to move on? It's so unfair that he's dead, and I'm going out to fancy dinners.

Without him.

I dream that night about a chess game between Mark and Trig. They keep making the wrong moves, and I yell at them both, but neither of them can hear me.

Because I'm dead instead.

When I wake up, I wonder what it means, but for the life of me, I can't figure out what.

12
TRIG

I love puzzles, always have. It may be one of the reasons I'm so good at my job. Which is why, when Geo handed me a puzzle piece, I jumped on it right away.

The Phineas Enrollment.

I spend two hours looking for anything that Geo could have been talking about and turn up nothing that might fit. There are public schools in Boston and California by that name, but even if she had a kid at fifteen, the child would only be eleven, so that can't be it.

Phineas is apparently a character in a dumb Disney cartoon, but how would that factor into anything? And what does that have to do with an enrollment? Some kind of Disney class or experience? Would that cost a small fortune?

I search medical trials for back surgeries on the off chance it has something to do with Rob, but honestly if it had to do with that, I'd have heard of it before. I've spent countless hours over the past few years obsessively looking up medical options for Brekka. Plus, Rob definitely acted like he was offering Geo a favor, not the other way around.

Finally I text Luke. HOW MUCH ARE YOU PAYING GEO FOR ORGANIZING YOUR WEDDING?

Maybe the amount they're paying her will give me an idea. Could it be some kind of college or course offering she wants to take herself? Maybe she has aspirations that differ from running her own event planning company. She said she knew Paisley from Emory, so she's probably already graduated from undergraduate. Grad school? She seems to love her job, but she's not exactly forthcoming.

Luke takes his sweet time to reply, which I assume means he checked in with Mary to make sure he could share with me. He's such a goodie two shoes. Be a man, Luke.

A HUNDRED GRAND. WHY?

COUSIN WANTS TO DO A WEDDING. WANTED TO KNOW THE GOING RATE. Lie lie lie. Can't let Luke know I'm borderline obsessed with his adorable wedding planner.

IN COLORADO?

I only have two cousins and they're both married already, so I hope Luke drops this or it might get awkward fast. I really should have thought up a better lie.

NAH, NEW YORK. At least that's true.

I THINK WE MIGHT BE OVERPAYING HER, BUT SHE WAS RELUCTANT.

Pay dirt. Reluctant to plan weddings, that I knew. But just because of the ex-fiancé and her own failed attempt? Or is there more? ANY IDEA WHY?

NO, BUT MAYBE MARY CAN FIND OUT. WANT ME TO PUSH?

I doubt Mary's going to be able to poke into this

Phineas thing without tipping my hand. In any case, I'm seeing Geo tonight, so if I need to push, I'll be better off doing it myself.

NAH, JUST CURIOUS.

HEARD YOU'VE GOT A DATE TONIGHT.

MAYBE I SHOULD POST DETAILS ON FACEBOOK, I text. MIGHT SAVE YOU ALL SOME TIME.

MARY'S EXCITED, WHICH MEANS I GET TO HEAR ABOUT IT. PART OF BEING ENGAGED. MAYBE YOU'LL FIND OUT.

NO RINGS FOR ME, OLD MAN. THANKS FOR THE HEADS UP, THOUGH.

A hundred grand. I tap on the desk of my hotel room with a pen. That could be tuition maybe. Or a multi level marketing buy in? Or a cult payment. Or the cost of a different type of clinical trial. But for what? What about an art institute? I search frantically for every stupid idea that strikes my brain, but still find absolutely nothing that looks promising.

Zippo.

After another hour of fruitless searching, I still have no idea what Geo could have been talking about. Nothing about this girl is easy. I call up one of my investigators from Nometry and explain what I heard and the few details I know.

"Find this," I tell him, "and keep your mouth shut about it, and there's a ten thousand dollar bonus in it for you. Feel free to use normal working time, but get it done without Brekka finding out."

"My son starts college next year," Scott says. "I'll figure it out, and I'll keep my mouth shut and my browser wiped."

"Thanks." I hang up.

Between prepping for my meeting in San Fran tomorrow, talking to Doug about the NASCAR bachelor party, which looks like a go, and searching pointlessly for the Phineas whatever, it's already time to shower for my date. I don't ask anyone what to wear this time.

I haven't been nervous about driving in years, but when I pull up in front of Geo's little condo, nestled at the edge of the woods along the Chattahoochee River, my hands are shaking.

I'm just going to help her loosen up, so why do I care? I don't, I remind myself. Not at all.

I force myself to walk toward her unit casually and rap on her door like it's just a casual Tuesday night.

When she answers, her hair twisted up into a complicated knot on top of her head, her eyes luminous, and her cheekbones so prominent I want to reach out and run my finger down the side of her face, every scrap of calm and cool I'd collected evaporates. She's wearing a delicate sapphire blue sweater that exactly matches her eyes, dark jeans, a black leather moto jacket, and flats.

"Is your knee bothering you?" I incline my head toward her shoes.

"No, but I was on my feet a lot today. I didn't want to push it."

"That's smart."

"Is that okay?" she asks. "I can change."

"Of course that's fine. You look amazing."

She beams up at me and my heart races. I close my eyes and breathe in and out once.

Geo grins. "Just let me lock up." She turns around to face her door and I can't help following the line of her back down to where her pants hug her backside. I lift my eyes up before she's turned around, so points for that.

I walk her out to my car, a little nervous about what she'll think. I offered her a ride home from the airport, but her car was parked in the lot, so this is the first time she's seen mine. I'm usually proud of my Vantage, but for some reason, it feels ostentatious and stupid.

Luke drives a truck. I should have bought a truck today instead of researching the Phineas whatever. A pickup truck seems like a normal guy car, something a guy might drive if he wasn't trying too hard.

"Holy moly, is this a Vantage?" she asks, running one hand over the hood reverently. "I've seen them on the road once or twice, but I've never been this close to one."

I cock my head sideways. "Any interest in driving?"

Her eyes widen. "Uh, no thanks. I'd be way too nervous. But feel free to gun it off the line." She winks.

"There's always next time," I say. "You can drive it whenever if you change your mind."

She gulps. "Maybe."

For some reason, at her acknowledgement there might be another time, my lungs fill with too much air. I open the door for her and she slides into the seat, rubbing her hand over the black leather. Her nails look different.

"Did you paint your nails?" I ask.

She blushes, and I'm kind of proud of myself for noticing. She cared enough to do her nails. That's a good sign, I think.

She squeals with delight every time I floor the gas pedal, even if it's only a hundred yards of acceleration. It's like I'm in high school again, and I love it.

"Rob is never going to believe this," she says.

My satisfaction melts away. "Why not? Can't he afford one?"

She shrugs. "Probably, but he's way too practical."

I knew I should've bought that stupid truck.

Her hand slides over mine. "I'm sorry I mentioned him," she says. "It seems to make you mad."

I shake my head. "Nothing will make me mad tonight.

I'm on a date with Geo. The girl who never dates. Talk about whatever you want." Like the Phineas enrollment. Or your innermost hopes and dreams.

What is wrong with me? I need my mojo back.

When we reach the churrascaria and I toss my keys to the valet, Geo squeaks. I turn to look at her. "What was that?"

"You valet this car?" She makes the sign for crazy by winding her finger around and around by her ear. "Maybe I will drive it after all. I can't possibly endanger it as much as that college kid will. He has braces. Did you notice the orthodontia?"

I grin. "Life's too short not to play with your toys, and I'm not going to hike all over the place just because I have a nice car."

"I guess so," she says.

I take her hand in mine as we walk into the restaurant, and she doesn't pull away. When I give them my name, the hostess tells us our table's already waiting.

"I guess you never have to wait for a table," she mutters.

"Not on a Tuesday night, I don't."

She glances sideways at my smirk and squeezes my hand. My heart races.

Her phone bings and her lips part. She lets go of my hand to dig it out of her tiny black purse. "Sorry, but I set it to silent unless it's from a priority client."

I shrug. "I don't mind."

She swipes to open it, and bobs her head. "It's Mary. I sent her the paperwork and my written evaluation on Vail and she and Luke are going to go another direction."

"Why?" I ask. "Did you hate it?"

She grins at me. "Not at all. I recommended it highly, actually, but." She swivels her phone toward me and shows me the text.

YOUR WRITEUP WAS GREAT, Mary says, BUT YOU GOT STUCK THERE. LUKE AND I HAVE BEEN TALKING IT OVER. WEATHER IN SNOWY PLACES IS TOO UNPREDICTABLE. I'D RATHER NOT WORRY WE MIGHT GET SNOWED IN ON EITHER END.

After we sit, she texts Mary back and forth for a few minutes. "I'm almost done," she says. "So sorry about that. We're just on such a short timeline."

"I think we're a go for the NASCAR weekend, by the way," I say.

She beams at me. "That's great news. Thank you so much for helping with that. I think Luke will enjoy it, and Mary said race cars don't make her nervous."

"Good news all around. Where are you taking the girls for the bachelorette party?"

"Probably Miami. Not completely sure, but something at the beach." She glances down at her phone and frowns. "Or maybe not. Now Luke and Mary want me to check out Hawaii for the reception. And Mary would rather not do a beach wedding and bachelorette weekend on the beach too." She waves the phone at me. "See? Weddings suck."

I laugh. "I bet you can handle it."

She rolls her eyes. "It's a pain, though. It's interrupting my first date in years."

"Where in Hawaii?" I ask. "Because I've got a meeting there on Friday morning."

"Maui, I think." She taps away on her phone. "Although they didn't say."

"I'd recommend Kauai myself, especially if they want scenic nature for their photos. Plus, that's where my meeting is and you could come along. Save them the price of a ticket."

She lifts one eyebrow. "You're going to be here in Atlanta until you leave for a meeting in Hawaii?"

I shake my head. "I have a meeting tomorrow afternoon in San Francisco. You'd have to come with on that little jaunt, but you could work from the hotel there."

She shakes her head. "I can't justify expensing extra hotel stays."

I don't bother pointing out that the hotel room would cost less than a flight. She could certainly stay in my room, but I don't suggest that because I don't want to scare her off. A better idea occurs to me. "I have scads of points. I can get you a room without spending a dime."

"You can convert those points, you know," she says.

I lift my eyes skyward. "I could trade them in for seven hundred magazines I don't want, it's true. Or you could just let me get you a hotel room so I don't have to travel all alone, bored and miserable. Plus we could have a rematch or two on that chess game. It's not often I find a competent opponent."

"Competent. What a glowing recommendation." Her scowl is so cute. "I wonder if Mary might consider San Francisco for a bachelorette weekend. Golden Gate Bridge, or Alcatraz, or something."

"Brekka loves the Kabuki Springs and Spa," I say. "That might be fun for a girls trip."

She taps her bottom lip with her perfectly polished pink fingernail and I want it to tap me instead. Which makes me think about kissing her. Senseless. Of course, she has no idea what I'm thinking. Which is probably good.

She taps on her phone and glances up at me. "Mary said I should check it out."

"Which it? San Fran, or Hawaii?"

Her lips curve up on the left into a half smile. "Both."

I don't bother hiding my grin.

The rest of the night flies by, a blur of steak, fish, sides from the salad bar, and limeade that tastes almost creamy. Geo can't eat very much, at least not compared to me. Our chairs inch a little closer, and then a little more, until her hand rests right next to mine on the table, and our knees brush against one another intermittently. Every single time her knee bumps mine, my heart lurches.

When the waitress asks whether we want dessert, Geo shakes her head and glances up at me to make sure I don't either. I stretch backward and groan. "Not for me either. I'm so full." I take advantage of having my arms outstretched to wrap one around her shoulders. She rests her head against me and I hope she can't hear my heart beating frantically in my chest.

"Check, then?" the waitress asks.

Geo nods her head against my chest. I don't want to shift, worried I'll dislodge her and she'll fly away like a startled sparrow. But when the waitress brings the check, I have to reach for my wallet.

She grabs her purse lightning quick and tries to give the waitress a credit card. "I'll pay."

I shake my head. "Absolutely not. This is a date. I'm not letting you re-characterize it in any way shape or form. It's not a work lunch, or payback for a contest you had already repaid, or anything else you might come up with."

"So you admit that I had already granted you that boon."

I grin. "I'm not above a little arm twisting to get what I want." I hand the waitress my credit card without breaking eye contact with Geo. "You're on a date with me. Bernard Thornton the third. And you agreed to do it knowing you didn't have to."

Geo huffs and leans back against me. "Oh, fine. Touchy, touchy. Probably for the best you pay anyway. I doubt I can make my car payment and cover this dinner in the same month."

I chuckle and she pokes me. "It's not a joke, Richie Rich. We can't all own a private island. Some of us have to grind it out one month at a time, turning the thermostat down when we have a rough month. Or eating ramen noodles for breakfast, lunch and dinner when our clients pay late."

That's a sobering thought.

"I'm happy to buy you dinner."

"Well, thanks. The food was amazing."

"I hope the company was okay too," I say.

She lifts her head up and meets my eye. "Well, that depends."

"On what?" I ask.

She lifts one eyebrow slyly. "On whether you're still okay with me driving your car home."

I nod my head. "Absolutely I am."

Her maniacal grin gives me pause, but I still wave her into the driver's seat when the valet pulls my car around.

"Why the Vantage and not the Vanquish?" she asks me from the driver's seat.

I shrug. "For one, I leave this in Atlanta, and I'm not here that often. But beyond that, when I picked this one a few years back, my dad already had a Vanquish."

"You didn't want to be just like good old dad? Isn't that where all your money came from?"

"Yes and no. My money came from the Thorntons, but my dad's not someone I strive to emulate."

"No?" she asks. "Why not?"

"We don't have that kind of time."

"Maybe on the plane ride to San Fran," she says. "While I'm decimating you at chess."

"Maybe so," I say.

Then she hits the gas and leaves my stomach back at Chama Gaúcha.

"It really can do zero to sixty in under four seconds can't it?" she asks.

I close my eyes. I've never been seated on the passenger side and it's a little disconcerting, not being in charge of the acceleration. "It appears so."

"You don't like it?" she asks. "Or do you think I'm a bad driver?"

She's a pretty good driver actually. "You should consider coming to the bachelor weekend NASCAR event," I say. "You'd probably do better than Luke and Paul."

"You think?" Her grin makes me a little nervous, but we make it back to her condo in record time.

I pry my stiff fingers off the armrest and force a smile. "And? What did you think? Worth the money?"

"I might have sprung for the Vanquish," she says. "But I guess I won't know until I drive one of those."

"I have one in Colorado," I say. "And Los Angeles."

"You said you didn't get one because your dad has one." She frowns at me. "And it turns out you have two?"

I chuckle. "This one's pretty old. I got it years ago, before I realized that if I excluded every car my dad owned from my list, I'd be stuck driving a Honda Accord. At that point, it seemed silly not to try the Vanquish. For the record, it is nicer, but I don't know if it's enough nicer to justify the bump in price."

"And yet you bought a second one."

I shrug. "I bought one, and Mom bought me another. I didn't have the heart to tell her I'd gotten one the month before. So I keep the one I bought tucked away in L.A. Mom hates it there, so she'll never know."

"Our parents really do not shop the same. My mom wouldn't even spring for the remote controlled Aston

Martin." She rubs her hands across the steering wheel longingly. "It's too bad you don't keep that extra one in San Francisco."

We could always hit LA next weekend, but I don't figure I should press my luck. "Maybe someday."

She tilts her head. "Who knows?"

I walk her to the front door of her condo, but before she can get her key out, I grab her around the waist and pull her against me. "You did admit this was a date."

When she looks up at me, there's an edge of panic in her eyes I don't like. "I did."

I reach up with one hand and touch her cheek. "Don't worry. I'm not asking to come inside. But it wouldn't be much of a date without this."

I lean down toward her slowly, one inch at a time, her eyes softening and her body relaxing against me. When my lips near hers, her eyes close, but I don't kiss her. Not yet. I pause. I want to make sure every bit of stress or reservation or whatever I saw is gone.

When she exhales, her scent washes over my face and I breathe her in. A light, flowery perfume mixed with some kind of cherry vanilla shampoo, and the mint from her gum.

Her eyes open, questioning me, wanting me, and that's when I finally press my mouth to hers. Her eyes close again and I hear a little moan. That's when I close my eyes too and give over to the feeling of her lips against mine. My hand on her waist tightens, pulling her closer to me, marking her as mine. My mouth presses harder when I think about Paul and Rob and every other man who sees her and wants her. They don't know how competitive she is. They don't know she taps her foot when she works on lists. They don't know how loyal she is to her friends.

They don't know she loved so deeply that when it

ended, her heart went into critical care. They don't know how to fix it, but I'm beginning to think maybe I can.

I don't say any of those things, but when I pull away from her, our lips parting, my hand releasing her hip, I worship her with my eyes. She deserves better than me, but I'm persistent and I'm here. That counts for something I hope.

"I'll be by around nine a.m. tomorrow to pick you up."

She nods and leans back against the door like her legs no longer support her weight.

I should wait and make sure she can get in, but if I stay, I'll kiss her again and I don't want to pressure her. I spin on my heel and head back down the stairs, one hand over my mouth. Tomorrow can't come soon enough.

13

GEO

The moment I wake up, I check the time. Nearly seven a.m. I meant to try and jog early today, but I don't even have time for that. Since I'm leaving with Trig later, my usual evening jog is out. I've missed it twice this week already.

I groan and move my thumb over my phone to check for messages, belatedly noticing the date on my lock screen.

January 26.

I bolt upright in bed. I should not have stayed up so late chatting with Paisley while I packed. My head's pounding. How could I have blanked on the date? What's wrong with me lately?

I blame Trig. I never should have agreed to that date. Or this trip either.

My phone rings. It's Rob. We haven't spoken since he told me he loves me. I close my eyes and consider screening his call.

But he deserves better than that. He had a broken back and he was still there for me.

I swipe to answer. "Hey Rob."

"We still on for nine today?"

He's supposed to be giving me a ride. I forgot he offered to do that. I should say no, but then he'll think I'm upset or something instead of just unsure how to act around him.

"Uh, yeah," I say. "I need to make the cobbler still."

"Cutting it close, huh?" he asks. "Well, I'll let you get to it."

I preheat the oven and pull a bag of sliced peaches out of my freezer before I even take time to brush my teeth. Whipping up a peach cobbler takes like three minutes, but it bakes for forty-five.

I don't want to text him too early, but I need to see whether Trig can wait for me. Honestly, it's probably better if he can't. I should just cancel, but part of me hopes he'll delay his flight.

I FORGOT I HAVE AN APPOINTMENT I CAN'T MISS THIS MORNING. I WON'T BE ABLE TO LEAVE BEFORE 11. I'M SO SORRY.

I want to hop in the shower, but I wait for a minute to see if he'll reply. My patience pays off.

I CAN PUSH MY MEETING A BIT. WHEN SHOULD I COME GET YOU?

ROB CAN DROP ME OFF AFTER.

WHAT KIND OF MEETING IS THIS? ROB'S GOING?

I sigh. ROB'S TAKING ME.

LET ME TAKE YOU. I HAVE NOTHING ELSE GOING ON THIS MORNING.

I don't want anyone else to know about any of this. NO, IT'S FINE.

ARE YOU SURE? I'D BE HAPPY TO DRIVE YOU.

I bite my lip. IT'S NOT ACTUALLY A WORK THING.

NOW I REALLY WANT TO COME.

Maybe a tiny part of me wants Trig along.

I text Rob. ACTUALLY I HAVE A WORK THING RIGHT AFTER. I'LL DRIVE MYSELF TODAY.

He texts back right away. YOU SURE? YOU AREN'T UPSET WITH ME, RIGHT?

I LOVE YOU TOO, ROB. JUST NOT THE WAY YOU WANT. I'M REALLY SORRY. BUT THAT HAS NOTHING TO DO WITH THIS. WE'LL BE OKAY, I SWEAR. I NEED YOU IN MY LIFE. I ALWAYS WILL.

I'M MORE WORRIED ABOUT YOU BEING OK TODAY.

I'LL BE FINE, I lie.

OKAY. IF YOU CHANGE YOUR MIND, I'M HERE.

I'm sure he's hurting right now, and waving him off from being there for me isn't helping. I doubt driving me around and being my shoulder to cry on is going to help him either, so I try not to feel too guilty.

Paisley calls right as I get out of the shower. "Are you so excited for Hawaii?"

I grin. Paisley always brightens me up. Her excitement's always so over the top that it's contagious. "A little bit, yeah."

"I was calling because I noticed the date."

My eyes tear up. I don't deserve my friends.

"You there?" she asks.

"Yeah," I say. "I'm here. How would you remember this date?"

"Last year it fell on a Saturday."

Right. Of course it did. And that was the first one so it was really bad.

"I'll be okay. Actually, Trig's going to take me to see her."

"Are you serious?"

Her reaction spooks me. "Should I not let him? I could still tell him never mind."

"No, no," she rushes to say. "I think it's great. I'm just surprised. You're many things, Geo. Many, many good things. But open and welcoming aren't really qualities I'd use to describe you."

"I'm hospitable," I protest.

"Sure, you offer people water when they come visit, but that's not what I'm talking about. You are about as closed a book as they come. I'm proud of you for letting Trig in, honestly. This is probably a bigger deal than a jaunt around the world to Hawaii."

My throat closes off because she's right.

"Well, I'll let you go. I wanted to make sure you didn't forget with everything else going on."

Crap, the peach cobbler. I rush into the kitchen, but it's fine. "I'll be okay," I manage to choke out. "Thanks for checking on me."

"Love you, Geo. Take care of yourself, okay? And call me if you need anything. Anything, seriously. Even if it's just to have someone cheer, or cry, or yell. Or I could totally take that spoiled rich guy off your hands if it comes to that. Unless he turns out to be a villain, and then I've got a concealed firearm and a shovel."

What the heck? "Are you serious?"

I hear her snort through the phone. "If you count a water gun, then yes. But my scowl can cross state lines. I mean it."

I hang up and notice a text came in while I was on the phone. From Trig. Because I forgot to text him after I told Rob I didn't need a ride.

HELLO? Trig says.

CRAP, SORRY. PAISLEY CALLED. YES, IF YOU DON'T MIND GIVING ME A RIDE, I'D LIKE THAT.

WHAT TIME? He asks.

It's already 8:20. 8:45 TOO SOON? I have no idea where he's staying.

I CAN TRY.

THANKS. I text back.

It's a good thing I was already packed. I'm just swiping on some mascara when I hear a tap at my door.

I scoop the photo albums into my tote bag, grab my rolly suitcase and slide the peach cobbler I transferred into a Tupperware into a sack and sling the straps over my shoulder.

I'm a little breathless when I finally answer the door.

Trig's leaning against the doorframe like he owns the place. I like it. I like him, probably too much. The thought makes me smile, but I feel a little guilty, too. Especially when I notice a photo on the entertainment center of me and Mark on a hike.

I shake my head to clear it and force a smile. "I'm ready. Sorry for the confusion and shuffling around this morning."

He shrugs. "No big deal. My meeting was easy to move. People are usually pretty accommodating for me."

"Wonder why," I say over my shoulder as I try to roll my bag past him.

He takes my tote and my roller bag. "You lock up. I've got this."

"Thanks. Billionaire Bell Hop audition?"

"Think I'll get the job?" He leans down and brushes a kiss across my mouth and my heart skips a beat. Or three.

"I'll consider you for it. I have high standards, and you were about two minutes late."

"Can't control traffic." He leans over me again, this time pulling me against him like he did last night.

When he pulls away I can't even remember my own name, much less what we're doing or where we are.

I glance around and recognize my front door. Right. I fumble around until I find my key so I can lock up. We walk down to his car, and I don't ask to drive. I'm too nervous and shaky to feel safe.

"Where to, boss?" he asks.

"Arbor Terrace on Burnt Hickory Road. I'll tell you where to turn."

His eyebrows rise, but he doesn't ask any questions. Which is good, because I don't really want to talk about it. When we arrive, I pull out the peach cobbler and the photo albums. He comes around and opens my door. I'm carrying so much that I let him. His car looks bizarre parked between a Lincoln Town Car and a Buick LeSabre, and near a fleet of Arbor Terrace Assisted Living vans.

He's got to be burning with questions, but he doesn't ask a single one. He takes the albums from me, and I snag his free hand with mine. He interlaces our fingers and squeezes once. I approach the front desk and wave.

"Geode," Megan greets me. "She's having a great day today. I'll sign you in." Her eyes slide sideways and seem to realize I brought someone other than Rob. Her eyes drop down to where I'm holding Trig's hand, and they cloud. "Wait, where's Rob?"

"He was busy. Trig brought me today."

Megan gulps and blurts out what I assume is the first thing that came to mind. "How many super hot boyfriends do you have?"

I shake my head. "Rob's just a friend."

"Pretty devoted friend," she mutters.

Did everyone but me know that Rob liked me? I feel like a complete imbecile.

"She just has the one boyfriend, Megan, and my name is Trig. It's a weird one, so I thought you might need to hear it again."

Boyfriend. I should be sprinting the other direction right now. But my heart swells instead. I want to kiss him on the mouth right in front of Megan for supporting me, for claiming me, and for being here with me, but I settle for bumping him with my hip and mouthing the word "thanks."

He shrugs. "It's nothing."

"We're going to see my mom," I whisper. "She's got early onset Alzheimer's and it's pretty bad. I hope Megan's right. I hope she's having a good day, because it's my parents' anniversary."

Trig's eyes widen and he wraps one arm around my shoulders. I feel something different then. Something I can't identify.

"And the Tupperware?" he asks.

"Peach cobbler," I say. "My parents didn't have much of a budget when they got married, so my Aunt Jane made them a cobbler instead of buying a fancy wedding cake. We've celebrated with peach cobbler every year since. It took them a long time to have me. My mom miscarried a lot. But even so, I've been around for twenty-six celebrations. This would have been their thirty-third year married if my dad hadn't passed."

He leans down and kisses my forehead. "I'm glad I can share this with you."

I march down the hall toward Mom's room, my shoulders squared. I'm prepared for her to have no idea who I am. Or at least, I'm as prepared as I can be.

When I round the corner and walk into her room, she's

wearing a bright yellow dress and her hair's brushed and pulled back. She turns toward me and her eyes light up.

"Geode! You remembered."

I will not cry. I will not cry. My mom's here today, here with me and I won't waste any time being sad.

I let go of Trig's hand to race across the room and hug her. "You look beautiful, Mom. Yellow has always been your best color."

She squeezes me tightly and then pulls back to look at me. "Every color is your color with those eyes and that hair. My beautiful, beautiful little baby." She turns back toward the doorway. "And who's this handsome man?"

"I'm Geo's boyfriend, Mrs. Polson. My name is Trig, and I'm happy to meet you." Trig strides across the room and holds out a hand to shake.

My mom swishes around me and pulls him in for a hug. "It's wonderful to meet you, Trig. Wait, Trig? Geo and Trig? You two sound like notes for a math class." Her laugh is warm.

"I never thought of that," I say. "I guess we do."

Trig slides his arm around my shoulders again. "We fit together really well. Names are just the beginning."

"I can see that," Mom says. "I've been so worried about her over the past few years. She shut down after Mark, you know, closed herself off entirely. You must be a pretty special guy to bring her to life like this."

Trig's eyes shutter and he nods. "Thank you, Mrs. Polson. I appreciate that. You have a very unique daughter."

"Of course I do." She notices the albums he's carrying under his free arm. "Have you seen her as a child yet? Maybe we should have let those agencies photograph her. We could have been millionaires if we had, I bet. She was much prettier than Shirley Temple ever was. And she can sing, too. Has she ever sung for you?"

I shush her, but Trig looks like he's not going to let that drop for good. I groan. "Mom, stop."

She reaches for an album and sits on her bed. I sit on one side, and Trig settles down on the other. If he's uncomfortable about sitting on her bed, he doesn't show it.

Mom wastes no time opening the old books. "Look here." She points. "Look at those eyes."

I'm three or four maybe in the photo, wearing a swimsuit that's clearly too small, my hair surrounding my face in a messy halo of ink. She traces my face with a finger, her eyes soft. My heart swells so big I can't take it, so I hop up, open the cobbler and flag down an aide for some bowls and spoons. "Happy Anniversary, Mom."

"Thanks, G. Your dad would be just as proud of you as I am. I wish he was here."

So do I.

"But at least his death brought you back home to me."

I shake my head. "I moved back when you got sick, Mom. Over a year before Dad passed."

"Oh that's right," she says, patting my arm. "I remember. I'm sorry you had to give up that big fancy job."

"I get by just fine, Mom."

"Fine, yes. Everything is fine." Her finger traces the photos on the next page absently.

I glance up nervously and sure enough, her eyes have become glazed. My throat closes up. Hang on a little longer Mom. I need you so much, especially right now. I want to know what you think about Trig. I want to tell you I'm finally planning a wedding, and even if it hurts like the slice of a blade sometimes, I'm doing it. I want to know what I should do about Rob, and how I'm supposed to talk to him now.

I know I'm not a baby. I'm not a kid. I'm a grown woman, but I need my mom more than ever right now.

But when I look at her, she blinks and blinks. "Have I had lunch already? Because I don't think I'm supposed to eat cake until I've eaten lunch."

I inhale several times. "No, Mom, it's me, Geo. And it's not cake. I brought cobbler because it's January 26."

"Of course it's cobbler, but that's in the cake family, isn't it? I'm not an idiot."

"You're one of the smartest people I know," I say.

She frowns at me. "How do I know you?"

I choke on a sob. "My name is Geo."

"Your name is Geo you said? I have a daughter named Geode, but we call her Geo sometimes."

I nod then. If I keep insisting I'm someone she doesn't know me as, she gets irritable. "That's amazing. It's not a common name. She must have been a special person."

"She *is* a special person. She's not dead."

"No, of course not," I say. "I'm sorry."

A tear forms in my eye and I wipe it away as quickly as I can. I should be happy for the fifteen minutes I had, but it's never enough, not really. It's never what I need.

So I try to be what she needs instead, because that's something I can control. Trig helps. He's completely calm and personable. Mom thinks he's a new employee and flirts shamelessly, but it could have gone so much worse. Sometimes she gets scared that she can't remember things and that makes her mad.

It's really hard when she's angry.

We look over her wedding album and listen to her recount details about her wedding day that I've heard a million times and could share myself, word perfect. I think back to all the times she shared the details with me as a kid, Dad stopping her to interject things here and there.

Once she's told the story of how they met, I stand up and thank her for sharing her peach cobbler with us.

"I'm not so sure I should have eaten that," she says. "I don't think I've had lunch yet, and they're very strict about that here."

"You haven't," I say, "but one day a year of sweets before lunch is okay. It's a special day."

She nods. "Yes, you only get married once." Her eyes meet mine. "I hope my daughter gets married one day. I really want to see that. She was engaged before, you know, but the fellow died off at war in Iraq or somewhere. I forget some of the details."

I pat her arm. "It's okay, Mom."

"Geode?" Her eyes widen. "Is that you?"

I hug her tightly and blink back more tears. "It's me, Mom. I came to wish you a Happy Anniversary."

I leave the albums there. The staff knows to collect them when she takes a nap so she won't get angry and destroy them. I'll collect them next Monday at my weekly visit.

Trig pulls me against him the moment we're in the hallway and wraps one arm over my shoulders. "You're brave, Geo. So brave."

He keeps his arm over my shoulders as we walk down the hall and out to the parking lot. He walks me to the passenger side of the car and opens the door, but instead of letting me slide into my seat, he pulls me against him, my face pressed to his chest.

Something breaks inside and I sob against his chest. "I wish you could have met her before."

"Me too," he says. "But even today, it was obvious she's a wonderful lady."

"It's gotten so much worse now that my dad's gone. He centered her somehow," I say. "In a way I can't, and he always knew what to say and do. Half the time, she gets so mad at me, and I make it worse."

"You're going. You're there for her. That's enough." He finally releases me and I slide down into the car, numb.

Once he gets in, he leans over and buckles my seatbelt. "Are you okay to head for the airport? Or do you want to stop somewhere? Get some tea, or maybe I don't know, a stiff drink?"

I laugh. "That's kind. I'm fine though. I'm sorry I've already made you as late as I have. Let's head for the airport."

He stares at me for a moment, but then he puts the car in gear and pulls out of the parking lot and toward the freeway.

"It seems like your parents were really happy," he says.

"They were. We all were."

"I'm sorry your dad passed. You're lucky to have had the time you did, though."

I don't usually think of it like that, and I realize he's right. A lot of people didn't get twenty-five really good years. "Are your parents both alive?"

He nods. "They are."

"And are they still married?"

He nods his head, lips pressed into a tight line, eyes flinty.

"That face isn't promising. Are they not happy together?"

He barks a laugh. "Not even anything approaching happy. I honestly have no idea why they ever got married. Lust, maybe. That might have been enough back then. Mom looked pretty enough in the photos of her early twenties, I suppose. The hair throws me, but I guess it was normal for that time."

I raise one eyebrow. "You don't sound like you like her much."

He shakes his head. "I know it sounds awful, especially to you. If you'd met my mom, you might get it. Mom's... a little hard to like. The only person I can think of in the world who sort of likes my mom is Brekka."

A deep sense of pity that he doesn't even love his own mother rises up within me. "Surely you have some nice memories?"

"None that I can think of. She hates my dad, and Brekka and I were always a major imposition. Mom and Dad are rarely in the same place anymore and when they are, there's a lot of alcohol to lubricate the space around them. Mom runs the company, and Dad, well. Dad runs up credit card bills."

What in the world? "Why don't they just get divorced?"

"You can thank the Thornton family trust's prenup for that one."

"I don't understand." But it reinforces my belief that prenups are a death knell for any marriage. I wonder whether Mary's signing one. I don't think I'll even ask. Not my circus, not my monkeys.

"Grandpa Thornton made Mom sign a prenup. Standard fare for my family. No prenup, no wedding."

"Okay, so your dad could still divorce her, right? Why wouldn't he?"

"That would be too easy," Trig says. "My dad grew up spoiled. He's a trust baby to the core. He spent every dime he was allowed every quarter and then asked his parents for more. When he married my mom, Grandpa and MaMa hoped he'd settle down and spend a little less on partying."

"Didn't happen?"

Trig shrugs and I wish I could reach through time and hug little boy Trig. His eyes look so hurt, even now. "Maybe it did, for a while anyway, but it didn't last. What they didn't count on was my mother. They didn't even know she had an MBA when Mom and Dad got married. Mom took an active interest in family finances, not in spending it so much, but in management of the trust corpus. She convinced Dad to give her half his allowance, and she tripled that in the first year. He gave her more the next year. Then Grandpa gave her some, too. Pretty soon Mom was running everything."

"She sounds like an impressive woman."

He nods. "Impressive describes Mom to a T. But she's also heartless, ruthless, and devious. Dad didn't realize how mean she could be until she caught him with a girlfriend the first time. I think Dad was relieved, honestly. I was seven. I remember because Mom was pregnant with Brekka, and everyone assumed she'd divorce him."

"Why didn't she?"

Trig's mouth twists. "She couldn't walk away from the empire. She could never amass anywhere near the money she was managing at that point, and she didn't have a job to put on a résumé, since she was managing family finances. Besides, for Mom it's never been about spending money. It's about controlling it. Doubling it. Tripling it. Growing things. If she divorced my Dad, she'd be reduced to a few paltry million."

"If your dad was relieved when she found out, why didn't he divorce her? Surely he could have."

Trig exhales in disgust. "Mom loved running things and feeling powerful, and Dad had grown accustomed to the boost to his allowance. If she left, he'd have to scale his life-style way back from his new normal. By then, almost every family asset was managed by Mom, who they all knew would never cheat them or steal from them. Besides not being able to part with the golden goose, no one else had any idea what to do with their assets now that she'd been handling them alone."

"I always thought being rich made everything easy."

He shakes his head. "I know, poor little rich kid. No one feels sorry for me because most people have things much harder. I'm not trying to engender pity, but my home life wasn't perfect, and that old adage is actually true. Money can't buy everything."

I take his hand in mine. "Marriage isn't always bad."

"My parents' certainly is. They're locked in some kind of Sisyphean cycle of earning and spending."

I gulp. Maybe I'm lucky my poor parents had each other. Even if I can barely afford to pay my Mom's nursing home bill each month.

"Can I ask you something?" Trig's eyes are focused on the road, but his voice is tentative, like what he says next matters to him.

"Sure," I say, thinking how Paisley said I'm a closed book.

"I know it's none of my business, but I've been wondering since you mentioned it to Rob. What's the Phineas Enrollment?"

I turn to look out the window. "Just the name I can put to my crushed hopes and dreams."

Trig's head whips toward me in concern. "What?"

I force a laugh. "I'm just being stupid and melodramatic. There was a clinical trial that's getting amazing results in California. Milton Phineas is the director. They're enrolling patients here in Atlanta, but I couldn't afford it. That's why I took the gig for this stupid wedding. I can finally afford to enroll Mom, but when I called to tell her doc to do it, the enrollment period had closed early. I guess they had an overwhelming response."

"What were the goals of the trial?" he asks quietly.

"They perform an injection that helps stabilize the patients. It practically ensures a lucid window of two to six hours once a week. They're hoping to figure out how to increase that obviously, but can you imagine?" I meet his eyes reluctantly. "My mom would actually be my mom. Every week."

"Time. The trial would have given you back some of the time Alzheimer's stole."

He understands.

14
TRIG

When I download all my emails to review on my flight, I notice there's an email from Scott. I glance at Geo before opening it, but she's engrossed in something on her laptop. I open the email.

No progress on the details of the Phineas enrollment, so I broadened the scope to investigate target's life for clues. List of possible matches attached. Dossier on target acquired. Scott.

My finger pauses over the file. I could open this and read almost every detail about Geode from birth to present day. Images collected from the web, her grades and school attendance, social media posts, everything. My finger shakes. I'm greedy, starving, and desperate to find out every detail that I can.

Then I think about Geo's face when she confessed that her mother was in a nursing home. The way her lip trembled and she blinked back tears. And when she told me she was too late for the trial. And when she confessed her fiancé died and she got the news on Valentine's Day.

I don't want to read all the secret details about her life.

I want to find out how things happened and how they shaped who she is today, and how she feels about them now. I don't want to dig up her secrets. I want her to share them with me in her own time, when she trusts me with them. I want to earn that trust. Not undermine it.

I delete the email.

And then I swear under my breath. I still need Scott to look into the Phineas Enrollment. Idiot. I shoot him an email asking him to get me every detail he can on the clinical trial for Alzheimer's in Atlanta.

I want details on how to add an enrollee, I tell him specifically, *and if it really is past entry time, I want to know how to widen that window so we can add a late enrollee.*

If I've learned anything in business, it's that it's never really too late, not until someone's dead. If I can get Geo her extra time, I'll do it.

"Drinks?" Ivy asks.

Geo glances at her watch. "It's early."

Ivy tilts her head. "I meant water or soda."

"Right. A sprite is great." Geo's cheeks redden, and I wish I could snap a photo of her in that moment. Eventually she won't be so surprised by everything in my world and the adorable blushing will stop, or at least slow down.

That thought makes me realize that I don't have a single photo of her or us.

"I'll take a coke with lemon," I say. "And Ivy, do you mind snapping a photo of the two of us?" I offer my phone.

"I'd like one, too," Geo says.

When Ivy holds up the phone and says, "Cheese," my smile is genuine.

"Chess?" Geo asks me as the plane taxis.

I shake my head. "I'd love to, I really would, but I've got a meeting almost the second we land, and I've got a lot of reading to do first."

She leans back in her chair. "You're just chicken. It's easy to be the winner when you've only played me once. But I could snatch that crown from your head any time. I'm the underdog now, and everyone cheers for the underdog."

I lean forward, my eyes never leaving hers. "I am a little scared, but not about chess." Then I move closer, my mouth nearly meeting hers. "You're not like anyone else I know." I kiss her then, our lips pressed close as the plane takes off.

I can't tell whether my stomach's lurching from the take-off or the feeling of her lips against mine. The feeling of her hair against my palm. I deepen the kiss, and slide my hand deeper into her hair, pulling her toward me until a tiny sigh escapes Geo's mouth. My hand trails down her neck to the space between her collar bone and throat, stroking her silky skin once. Twice. This time her sigh isn't small.

Ivy clears her throat.

Our drinks, right. She doesn't bother hiding her smirk when she hands me the coke. "Be careful you don't make a mess with that on this flight," she says.

I scowl at her and she giggles. No respect.

"Well, that was embarrassing," Geo says when Ivy's gone.

I shake my head. "I'll never be embarrassed about kissing you."

She blushes again and I wonder whether I could snap a photo of her adorable blushing face without freaking her out. Maybe if I install a security camera on the plane? No, that's too far. Like Macaroni Grill far.

"Aren't you supposed to be reading?" she asks.

Right. "Yes, thanks. I really do need to finish preparing for this meeting. Brekka's counting on me to be her man on the ground, and I've got a few more calculations to review."

She grins and I almost forget why being prepared matters and lean toward her again. Geo breaks eye contact and picks up her laptop, so I do as well, reluctantly.

We're on the ground, waiting to deplane, when I notice an urgent text. From my mom.

I'M IN SAN FRAN. BREKKA SAYS YOU ARE TOO. DINNER. 7 PM. SORREL.

I groan. Why would Brekka tell her I was headed for San Fran?

I text back. CAN'T GET TO PACIFIC HEIGHTS THEN. TOO FAR.

FINE. She replies. 9 PM.

I sigh. Two mothers in one day. I wish mine would lose her memory. Guilt immediately follows that though, but in so many ways it would improve my life.

SEE YOU THEN.

TABLE FOR TWO OR THREE? She asks.

I nearly drop my phone. My fingers fly as I text Brekka.

WHY IS MOM ASKING ME IF I WANT A TABLE FOR TWO OR THREE?

SHE MIGHT KNOW ABOUT GEO...

I'm going to kill Brekka.

IT'S NOT MY FAULT. SHE SAW A PHOTO OF YOU TWO KISSING AT VAIL. HOW'D THAT GET OUT?

It had to be Natalie and her insane obsession with social media fame. I groan.

"Everything okay?" Geo asks.

"Just normal business hiccups," I lie.

"I know zero about business, but would it help to talk about any of it?"

Would it help for me to talk to her about my mother

planning to grill me? Sure, like bubble gum would help with a root canal. "No, I don't think so, but thanks."

She shrugs and I hunch back over my phone to press Brekka for more info. WHAT DID YOU TELL HER?

Mom texts again. INTERROGATING YOUR SISTER NOW?

I grit my teeth.

Brekka finally replies. I TOLD HER YOU'RE DATING A WONDERFUL GIRL, AND THAT I LOVED HER. I GUESS MAYBE I SHOULDN'T HAVE ADMITTED TO MEETING HER BECAUSE SHE CALLED ME WITH EVEN MORE QUESTIONS. SORRY.

I close my eyes. This couldn't be worse. Mom's more obsessive than the tabloids when it comes to my love life. Or lack thereof. Only, unlike all those movies where the moms want grandkids, my mom's always telling me not to settle, not to worry about it, and that I have loads of time.

Maybe I should have clicked on that dossier after all, because there's no chance Mom's not reading one as we speak.

TABLE FOR TWO MOM. NO WAY YOU'RE GETTING ANYWHERE NEAR GEO. WE FLY OUT IN THE MORNING.

I'M NOT SURE WHETHER I'M GLAD YOU DON'T WANT TO INTRODUCE HER TO ME, OR OFFENDED YOU'RE HIDING HER.

I roll my eyes. Classic Mom.

TAKE YOUR PICK. SEE YOU AT 9.

"I've got an Uber lined up to take me to the spa," Geo says.

I try not to breathe a sigh of relief. I'm due at my first meeting in half an hour. It's already going to be tight with Bay area traffic. "Well, you're self sufficient, aren't you?"

"We can't all be billionaires," she says with one cocked eyebrow. "We little people have to learn to get by without chauffeurs and private jets."

She may think I don't live in the real world, but when I lean over to kiss her, she leans toward me and wraps one arm around my back. It's hard to pull away and head in opposite directions, but I force myself.

"I've got meetings until really late tonight," I say.

"I'll see you in the morning then," she says.

I nod.

"Your assistant sent me booking info on the Hyatt."

"Perfect," I say. "I was thinking if we leave really early tomorrow, like six-ish, we should get to Kauai around 2 pm. We'd have time to hang out a little before my first appointment, which is supposed to be a dinner meeting."

"I'll be ready to go by five a.m. then?"

"Sounds good. Steal a pillow or two and you can sleep on the flight."

She lifts one eyebrow. "You don't have pillows on your fancy jet?"

I shrug. "I do, but they're kind of hard and flat. I complain a lot, but never remember to replace them."

"You poor little rich kid, with no one to take care of you. I'll bring two tomorrow morning." She winks and again, I wish I could keep that image forever.

I set the photo of the two of us as my lock screen, and smile every time I see it during the meetings.

By the time I finish, it's nearly eight p.m. already. I lean back in my chair and stretch, wishing I could head back to the hotel and pull Geo into my arms. I do not want to go fight with my mother.

But, ever the dutiful son, I go.

Mom's early, already tapping her red soled Louboutin against the marble floor when I walk inside. Her sheath dress hugs her curves a little tighter than I'd think a sixty year old woman would want, but Mom's always been at the height of fashion and I grudgingly admit that she's fit enough to pull it off.

She spends most of the winter in San Francisco every year. She hates the snow of Colorado, but abhors the 'infestation of spray tanning and implants' that infects LA. That keeps her from truly going south. Mom loves Sorrel, and they love her, too. She's chatting with the hostess when I arrive.

"No," she says, "I think that color brings out your eyes, dear. Truly."

The hostess is wearing a white button down shirt, so I have no idea what color she could possibly be talking about. Even on pain of a hot poker, I'd never ask.

"Oh, Mr. Thornton's here." The hostess coos at me. "Could I get you anything from the bar, sir? We're so happy to have you here with us again."

I roll my eyes at Mom, because she only tries to shove hostesses and the like at me when I'm dating someone of whom she doesn't approve.

"Let's just get this over with." I stomp behind the hostess, who keeps swaying her hips and glancing back at me. I hope she doesn't trip and break her foot, but that's probably the only way she'd get more than ten seconds of my attention. I don't bother pointing out that she has red lipstick on her teeth.

When the hostess walks off, Mom tsks in disapproval. "You didn't have to be so rude to her, Bernard. She's a lovely girl, you know."

"Why did you want to meet, Mom? It's late, and I'm not even hungry." Not anymore, anyway.

She reaches over and places her hand over mine. Which she only does when she wants something. I think about

Geo's mom and soften a little. At least she knows my name, and she did teach me a lot of the things I know about business. I owe a lot of my own success to her.

"You're my son. I missed your handsome face."

"I'll send you a photo so you don't have to drag me all the way across town next time." I text her the photo from that morning with Geo. "Or did you already have a photo that looks something like this?"

Mom picks up her phone, and glances down. She sniffs. "Well, she looks better detached from your face, at least."

She can't possibly have anything negative to say about Geo's looks. I lift my eyebrows in a silent dare to try.

"I didn't realize you liked your women to have eyes that resemble characters from anime cartoons, or I'd have been looking for that all along."

I should never have doubted her. There's no one my mom can't criticize. If Geo were here, I'd shut that down, but it's not worth engaging with her while we're alone. "Mom, can you get to the point?"

"There wasn't any one point," she says. "But I did need to discuss the details of the Free Fall merger with you. Your father's useless, as you know."

She orders my food for me like I'm ten years old, forcing me to eat duck, which she knows I hate. "It really is the most flavorful of all poultry." She always tells me that. "One day you'll realize that."

I doubt it, but I have to pick my battles with Mom.

She spends the next hour discussing the merger she's handling, which I'm mostly up to speed on thanks to her weekly emails on the Thornton trust assets. I help her make a few decisions, but we could have done all of this on the phone. I don't argue or pick any fights with her, which takes some real discipline on my part. Mom loves a good fight, and she's obviously spoiling for one.

She voices her unsought opinion on the tech company I met with today, telling me I'm undervaluing their largest asset. She's a brilliant businesswoman and I should be listening, but I'm so annoyed it strengthens my resolve to pass.

She suggests I buy a vacation property from one of her bridge club friends in Miami, even though she knows I hate the insane colors and complete melee of that city. I don't express interest in the house, but I agree with her that the stone crab in Miami is phenomenal. She clicks her tongue more and more often as she grows increasingly annoyed at my refusal to argue. Over anything.

Finally, when the waiter brings us dessert, I'm sick of pretending she brought me here for business reasons.

"Brekka told me you called her about Geode. I'm in San Francisco with her now, and I'm taking her to Hawaii tomorrow. I like this girl Mom, and I don't need any advice from you, or any warnings either. I'm thirty-four years old, so maybe have a little faith in my ability to make decisions on my own."

Mom's lips compress and I realize I've thrown down a gauntlet here. Which surprises me a little, since I have no plans to ever propose to Geo. Quite the contrary, I'm just trying to help her. I'll open her back up again so she can take risks and then I'll bow out. I'm not even going to sleep with her, since that would make things harder for her. What did Geo say? I'm saintly? I'm like the saint of nearly widowed women.

I like the sound of that. Saint Bernard. Crap. Maybe not.

The point is, Mom has nothing to worry about. So why am I taking such a hard stance with her? Maybe I'm secretly spoiling for a fight too.

"You know nothing about her," she says.

"I'm sure you could send me an extensive file." I cross my arms.

She feigns shock. "I have no idea what you mean."

"Cut the crap, Mom. Tell me what you want to tell me so I can go back to the hotel where Geo's waiting for me." I don't bother mentioning we're not sharing a room. Let my mom choke on her concerns with no idea how far along we actually are.

Mom reaches into her huge purse and pulls out a thick stack of paper. "The Thornton Trust Prenuptial Agreement," she says. "You should have a copy. So you're prepared."

I recoil. "What are you talking about?"

She slides it across the table toward me. "You don't want to take her by surprise. I'd suggest you leave it out somewhere she can find it. Maybe on a desk or at the top of your luggage."

"Hold on. Are you *encouraging* me to propose to her?"

Her head shake is so small I can barely see it. "I never wanted this for you. In fact, marrying is my biggest regret of the life I've chosen. You and Brekka don't really have a hope of being happy in marriage with your dad and I as your role models. But I know it's hopeless to fight with you about it. I always pushed against any girl you liked and until today, you've never pushed back."

What does that mean?

"The material point is that you're just like me. You're going to do what you want no matter what I think, and if you're serious, I want to give you the best chance of success."

"I've never even considered marrying thanks to you," I say. "You and Dad broke us, me and Brekka both. We'd have to be blind and stupid to want anything resembling what you have."

She flinches, but holds her head high. "I don't expect you to understand the decisions I've made, or acknowledge the sacrifices. The world has changed in the last forty years, and women have opportunities now they never had back when I was young. Maybe today I'd make a better decision. Maybe I did the best I could with the options presented. Besides, when I met your father, he wasn't—" she chokes and dabs at her mouth with her napkin. "The point is, this will be much easier if your, err, if Geode is prepared. She needs to know what she's getting into."

I take the stack, knowing Mom won't relent until I do.

"I sent you an e-copy as well, in case something happens to this one."

I sigh. "Mom, I have no idea why you even think this is serious, but you've been misinformed."

She frowns. "Brekka's my source. She told me this girl is different and she hears wedding bells."

My jaw drops. "She didn't."

Mom nods.

"Did she mention that I barely know Geo?"

Mom narrows her eyes at me. "Sometimes love hits like a lightning strike."

"You knew dad for years."

She nods. "Your dad and I were a slow burn that eventually went out. But not all fires burn the same. And even infernos die down eventually." My mom leans toward me, her eyes bright. "Don't forget, son. You may like her face or her body. You may even like some of the things she says and does, or how she makes you feel, but marriage shouldn't be about love or lust, not for us. It's a contract that will impact you for a long time. Be smart about this. You offer marriage and if she takes that ring, she's accepted that offer. We aren't like normal people. We don't have the luxury of wandering around and making declarations and decisions without the proper thought. The only good reason for you to marry is to create an heir for this family, and unless that's your reasoning, unless you think her genetic code will produce a smart, capable child who could properly run this family in fifty years, then don't propose."

I stand up then. "You've fallen into some kind of delusional time warp, Mom. You said things have changed in forty years, but you're talking like it's 1757. I'm not Lord Wattingham, required to produce a male heir for our entailed estate."

She stands too. "Laugh if you want, but I'm serious. Children are the only real reason to marry. The only reason to propose now is that she'll have too much leverage once she's pregnant. Make her sign this first, and don't worry. There's an escape hatch if she's barren."

I don't swear. I don't argue. I simply turn on my heel and walk out. I don't even realize I have the stupid prenup in my bag until I've reached my car.

I drive a little too fast on the way to the hotel, but I don't call Brekka and wake her up to yell at her, or tell her how insane our mother really is. I'm proud of my restraint.

The hotel clerk hands me a keycard, and mentions my room number. And the room number for my guest. Two doors down.

I take the elevator up to the eighteenth floor and exit, bag slung over my shoulder. I open the door to my room and toss my bag inside. I glance at my watch. Twenty minutes to midnight. Five a.m. departure time. I'm sure Geo's asleep, but for some reason my feet walk down the hall anyway.

I look at her door, room 1817.

I lift my hand to knock, but pull up short, my hand suspended in the air. I close my eyes. I want her to open the door in nothing but a night shirt. I want to pull her close to me, and forget myself in her smell, in her lips, in her eyes. I want her to erase my mom's talk of heirs and prenups. I want to sink into the sight and smell of Geo and forget about the rest of the world.

But I think about the prenup anyway. The document that destroyed my parents. My mom must have loved my dad at some point. My dad clearly loved my mom at the beginning. But Mom wanted to build an empire, and Dad was wired to spend, spend, spend. Mom stayed with him because she couldn't leave him, not without losing what really mattered to her.

I wonder for the first time in my life how my dad felt, knowing Mom stayed with him for his money, not for him. He knew she'd leave him in a second if she could keep running the company he only owned thanks to luck and some words on important papers.

I wonder how my mom felt when my dad brought his girlfriend to company parties. I drop my hand and turn around. My mom's a workaholic, a power-hungry, manipulative lunatic. But she might be right. Why would I ever propose to anyone, knowing they'd need to sign a prenup, which would send me down the same path of misery I've already witnessed firsthand?

I head back to my room, but I don't sleep well that night. I toss and turn, haunted by blue eyes and prenup clauses, with a voiceover of my mother's laughter.

15

GEO

My eyes burn the next morning when my alarm goes off, but I pop up anyway. I've wanted to go to Hawaii for more than ten years. I can't believe I'm going today. In a private jet. It feels a little surreal, actually.

I shower quickly and blow-dry my hair, swiping on some mascara just as I need to leave. I knock on Trig's door quietly, unwilling to wake him up if he's sleeping. After all, it's not as if his jet will leave without him.

I may also be a little nervous, knowing Trig slept just behind this door last night.

He opens the door seconds after my knock, his hair still mussed, his bed sheets rumpled behind him, but at least he's already dressed. I pretend I'm not disappointed.

I reach up without thinking and smooth his hair back. "Long night?"

"Short." He captures my hand and brings it to his mouth for a kiss. "Too short, but you look amazing anyway."

I roll my eyes. "If you like bloodshot eyes and hardly any makeup."

"You don't need it, clearly."

Says the guy who doesn't realize I'm wearing eye shadow and mascara already. "It was your brilliant idea to head out so early. You have your own jet you know, so we could be leaving at noon."

He whispers the next words, tugging me closer with the hand he never released. "I can call my pilot right now and tell him to bump our time back."

I'm tempted, actually, especially looking at that messy bed. "I doubt we'd get any more sleep."

"No," he agrees in a husky voice. "We probably wouldn't."

The guilt about sending a pilot who's probably already at the hangar, and Ivy the flight attendant back to wait on us would eat at me. I shake my head. "You have a meeting set up already, right? And I have at least two resorts to talk to and tour, and a botanical garden. I'd love an extra day to see them."

He exhales and bobs his head. "Fine, fine, you're right of course." He ducks back in his room, presumably to grab his bags.

"How'd the meeting go?" I ask, casting around for anything to make my wait here in the doorway less awkward. I don't dare step inside, or I might tell him to delay that flight. "You're about to fund another venture?"

"Probably not the one I met with yesterday," he says. "It's not a numbers thing. Those add up, but I got a weird vibe from the lead. He's a little too eager, honestly."

"Aren't they all excited to meet with you? You're their golden ticket to make something out of their business, right?"

"Sure," he says, "I guess, but this guy seemed desperate."

"He could be dealing with a bad divorce, or have a special needs kid, or suffer from insomnia. Or a hundred other things, but maybe his idea's solid and his company still a good bet."

Trig shrugs. "Maybe. Just like you, Brekka's going to press for more than a hunch to make this decision, but I've got some people digging deeper into his background already. You'd be surprised how often I turn up something we missed on the first pass. I never ignore my intuition, but until we find more details one way or another, we don't move."

I think about the poor eager guy. I feel bad for him, but Trig's probably right to hold off. After all, numbers only get you so far. The rest is about people.

"That's smart. Sometimes I have to make guesses about caterers and other vendors. My very first large solo job, I took a chance on a new baker who came highly recommended by a friend. He made my skin crawl, but he was cheap and had good samples. As a newbie, I figured my feelings didn't matter and my clients would appreciate the price break."

"And?" Trig asks.

"He took the deposit and never delivered the cake. It was a disaster. I ended up serving donut towers and grocery store cupcakes at the kid's fifth birthday party."

"I bet the kids liked it." Trig raises one eyebrow. "But a kid's birthday party was a significant event?"

"For this particular child, yes. His parents owned the largest privately owned shuttle company in Miami," I say.

He frowns. "When were you in Miami?"

"After college, I took a job for the biggest event planning firm in Florida. I wanted to live somewhere other than home and see the world. Mark and Rob were stationed at

United States Southern Command, so it was the obvious choice."

There's no traffic to speak of this early in the morning, even in San Francisco, and my mention of the dead fiancé effectively kills the conversation, so the rest of the ride to the airport is pretty uneventful. Luckily, it's not a long drive. Of course, the M6 might have something to do with that.

"This is a pretty reserved car for you," I say. "Compared to the Aston Martin, that is."

He shrugs. "Well, I try to avoid San Francisco whenever possible."

"Why's that?"

"My mom lives here almost half the year."

"Oh?"

"When I come into town, she tends to pounce on me. In fact, I saw her last night."

My eyes widen. "And how did that go?"

He grimaces. "About like it always does. She asked my opinions on things and when I gave them, she told me how stupid they were."

"I'm sure she's proud of you," I say. "What mother wouldn't be?"

His eyes stay trained on the road. "She's not the kind of person to be proud. My dad thinks I'm amazing and always has, but my mom thinks that telling me I did well at something won't motivate me to try harder. Which means she never praises me, no matter what I accomplish. It took about six months of therapy to get that worked out and then I quit. The therapist was almost as bad as my mother."

"I'm sorry." I have no idea what else to say. That couldn't be further from my own mother, who was always proud of everything, including the time I drank a gallon of milk in twenty seconds. Never mind that I spent the next twenty minutes puking it back up.

"How did your meetings go yesterday?" Trig asks.

I beam at him. "Kind of perfect. Thanks for the Kabuki spa recommendation. It's amazing and Mary jumped after she saw some photos. We've got the bachelorette party booked, a girls trip to San Francisco."

He reaches over to take my hand. "Are you going on that trip? Because I could tag along, you know."

I let go of his hand to swat his arm. "No boys on a bachelorette trip, plus you'll be troubleshooting the bachelor party for me, right?" I slide my hand down his arm and place my fingers back over his. "I'll probably be here in San Francisco since this one's out of town. I can handle most details for the Bachelor party before I leave, thanks to all your help."

"Happy to do it." His words proclaim he's happy, but he seems closed off to me today. I wonder whether it has to do with his mom. I almost wish I'd met her, which is crazy since I've known Trig for a week.

A week? It feels like so much longer. I shake my head and force myself to pay attention to the skyline, which is breathtaking.

On this flight, Trig sets up the chess board without even asking me. He beats me again, but I notice he takes a long time between each move.

"How about a timed game?" I ask.

He frowns. "Why?"

I try not to show my hand. "No reason. Just to change things up."

"Sure," he says. "Why not?"

Once we're on a timer, I beat him three times in a row.

He swears after the third time. "How are you so good at chess?"

"I might have been a child chess prodigy."

"Are you serious?"

I shrug.

He whistles. "I should've known. I think hearing you were a cheerleader threw me off. But you're always looking for ways to mitigate risk. I might have a good position for you at Nometry if you ever decide you're sick of planning events."

"Might?"

"Well." He leans toward me and places one hand next to my thigh. "It would be harder to do this if you're working for me, but easier if you lived closer. So it's a tradeoff." He leans over and kisses my cheek. And then he kisses the spot between my cheek and ear. And then my temple. My forehead. My nose. And finally, when I'm ready to scream, his mouth closes on my lips.

We should have delayed this flight.

As it is, I'm far too aware that Ivy might walk back in here any minute. After a few moments of no thinking at all, I slide away and press one hand to his chest. "Have you done your reading for tomorrow's meeting?"

He blinks several times. "Excuse me?"

I laugh. "I don't really plan to join the mile high club today, and we're headed that way."

He yanks back like I've scorched him. "No, that wasn't —I'm not—"

I place a hand against his cheek and almost pull him back down toward me. "I like you a lot, Trig. Maybe too much. I haven't liked anyone since—" I think about how any mention of Mark seems to shut him up. "Well, in a long time. A very long time."

He gulps. "I get it. It's a lot to process. We've been in three states in a week, and we're headed for an island in the middle of the Pacific. I'll go do my reading." He presses a kiss to my hand and shifts back into his seat.

But I catch him looking at me almost every time I look up. And I look up a lot. Too often.

By the time the flight finally lands, I've finished my novel.

"Who did it?" Trig asks me.

"Huh?"

"In your crime novel. Who killed him?"

I glance at the title. *Widowmaker's Justice.*

"The groomer," I say. "Over a poodle."

He shakes his head. "You like those?"

I shrug. "I like trying to work out the ending. It's a puzzle."

"The real world is infinitely harder," he says. "Books limit what information you have, so the answer is obvious."

I shake my head. "They throw in red herrings, too. At least in real life you've got the ability to pursue any lead, and to see and evaluate people yourself. With a story, you're in a partnership with the author, and you're trying to outwit them."

He laughs. "Reading's just another chess game to you."

"I struggle to find partners, so I guess it is something like that."

"I didn't peg you for a crime novel aficionado, but that makes sense."

"I love all books, but I figured you'd mock me less for that than for this." I slide a paranormal shifter romance out of my bag.

He snags it and reads the title, his eyebrows sliding up to his hairline. "*Breaking the Horse Lord*? Really?"

I snatch it back. "It's a really good series, actually. There's this witch's curse that—"

He's laughing at me silently, his chest shaking.

"You know what?" I ask. "Shut up. It's better than your boring reports."

"Nope," he says. "I'm basically searching for buried treasure. Or, you know, the modern day equivalent."

I roll my eyes. "You don't get to make fun of my choices for free time. These make me happy."

His eyes soften. "Then I won't make fun of them again." He makes an x shape over his chest with his index finger. "I promise."

"That's better," I say. "If you're really good, I might even let you read it. It's an advance copy. I'm friends with the author, or I'd have to wait until April first to read it."

"Oh?" he asks. "You don't say?"

"She's this awesome lady with five kids who's a lawyer and kick boxes and writes. Even you'd like her."

"What does that mean?"

"Just that you're a little judgmental, but she'd pass muster with you I think." I grab my bag, but Trig takes it from me.

"I've got this."

I don't argue. I kind of like watching his biceps bulge as he carries my bag and his.

"Another Land Rover?" I ask when we reach the car.

He shrugs. "I like having cars I don't need to think too much about driving. This was a good fit for beach crawling and whatnot."

Makes sense, and as I climb into the Range Rover, I can't even fault him. It may not be as fast as the sports cars, but it's at least as luxurious. "So what time is your meeting?"

"They're coming to my place at five," he says. "I figured we'd head that way now. There are plenty of things to do and see on the way."

"Wait," I say. "Your place? You didn't say anything about

staying at your place. In fact, I distinctly recall you said we'd use your miles."

"We did in San Fran, but I own a house here."

Of course he does. And there's no built in chaperone this time.

"I hope that's okay," he says. "I figured you'll be able to relax while I go over the nitty gritty with the lead before tomorrow's barrage of meetings."

"What are you evaluating?" I ask.

"Surfboard tech. It's supposed to revolutionize the stability of the board."

"Wait." My eyebrows draw together. "Tomorrow's barrage of meetings?"

His sideways smile tugs at my heart. "A few of them might be out in the ocean."

"You're surfing tomorrow?" I ask.

"You're welcome to come. I feel obligated to test out the tech myself."

"I bet you do," I say. "Speaking of. I've been meaning to ask why do you do all the crazy stuff you do. Don't you worry about getting injured?"

Or dying? I wonder whether Trig's antics make Brekka nervous.

"What do you mean?" he asks.

"You know, all the skydiving, cliff jumping, extreme skiing, motocross and NASCAR. Aren't you worried you'll break a leg, or worse, your skull?"

"How do you know about any of that?" he asks. "We haven't talked about it."

Uh. Crap. "I might have googled you."

He laughs. "Why would you do that?"

I turn toward the window where we're hugging the coast as we head north. I can see people surfing right now.

"I might have missed seeing your face after I told you not to call me again."

I expect him to gloat. Or maybe to tease me. I brace myself, preparing for what I deserve.

He reaches over and sets his hand on my knee. "I miss your face when you're gone too."

My heart eases, which makes me more desperate to know the answer. "You never answered. Why do you do it?"

He pats my knee. "Do what?"

"Why risk your life all the time?"

"Look at me, Geode."

I turn and meet his eye briefly before he glances back at the road. "What?"

"Why do you care?" He turns to face me again. His eyes bore into mine and I'm exposed.

My broken pieces and parts are all on display. He'll realize how shattered I am, I know it. "I care."

He smiles. "I'm glad you care. And I don't know how to explain it." He turns back to the road. "I didn't used to do any of it. Brekka was the force of nature, the one who couldn't be contained. She was always the one who risked everything, but feared nothing. But then." He swallows hard. "She broke her back, and she couldn't do anything. I felt so guilty."

His voice drops and his hands grip the steering wheel at ten and two. "It was my fault. The car that night. I was driving."

"We've been over this. That wasn't your fault. You know it, I know it. It's simple fact."

His lips compress into a line.

"I can ask Brekka if you'd prefer," I threaten, not really meaning it.

"I wasn't drunk, but I was on my phone," he says. "I was negotiating the details of a deal Brekka had found. If I hadn't been distracted, I'd have seen the semi crossing the midline. She'd still be fine."

"No," I say. "That's not your fault. I already told you. We make decisions, we do our best. I bet you don't talk on the phone while driving anymore."

"Never," he says. "But it's too late."

"She was a risk taker, huh?" I think about Brekka's delicate bone structure, her tiny frame. I don't see it.

His eyes light up. "Brekka was..." He pauses. "I don't know how to explain it. Have you seen footage of wild mustangs?"

I nod.

"Or maybe dolphins spinning through the air in the open ocean? Or an eagle diving? She was like all of those things and more, because in addition to that complete ease of motion, she also possessed an intelligence that as far as I can tell is unrivaled."

His admiration for his sister almost makes me jealous. Which is nuts. "She was smart and graceful. Got it."

He shakes his head. "It was more than that, especially on the slopes. The first time she skied, she was three years old, and Mom told me I had to watch her. I was ticked off, actually. But then I watched her on her first run, and it was like she'd been missing an extension of her body for years. I don't think I ever saw her fall. She had complete body control. Watching her was like what I imagine it would have been to watch Van Gogh paint. Did you know he did many of his later paintings in an hour or less? Before he lost the light on location. Brekka was like that. Like she knew her mobility had an expiration date, so she pressed everything to the limit."

"Why does that perfection mean you have to skydive? What am I missing?" My heart goes to my throat, thinking of Trig breaking his neck, or worse, his head. I think about the images the Marines finally released of Mark and shudder.

"I promised her," he says simply. "At first after the accident, I stuck to her side like glue, but one day she begged me to do what she couldn't. I vowed I would, every single thing she would have done if she could. I've done it all ever since."

His eyes plead with me to get it. He was truly understanding about my mom and I know I should try to cut him some slack on this stuff. I get his reasoning, I really do. I can relate to the desire to do anything you can to atone for a mistake you feel you made. I've even felt obligated to someone who suffered for me.

But knowing he's never going to stop flinging himself out of airplanes and driving across the ridge of mountains on a dirt bike?

I've got my own baggage, and I'm beginning to think it's incompatible with his.

16

TRIG

Geo doesn't say a word for almost half an hour, staring intently out at the waves and surf on the East Shore. When she does speak, it startles me.

"Is that the Na 'Āina Kai Botanical Gardens?"

"Yeah," I say. "It's like a mile from my place."

Her eyes widen and she claps her hands. "That's top of my list for wedding venues. Do we have time to stop and take a look now?"

I want to get home and drop off my stuff, as well as make sure everything is lined up, but I glance at my watch. It's nearly three, but that's probably plenty of time. I've got dinner being brought in for the meeting at four-thirty. If we go drop things off, we won't have time to backtrack. "Sure."

I turn around and take Wailapa road to the Gardens. I glance over at Geo as often as I can because, as gorgeous as the scenery is, her reaction to it brings me more joy. I could almost stare at her all day, but when she's excited? I can't look away. Her wide eyes glisten, darting to and fro as she takes in the lush vegetation blooming wildly in front of the oceanic backdrop. Her lips part slightly when we pull up alongside the Poinciana Maze to park.

I'd love to witness it when she takes in the Garden for the first time, but I really ought to make sure everything is ready at the house. It leaves me torn. "Would you mind if I drop you off and come back in thirty or forty minutes? Maybe you can get a preliminary feel for this as a venue option and if one of the ones they have here feels good, set up a meeting for tomorrow?"

"Absolutely," she says. "That's perfect. I'm sorry for forcing you down here so last minute."

I shake my head. "I don't mind at all." This is where I should walk away, but I can't quite bring myself to miss her reaction. Five minutes won't kill me. I could walk her inside and then head to my place.

I open my car door and walk around to her side as she's climbing out.

"I thought you were dropping me off," she says. "Which is completely fine. Go and be fancy. I'm actually pretty competent at what I do."

"I know that." I take her hand in mine. "But I know the owner, so if you run into any issues, I can lean on him."

She hugs me suddenly, squeezing me tightly around the chest. I wrap my arms around her too, always happy with the feel of her in my arms. She's not tiny like Brekka. She's just right.

Geo finally pulls back, but I keep one arm around her shoulders and we walk toward the entrance.

A man's voice calls out behind us. "That cannot be Geode Polson? Is that really you?"

We both spin around, my arm falling off her shoulders when I see my old family friend, Ethan Trainor. He looks like a stereotypical surfer dude. Streaky blond hair, bronzed skin, rippling muscles that are easy to see from under a shirt with the top few buttons undone.

"Ethan?" I ask.

"Ethan!" Geode says at the same time.

My head swivels toward Geo and our eyes meet, hers reflecting the puzzlement in mine. "How do you know Ethan?"

Ethan has reached us, his arms outstretched. "Geode, I can't believe you're here." He turns to face me. "Geo broke my heart for the very first time. Actually, probably the only time."

Geo rolls her eyes and steps away from me to hug Ethan, who holds on a little too long for my taste.

The pieces click for me. Ethan went to Emory, and he's several years younger than me. Of course he would have gravitated toward her in school. From what Brekka says, women badger Ethan. If he was interested in Geo and she passed... she must care even less about money than I thought.

"It's been too long," Ethan says, "but all is forgiven now that you've flown all the way out here to see me."

Ethan's always been a ridiculous flirt. His 'chill dude' and 'hang ten' slang always annoyed me, but he's a nice enough guy for the most part. When he grins his toothy grin and Geode smiles right back, her eyes sparkling with genuine warmth, I grit my teeth.

"I'm actually here for work," she says. "I'm planning a wedding."

Ethan glances from Geo to me and back and comes to the wrong conclusion. "Are you getting married, Trig?"

For the first time in my life, I want to say yes. I want to grab Geo's hand and pull her against my chest. But that would be past crazy and inching toward clinically insane. "No, not me. I'm just the Best Man."

"That makes so much more sense." Ethan puts his arm around Geo. "I looked up to Trig for years, you know. I even wore the same jacket he did for over a year, and the same sneakers. But I wouldn't recommend him as a potential spouse." He winks at me and I push my irritation down. He really did dress just like me for years. It was kind of adorable, in an obnoxious way.

Ethan walks a few steps ahead, arm still draped around Geo's shoulder. "You've come to the perfect place for a dream wedding. We actually have four distinct venues available. I'll shuffle around whatever you need to get you the dates you want."

Geo bites her lip, which only emphasizes the whiteness of her teeth. When I notice Ethan staring at her mouth, I clear my throat.

"Oh, sorry Trig." She turns to Ethan. "He's got a big meeting at five. He was going to walk me in to introduce me, well..." She glances my way. "To introduce me to you, I guess."

She created the perfect opening for me to bow out, but my feet aren't walking back to my car now, not while Ethan's basically hugging her.

"I'm still a little confused on how you two know each other," I say.

"I studied hospitality at Emory," Ethan says.

"I knew your family owned resorts," Geo says, "but I didn't realize you had holdings in Hawaii."

"Well, the Gardens used to be a non-profit, but you know how that goes," Ethan says. "No profit, not much success either. It was about to be sold at auction and we picked it up for a song. I've been here ever since. I'm even doing a decent job, thanks to what I learned at good old Emory."

"Little Ethan Trainor and studying aren't compatible concepts in my brain," I say.

Ethan ducks his head a little. "Well, that's where Geo came in. She helped me quite a lot. She was my study partner, and I liked her enough that I wanted to impress her. I even took her out a few times before that big beefy guy stepped in and stole her from me." He glances at Geo's left hand and raises his eyebrows. "But I guess that didn't work out? Somehow I missed that memo. Last I heard you were getting married."

Geo blinks quickly and gulps air, but before I can figure out what to say to save her, she speaks. "I was, but actually Mark died almost four years ago. Killed in action."

Ethan's face crumples. "I'm so sorry to hear that."

But his arm tightens around her shoulders, and I realize that while he genuinely feels sad for her, he's not really sorry. I wonder how many of his earlier jokes were constructed on an underlying element of truth.

"I'm sorry if I made you uncomfortable," Geo says. "There's never an easy way to tell people."

"Not at all," Ethan says. "He was such a good guy. I feel bad for making fun of him now. I was just jealous."

He managed to hit on her and express condolences in the same breath. I'm rethinking my prior impression that Ethan was an empty headed trust brat. The surf bum image might be hiding more.

She shakes her head. "You didn't know. It's fine."

"I honestly had no idea, or I'd have expressed my condolences a long time ago. I'm pretty out of touch out here," he says.

Geo glances my direction, and then down at her watch. "Oh no, I almost forgot. Trig has that meeting later, and he's cutting it a little close I think. He only stopped here because he's too much of a gentlemen to turn me down."

"I can bring you back tomorrow," I say. "Is there a good time for you, Ethan? Or if you're busy, maybe one of your people can show her around?"

He snorts. "Oh please. I'll reschedule whatever it takes to catch up with an old friend." Ethan beams at Geo. "I'm completely free right now, though. I'd be happy to take her back to her hotel after she's looked around. Or if she needs some hotel recommendations, I have several I could show her during your meetings. We have affiliations with three."

A few days ago, I'd have wanted to punch Ethan in his tanned surfer face, but not today. Today his offer and obvious interest doesn't make me angry. I'm completely calm.

"She's not staying at a hotel. She's staying with me." Pride swells up inside me for some reason. "Geo's my girlfriend."

I said it before back at the nursing home, but that was different. It's not like anyone there would know, but Ethan knows everyone I do. Which means the word will be out twelve seconds after we leave. I've never called anyone my girlfriend before, not in thirty-four years, but I'm not panicking. In fact, it's as though for the first time, I'm not afraid. Like I've freed myself from my parents, somehow.

I haven't known Geo long, but she's everything I want. She's organized and reserved and classy. She's loyal to friends and family. She moved back home when her mom became sick, weathered the storm of losing her mom, for all intents and purposes, and her dad in the same year. She's forgone the easy path of relying on her looks to make something of her life that's unrelated to appearance. She eschews all drama in favor of modesty. She's got a quick mind that maneuvers through chess and risk assessments easily.

Possibly most important of all, I love talking to her, even when she's miffed at or annoyed with me.

It's like the dust has cleared from my brain and I realize something. Geo's the only girl I want to kiss. The only girl I want to talk to, other than my sister. Geo's the girl I care about the most in all the world. Something in my chest explodes and I breathe easier, like I've pulverized an anvil that had been weighing me down.

Because my thoughts force me to acknowledge something. Something I haven't ever said to any woman outside my family.

I love Geo.

I want to take her in my arms right now and tell her a thousand times. But it's not the best timing for my epiphany, I guess.

"I can give you my address," I offer. "If you want to stay Geo, and Ethan can give you a ride, that's great."

Geo steps toward me without hesitation. "I love what I've seen Ethan, and I think this may be exactly what Luke and Mary need for their wedding, but can I come see it tomorrow? I really ought to head to Trig's house in case he needs help preparing for his meeting."

I never understood that stupid Dr. Seuss line about the Grinch's heart. Until that moment. The heart I just discovered grew at least one size with Geo standing next to me. No melodrama over collecting men who worship her, no attempts at making me jealous like every girl I've ever dated until now.

Simple support.

"That's completely fine," Ethan says. "I have a meeting at ten but it shouldn't take all day. Can we do eleven? Then if you need more time, we can eat lunch at one of the local resorts. It would give you a chance to check those out, too."

"That's perfect." Geo leans against me, her face pressed

to my chest. “It was wonderful seeing you again Ethan, and I apologize if I seem tired. We had to wake up early this morning, and it was a long flight.”

Ethan shakes his head. “Not at all. If anything, you look more amazing than you did back at Emory.” He turns toward me. “Looks like I’ve lost my chance with this one again, but I don’t think I’ve ever seen you look happier, man. Good for you guys. Maybe you’ll be planning a wedding here next.”

I look down at the shiny, ebony top of Geo’s head. Maybe we will.

17

GEO

Trig doesn't say much on the short drive to his Kauai house. When we pull up to a large wooden gate, I scan the area. "Is this like a condo?"

He turns toward me, his eyebrows drawn together. "Are you kidding?"

"Totally," I lie. "But seriously, is this your place? Or another family cabin?"

"Not that it matters really," he says. "Mom and Dad don't care where we go or when. But Brekka and I bought this one ourselves."

"Together?" I ask.

"Yep." His eyebrows draw together. "Well, yes and no. Technically at first we didn't."

"I don't understand."

"I'm thirty-four," Trig says. "And Brekka's twenty-seven."

"Okay," I say. "What does that have to do—"

"I'm getting there, Miss Questions."

We pull through the gate and I gasp. "Is this on ocean front acreage?"

He bobs his head. "Three acres."

Even the driveway is sculpted. Flagstones lead to three garage bays, the entire thing overlooking a verdant green field that drops to the ocean below. "This place is amazing."

"Thanks. Mom and Dad bought it for me and Brekka as a graduation present. She graduated high school the same time I got my MBA."

"I thought you said you bought it?"

He reaches back and pulls our bags out of the rear of the car. "I'm getting there. Be patient."

"It's not one of my strong suits," I mumble as I climb out.

"I'm gathering that, but this isn't a chess game. You don't need to figure this out. I'll tell you."

I sigh and try to take my bag from him. "Then get on with it already."

He tugs on the bag until I flop against him, and then he kisses me briefly. "I was worried back there for a minute that Ethan would kidnap you and paddle you out to some private island, never to be seen again."

"Does he have a private island? Because if so, maybe I'm rethinking this whole thing." I gesture at the door that leads into the enormous beach house behind us.

He shakes his head. "I knew I should've bid higher on that island."

"Wait, is there really an island?" Who knows with him?

Trig laughs. "Ethan's family only has a few hundred million. He probably lives in a hut outside the botanical gardens. Which is why if he kidnapped you, I might never find you again."

I smile against his mouth. "He could have kidnapped me years ago and didn't. I'm sure I'm safe."

He shakes his head. "I think he only recently realized what he lost."

I roll my eyes. "Oh please. We only went out like three times."

"Which is technically two more times than we've gone out. But to answer your earlier question, when I decided to start Nometry, Brekka convinced me to sell this house and use the money as my startup capital. She was a freshman in college, but I made her a half owner anyway."

"You didn't have other funds to use?" I ask.

"Only my trust fund, and Brekka pointed out that I didn't want my company to be owned by the trust."

"Smart," I say. "But how are we staying here now if you guys sold it?"

"Two years ago it went on the market, and we decided to buy it again. With our own money this time."

"Nice," I say.

He straightens. "I value it more now that I paid for it myself."

"I bet you do." I finally grab my bag. "I mean, when I graduated, my parents gave me a new flat iron for my hair. It was a really nice one, salon quality. It cost almost two hundred dollars. But when that one eventually gave out, I bought the replacement myself." I walk up the steps toward the door into the house. "And I've got to say. I value my sleek hair much more now, knowing I paid for it myself."

Trig chases me up the stairs. "Mock me if you will, but this was a big deal to me."

"I believe you," I say. "I'm not actually mocking you. I'm more mocking me."

"You shouldn't be. You've done really well. You own a business."

"I can barely make my monthly payment on a one bedroom condo," I say.

"But surely you're saving."

I look down at the floor of his garage, which is nicer than the floor of my kitchen. "Not really."

"What are you spending your money on, then? Manicures?" He takes my free hand. "Because I'd say that's totally worth it."

I shake my head and force the words out. "My parents wanted kids really badly." I still think about all the siblings I never met. Mom lost them all before I was born. "They spent every extra dime on trying everything available at the time, but none of their children survived. Until me. My mom was almost forty when she had me. When I was growing up, we never had much left over after they paid the bills. Then Dad's company laid him off before he vested in his pension. So when he died, Mom's decline accelerated, and well. Her social security doesn't cover the costs of her care. Or at least, not at any place I'd be willing to leave her."

It's so embarrassing to be telling this multi-billionaire that I have basically nothing, other than a mother I'm caring for alone.

"You pay for your mother's nursing home."

I can't meet his eyes. It's all so pathetic. I can barely make my condo payment and my car payment with enough left over for Mom's nursing home. Well, except now I have almost a hundred grand I could spend. If it wasn't already too late.

Trig's hand touches the bottom of my chin and lifts my head upward until my eyes finally meet his.

"I love you, Geo. When we first met, I thought you were the most beautiful person I'd ever seen. You floored me. Your hair, your eyes, that body." His eyes widen and he shakes his head. "But you're so much more than a knockout. The more I got to know you, the more I realized that you glow, not because of your outward appearance. Because of the sacrifices you make for others. You make the world around you a brighter place, and that inspires me. Your worth isn't tied to your bank account balance or some stock portfolio. Not to me. I love the inside of you, the light you give."

He leans over and kisses me, his lips soft but urgent, and I drop my bag. It topples down the stairs and crashes against the ground. The sound jerks me back to reality and I glance down at the resultant mess. My clothing spewed out all over the floor, and I breathe a sigh of relief that his garage floor is so clean. But I wish my pink lacy bra wasn't lying on top of a heap of beach gear.

"That is so not how I thought I'd see your undies for the first time," Trig says.

I swat his arm, and he catches my hand. "But I do want to see them. And the rest of you, every single day." He drops down to one knee, in the middle of the garage. "Marry me, Geo. Shine with me forever."

I splutter.

He loves me. He wants to marry me?

It's way too much, way too fast.

But I think about what I've learned about Trig. He adores his sister. He finds companies and props them up, working with them to succeed. He's best friends with Luke, who from what I can tell is one of the truly good men out there. He detests the miserable marriage his parents have. He met my mom, and now, after seeing me with a sprained knee, after seeing my tiny condo, and going with me to deliver a pathetic peach cobbler to my sometimes-there mother, now he's proposing.

In Hawaii.

I'd be a moron to say no. So I surprise myself by saying, "Yes."

"Really?" He laughs, but it's not a mocking laugh. It

sounds like sunshine pouring out of his mouth. He swings me in a circle and sets me down, but keeps his hands around my waist. "Let's not wait. I don't want a long engagement. I want to marry you soon. Tomorrow even."

I laugh this time. "Maybe not tomorrow, but I don't want a long engagement either."

He leans down until our foreheads press together. "Next week."

I look up at him. "I'd like time to pick a dress and prepare my mom."

He closes his eyes. "Of course. While you're doing that, can we figure out how to keep my mom in the dark? Because she's sure to wreck this if she possibly can."

I roll my eyes. "I've dealt with some mothers-in-law in the past. I'm sure I can handle yours."

"Fine, fine. No rush then. I know this part isn't about me, but you should know that I'm excited. And this is sudden, I know, but it feels right to me. So right. Maybe the first really right thing I've done since starting Nometry."

"It feels right to me too." I actually mean it. I don't feel any panic, just a sense of baffling peace. As though I'm finally doing what I should have been for a long time.

The door separating the garage and the front door opens without warning and I almost follow my suitcase to the floor of the garage. Trig's big hand clasps my forearm, steadying me at his side.

"Mr. Thornton?" a woman in a white apron asks. "The caterers will be here any minute."

Trig stands up and takes my hand in his. "Bonnie, you're the very first person we get to tell."

She frowns. "Tell what? Do we not need food for twenty? Because if so, I should call my cousin right now."

He laughs. "No, I think the meeting is still on." He glances my way. "Is it?"

I nod.

"But you're the first person I am telling that I'm engaged to marry this superwoman, here. Bonnie, meet Geo."

Bonnie's eyes widen. "Congratulations, sir. That's the best news I've heard in months."

A white van pulls up behind us.

"We better get things ready," I say. "You've got a lot of people coming, and soon."

Trig beams at me, and then proceeds to tell every single person, starting with the caterer and house staff and continuing with the men from the venture he's investigating. His enthusiasm only grows, if anything. I stick around for the dinner portion of the meeting, but after that, I beg off and drag my luggage into one of the guest rooms. We may be engaged, but I don't want to be presumptuous.

I call Paisley, who screams into the phone for a full minute before I can understand a word she says.

"I am so happy for you," she finally manages to say. "This is the best news I've ever heard in my entire life. I mean, don't get me wrong, I love Mary, and Luke is great, but Geo, oh my goodness! I am just so!" More incomprehensible screaming.

I hold the phone away from my ear until it abates a little bit.

"Pais," I finally say. "Pais. I can't understand a thing you're saying."

"Sorry," she says. "But could this be more of a fairy tale? You have this epic love story that ends with unbelievable heartbreak, and you completely go hide in a tower. Then you finally let your hair down and you meet a gorgeous *GAZILLIONAIRE*!"

"How do you know he's gorgeous?" I ask.

"I have the internet, duh. I googled what he looked like twelve seconds after you told me he met you for lunch."

I love Paisley, but I know her too. "You knew before that."

She sighs. "Fine, I knew before that. I've followed him for a few years. There aren't very many hot billionaires out there, okay?"

"Since when do you care whether a guy's loaded?"

"I can't marry anyone who isn't mega rich," she says. "My mom and dad would never allow it."

Paisley searches her car seat cushions for change almost every time we go to lunch. She's my one friend who's actually poorer than me.

"Whatever," I say.

"But seriously, you're engaged. I just can't even wrap my brain around it. Is the ring like a hundred and fifty carats? Did he hire someone to walk around and hold your hand up? Why haven't you sent me a photo yet?"

"I might need to hire someone to answer all your questions."

Paisley laughs. "You can answer in order. I'll wait."

I snort. "You are ridiculous. He proposed a few hours ago, about five minutes before a huge meeting started here at his house. I don't think he planned to propose, so I don't even have a ring yet."

"Well that's crap."

I giggle. "I'll be sure to send you a photo the second it's on my finger. And I'll make sure he gets one big enough that we need to hire a ring holding lackey."

"Mock me if you want, but the struggle is real. I haven't had a decent date in over a month. Some of us are living vicariously here, and you're expecting me to subsist on wafers here."

Oh Pais. "Your happily ever after is out there. I know it. Be patient."

"After this, my hope is restored," she says. "In all seriousness G, I am so so happy for you. Like I know you think I'm dumb, but I am totally crying right now. More than I cried during *Me Before You.*"

"I'm glad my actual engagement rates higher than a fictional tale. And one with a horrible, terrible ending, I might add."

"No, don't say that. You know how much I love that movie. She changed his life, and then she lost him. He loved her too much to hold her back."

I roll my eyes, which is a complete waste because she can't even see it. "I can't get into this with you again. Agree to disagree. But I love you, Pais."

"Love you too, G. Call me tomorrow. For reals. And photos, so many photos, I absolutely insist."

I change into the silk nightgown I brought and slide under the covers. Sometime after ten p.m. local time I fall asleep, a smile on my face.

18

TRIG

Between the early morning flight and the time change, by the time my meeting ends, my brand new fiancé is fast asleep. In one of the guest rooms. I'm not sure what that means, so I give her space. I finally drift off myself, way later than I imagined I would, but when the first of the sun's rays hit my face, I wake up smiling.

When I peek in this morning, her face looks even more angelic than usual. I pull out my phone to check the time, and it's early. Like, seagulls are my only companions early. I tiptoe into the family room so I won't wake up Geo.

I notice that Brekka texted me late last night. HOW'D THE MEETING GO?

I told everyone I met yesterday about our engagement, but I haven't mentioned it to family or friends yet, and I'm not sure whether to wait and tell them in person, or call now. It's strange I haven't called Brekka already, honestly. She usually knows everything about me before I do.

I'm probably still mad she told Mom about Geo. Which is a lousy reason not to tell her my happy news. Withholding information from my mom is like stonewalling the Gestapo. It's only a matter of time before Mom pries the info she wants loose, so you may as well spare yourself the finger screws and water torture.

I pull out my phone and text Brekka back.

IF YOU'RE AWAKE, I HAVE SOME NEWS.

Immediate response. MEETINGS WENT WELL? I SAW THE PROPOSAL THEY SENT. IT'S TOO BAD ABOUT SAN FRAN, BUT WE DON'T REALLY NEED TO ADD TWO IN THE SAME WEEK.

NEWS ABOUT GEO.

My phone rings three seconds later.

"You slept with her!" Brekka practically cheers. "And?"

I choke. "When have I ever called you about something like that? Gross! What is wrong with you?"

"What other news is there? Did she dump you? Because you could have texted me that in like three words, B."

I sigh. Why do all the women in my life talk so much I can't get a word in edgewise? "I proposed."

Complete silence.

"Brekka?" I walk outside in case the reception's bad. "Are you there?"

"I'm here."

"Uh. This is where you tell me how excited you are."

"You screwed this up," she says.

I grunt. "That's rude. Besides, you aren't even here, so how could you possibly know?"

"Where did you propose?"

"What does that have to do with anything?" I ask.

"What does the ring look like?"

"Stop," I say. "You're not supposed to be grilling me. You're supposed to be congratulating me. Unlike Mom, you've been shoving me at every woman under forty for years. I finally found one, a girl you actually adore, and I proposed. She said *yes* by the way, and you think I screwed up? I ought to hang up on you. You obviously woke up too early and you're cranky."

"Where did you propose, B? Were you lying in bed? Or on a plane? Or had some guy just hit on her and you were jealous? Because contrary to pop lyrics that may teach you otherwise, when you're dating a quality girl, you don't have to 'put a ring on it' to make sure you don't lose her. It's been a week."

I wish she could see my scowl. "A week and two days."

"You sound like a toddler right now. Where did you propose?"

I grunt.

"The longer you fail to answer me, the worse my imagination conjures the scene to be. Please tell me she's not secretly a foreigner. Because if she needs to get married to stay in America, I am hanging up on you right now."

I laugh then. "No, nothing like that. Look, I was standing in the garage of our house in Kauai, okay, and that doesn't sound super romantic when I say it out loud, but she had just dropped her bag and you know what? You weren't there. You don't get it. For the first time, I want to be with someone every single day. I want to wake up and see her face in the morning and go to bed at night and guess what? We haven't even had sex. So there."

"Umm, you're saying that like it will convince me this is a good idea."

"It's clearly not about lust," I say. "That's my point."

"So you're waiting until the wedding?" The incredulity practically seeps through the phone.

"I didn't say that, but if she wants to, I would. Look. The point here is, I *love* her and she loves me back. I really didn't expect to be having this conversation with you."

"I'm assuming you didn't get her a ring," Brekka says.

"And if this is for real, you better do that quick. And don't take her to pick one. That's lame, and knowing her the small amount I do, I can tell you she will pick something tiny because she's uncomfortable with wealth. Get her something now, and make it nice enough that it's obvious to everyone you love her."

I sigh. "It's six twelve a.m."

"You know how to get things done. Track down the owner of some place and wake him or her up. They'll come in early with a goldsmith for a ten carat diamond."

I did buy a bracelet from a local shop for Brekka last Christmas. I think the owner scrawled his number on the invoice in case I ever wanted another custom order. Could I call him at six a.m.? I think about surprising Geo with a ring when she wakes up.

Sure, I can call him.

It takes me twenty minutes to dig through all the junk from the cloud for last year's taxes, but there it is. The invoice. With a number.

An hour and forty minutes later, I'm headed back to my house. The owner of Van Balen Fine Jewelry, Pete Fisher, can send his kids to whatever ivy league school he wants after my morning interruption. He insisted on saving his number in my phone before I left. I guess I don't blame him since he just sold me a string of Tahitian pearls, a canary yellow diamond bracelet, and an eleven carat oval solitaire engagement ring with tiny blue sapphires on either side that I think exactly match Geo's eyes.

I might have gotten carried away. I don't buy much jewelry, but I doubt Geo has anything nice, and I got a little excited.

When I open the door from the garage, the bag with the jewelry boxes inside clutched in one hand, I smell bacon. Which means I missed my chance to wake her up with a second, better-phrased proposal.

As beautiful as Geo looked asleep, she looks even more breathtaking in a cotton print sundress covered in daisies and leather sandals. She's singing a pop song while she cooks eggs in a pan and I stop in my tracks. She sounds like Celine Dion. Brekka might be right. I barely know her. But every single new thing I discover makes me love her more.

She turns around to grab a bag of grated cheese and freezes. When her eyes meet mine, a shiver of excitement runs up my spine. I cross the room in five steps and throw my bag on the counter, shoving the food over in the process. I wrap my arms around my future wife and pull her tightly to my chest. There's nothing slow about my actions this morning. My head drops down to hers and captures her lips in one smooth movement.

She gasps against me and wraps her hands around the back of my head, pulling me even closer. I kiss her urgently, little nips against her mouth, and then longer, deeper. Until she shoves against my chest and breaks away.

"What?" My heart accelerates. What did I do wrong?

She groans. "The eggs."

Smoke billows from the pan on the stove.

I scrunch up my nose. "Whoops?"

She shuts off the stove and leans back against the counter. "So much for impressing you with my cooking."

I grin. "We may not have gone about any of this in a typical way, but believe me. I'm impressed."

The side of her mouth curves up. "I've only known you for a little over a week, so I still get a little nervous when you walk in the room. I'm trying to show off for you this morning, and I'm not ready to let you see me without makeup. Are we being stupid?"

"If we are," I say, "it's not just you. I'm all in, G. In fact, maybe you're wondering where I was so early this morning."

"I did wonder." She bites her lip. "But I tried not to worry you panicked and freaked out and went to a hotel or something."

I can't look away from her eyes, so open, so vulnerable, so caring, but I need to get the ring. I fumble around behind me and knock my bag sideways. My hand bumps around until I feel the ring box and I pull on it behind my back.

"Brekka says I screwed this all up last night. But I believe in second chances." I drop to one knee. "I'm sure that I've done a lot of things wrong this week. Like stalking you on your Macaroni Grill night."

Her lips curve all the way into a smile. "I thought that seemed too coincidental."

"Of course it was me. Paul's clueless. I had to scope out my competition."

"How'd you know which location?"

I sigh. "Paul gets credit for that. He was too lazy to go to the one I suggested. Maybe that means fate wanted us together."

She reaches for me, but I'm not ready to stand up yet.

"No, let me get this right. I have to report back to Brekka, you know."

"I'd never dream of interfering with that. I don't want you to lose your job, after all."

I frown. "We're equal partners, but I'm older than her. And when we started the firm, she was a freshman in college. That means if anything, I'm her boss."

"Uh huh." She shrugs. "If you say so."

"Stop talking so I can propose to you, woman."

She air zips her lips in mock solemnity.

"Like I was saying back before my knee started to

hurt on this stone floor, I've done a prodigious amount of screwing up in one week. I imagine I'll cram in even more mistakes in the next fifty or sixty years, but I hope you'll take the time to correct and forgive me, and I'll try not to make the same mistake more than four or five times."

"What a reassuring promise."

"Geode Polson, will you marry me? Please?"

She looks sideways and says, "Hmm. Well. Let me think."

"My knee! Think of my poor knee."

She reaches one hand down to cup my face. "Bernard Thornton the third, yes. I will marry you, in spite of your old man knees." She grabs my collar with both hands and pulls me up to her. I don't waste any time kissing my fiancé. She tastes like strawberries.

Which reminds me of the eggs, which interrupted our last kiss. And now here I am, distracted again. I've got one more step I need to complete.

I pull back a bit and open the ring box. "I was out this morning trying to find a sapphire that exactly matched your eyes." I hold the ring up next to her face. "I got close, but it's not quite right. I hope you'll let that slide. Honestly, I'm not sure any rock can compare to that pigment."

A single tear forms in Geo's eye. "It's beautiful."

I slide it on her finger and it's a tiny bit too big, but I'm proud I'm not too far off. "Not bad for a whirlwind romance, right?"

"And nine in the morning. It's almost like you know how to pull strings." She turns her hand right and then left, inspecting the stone. "Paisley will be pleased I think. I imagine I'll need at least one assistant to help hold up my hand."

"You told Paisley already?" I want to clap or cheer. So

far, I've told everyone and Geo told a soul. I didn't realize how much her lack of animation worried me until now.

"She says Congrats." She giggles. "Actually, she more or less screamed it for five minutes. She's already asking me about wedding colors." She spins her phone around toward me. "She's sent me twenty or so options for a maid of honor dress." She shakes her head. "You'd think she was the event planner."

"You already asked her to be your maid of honor?"

Geo smirks. "You've never met Paisley so I'll forgive that question. I didn't even have an opportunity to ask. I'm going along with it, since I want to survive until the wedding. She's like a tornado of energy and glee, but like the Tasmanian Devil, she can turn nasty when she's upset."

"We definitely need to go to lunch with her next week when you head back to Atlanta."

Geo's face falls. "When I head back." She gulps. "Because I live in Atlanta and you live in Colorado."

"I travel all the time, and you're always welcome to come with me by the way, but it means I don't care much where my home base is. Nometry is based in Denver, obviously, but Brekka won't mind holding down the fort for the main meetings and letting me call in. That's our usual setup anyway."

"So you're saying you'll move to Atlanta?" Her enormous blue eyes look up at me, eyelashes batting, and I wonder if I'd have been able to say no even if I wanted to.

It will be nice to be close to Luke. And it's warmer than Colorado. And further from San Francisco. "I guess that's what I'm saying. You can pick the house, of course, but I'd like to come with you to check out our options."

"What about my little condo?" she asks.

He shrugs. "You can rent it, use it as a storage room, or

let Paisley stay there. Whatever you want, really." She doesn't look as excited as I expected. "Are you okay?"

She nods. "Yeah, totally. It's just a lot to think about." A beeping sound fills the room.

"What's that?"

"I made biscuits." She grabs a towel and pulls a pan out of the oven.

They aren't even the canned kind. They're fluffy and golden and I can't believe I didn't notice the smell before. I guess burned eggs kind of block out everything else

"Bacon and biscuits for breakfast?" she asks. "Or I can make more eggs."

"That sounds great," I say. "And for the record, I'll always forgo eggs to kiss you longer."

She rolls her eyes. "For the next few months maybe."

"Forever," I say. "And that's a promise I can keep because I don't really like eggs much."

She laughs and shifts things around so we can sit at the bar. When she picks up my bag, papers slide even further out across the counter. I reach over to help her, but notice she's gone utterly still.

"What's this?" she asks.

I shift until I can see what she's holding, the Thornton Family Trust Prenuptial Agreement.

I close my eyes and rub my face with my hand. "It's nothing."

She looks up at me. "Nothing? Just a prenup in your bag, no big deal."

I open my mouth and close it again. How do I explain my mother to someone who's never met her? Especially to someone whose mother probably made her lunches every day and tucked her in at night with a kiss. How can I convey the sheer, overpowering force that my mother exerts daily? Part of me wonders whether Mom incepted this whole idea. I hope she didn't. I mean, it's not like she wanted me to propose, and it's not like I'd do it even if she did. But she handed me a prenup, and here I am, engaged two days later.

I open my mouth, not quite sure what might fix this. "My mom—"

"Is she here right now? In Hawaii?" she asks.

I shake my head. "No, no, I saw her in San Francisco."

One eyebrow rises. "And you were planning to propose to me then?"

"No, look, I wasn't even planning to give that to you now, okay? It's an accident you're even seeing it."

"So I don't need to sign it?" She backs up a step, the prenup still in her hand. Her eyes drop down and start scanning. She flips to the second page, still reading.

"No," I say. "I mean, yes, I guess. Eventually you'll have to sign it. It's not my thing; it's the family trust paperwork. I don't even care about that stuff, but the lawyers will require it."

She glances up at me, her eyes hurt. "So I do need to sign it, just not this morning? Can I wear the ring before I sign it? Or should I surrender it to you until you've got an executed contract in hand?" She slides the ring off and holds it out to me.

What is happening?

"No," I say again. "That's not at all what's going on. Look, my family's complicated, okay? Believe me, I hate it too, but I was born a Thornton. It's not like I can just quit. Part of the madness of my family stems from the paperwork. I deal with piles of crap like this on every single trust transaction. It's a pain."

She plonks the new ring I bought her down on the counter and waves the thick document at me. "This says I have to list my net worth, and every item I own. My bank account balance, my debt. You said you didn't care about that, but I guess that wasn't true. I should warn you. I don't look very impressive on paper. In fact, I might be upside down, once you include my extensive manicure related loans."

Funny, she's funny, but I worry if I smile right now it'll be misconstrued like everything else in the last five minutes.

"It's not like you're applying for a credit card. You can't be declined. You just sign at the bottom and pretend we never even had this discussion."

"We didn't have this discussion," she says. "You didn't tell me about it, or ask me, or even give me the courtesy of reviewing it."

"I haven't even reviewed it!"

"But for some reason, you think I should just sign it and pretend I never saw it? Is that what you do with contracts? Somehow I doubt that."

She flips the prenup around toward me and points at a spot halfway down one page. "How about this? There's a barren woman clause. I didn't realize you were marrying me so I could be a walking baby incubator. But I can rest easy knowing that if I can't provide a blood heir, I walk away with the same bunch of nothing I'm bringing into this marriage."

I can't even act shocked, because Mom warned me that horror of a provision was buried in there. How did Geo spot it so fast? I close my eyes and reopen them. I need to de-escalate this fast.

"Calm down, okay? You're not listening to me and you're blowing this all out of proportion. I'm saying that my mom gave me that when Brekka told her how much I liked you, and she told me to make sure I get it signed since marriage is a contract. I didn't—"

"Marriage is a contract?" Her eyes are flat, almost flinty.

"No, not to me, but legally it is."

"So I shouldn't mind that I will be entitled to nothing but my own twelve cents when you get tired of me? That worked well for your parents, didn't it?" She shakes the pages at me. "Do I get to keep the jewelry you buy me? Or at least whatever I'm wearing when you deliver the news we're through? Maybe I can follow you around from meeting to meeting decked out in my nicest Prada boots and fanciest jewelry you've given me so that when you tire of me, I'll get to keep it. Or is that a carve out on page nine hundred and sixteen?"

I roll my eyes. What a diva. "No, that's not what I'm saying. I have no idea what it says about that, but be reasonable. It's not like the trust is going to be buying you jewelry. I did, however." I pull out the necklace and the bracelet and shove them at her. Which might not have been the right way to give her the presents I bought with such excitement.

She shoves the boxes back at me. "I don't want more rocks from you. Do you know me at all? Why did you even propose?"

"Huh?" This has officially spun out of control.

"What made you ask me to marry you in the first place?

"I realized that I love you, and I never want to be without you."

"You proposed half an hour after we saw Ethan, a guy I used to date who's part of your world. You didn't seem too keen on him putting his arm around me, as I recall." She puts her hands on her hips, her ring finger conspicuously empty. "You sure this wasn't all a reaction to that?"

"I can see how you might misconstrue things, but actually I wasn't mad at him, not at all. It was my lack of anger, my desire to spend time with you that told me it wasn't jealousy or wanting someone else's toy. I only want to be around you. Now. Forever."

I hold my hand out to her, willing her to drop this fight and come to me. She steps forward and I pick up the ring. "Put this back on, okay? My feelings are real. I want to marry you, now. Without signing that paper."

"Your mom would hit the ceiling, and she'd make me sign a post nuptial agreement."

I shrug. "Probably, but that's not the point. You're not mad about anything that involves you and me. This is all family stuff." I slide the ring back on her finger. "Now the whole world will know you're mine."

She shoves away from me and I want to scream. Why is everything I say today wrong?

"I'm not a land claim Trig, and even if we get married, I'm not your property. You can't pee on me to keep the other dogs away."

Pee on her? What in the world is she talking about?

"People aren't fire hydrants for you to mark your territory with huge diamonds and whatever this other stuff is." She gestures at the jewelry boxes that I thought she'd love.

It never occurred to me she'd hate it without even seeing it. Note to self, in the future, buy Geo boots, not rocks.

"I'm not trying to own you," I say. "Can we just put this behind us? The one thing I really don't want is to have my parents' nightmare become mine." I swallow hard. "Not every family has peach cobbler and photo albums full of smiling memories. My family has one, very forced, very staged, Christmas card image every year, okay? Once we all posed in different states and they superimposed our images together on the beach. Our families aren't the same, and you're taking everything I say the opposite of what I intended."

"You may think peach cobbler at a wedding is stupid," she says, "but it means something to me. It means that people matter more than diamonds. People matter more than cars. More than houses or paperwork. My family thrived *because* they had nothing when they met, so every dime they earned, they earned together."

"So you wish I was poor now?" She pities my family and thinks her is so much better than mine? Well, her dad died and left her to care for her mom alone. My family may have its issues, but we take care of each other. "You wish I only had two dollars in my pocket so we could build our life from nothing? Because that didn't work out so great for your parents, did it?"

The second the words leave my mouth I want to snatch them back, but I can't. The injury in her eyes slices me like a rusty razor blade.

"Valentine's Day has been the worst day of the year for me for four years now, but this morning I was looking forward to it. A day of love, to celebrate that someone cares about me. I was giddy that someone loves me more than anything else in the world."

She collapses with her elbows braced against the counter, her eyes on the biscuits she just made. "I hated stupid fat Cupid. Why would he shoot me with an arrow and leave me hopelessly in love with the kindest man I had ever met, only to let him get blown to bits right before my happily ever after began?"

I'm afraid to say anything right now, but in this case, I have no idea what to say.

"But now, thanks to my high hopes, this year's shaping up to be my second worst. Because I was stupid enough to fall for a charismatic, electric, pretty boy billionaire. I thought he cared about me. Cupid shot his arrow, and I knew I should dodge it. I knew I should duck and run. But

I stood still and watched it happen. You melted the walls I'd put up and I let you in."

"I do love you," I whisper.

It's true, even though she's mad. Even though I've hurt her.

"That's not enough. You of all people should know what happens when you put money and paperwork ahead of the people you love. You've been telling me about your parents with enough contempt that I didn't think you wanted to follow them right down the same road. I sure don't. My parents may not be alive and well anymore, but I would pick peach cobbler and credit card debt over golden plated shackles every day of my life. And twice on Sunday." She tosses the paperwork on the table and walks back to the guest room.

I sink down on the couch, exhausted. I'm supposed to be surfing in half an hour, but now all I want to do is curl up and go back to sleep. Maybe I can get a do-over on the morning. I think about that movie, *Groundhog Day.* I wonder how many times I'd need to redo this interchange before I could get things right. Minutes tick by, and I run her words over and over in my mind.

The growling engine from an old Land Rover Defender pulling up in front of the house brings me back to my sense. I stand up to squint at the car. Who in the world could be here?

Geo breezes past me, bag in hand. "Ethan's going to show me around today, and I've booked a flight home that leaves at six p.m."

My eyes widen. "Wait, what? We had one little fight. You're bailing because my mom shoved some document in my bag? Are you kidding me right now?"

She inhales slowly through her nose. "It's not one little fight, Trig. Your proposal was the one off. This whole thing was insane from the start. You got jealous, you figured, why not? It's not like there's anything at risk for you here, thanks to all your chain mail of paperwork. I'm not going to take over your business and get stuck running an empire. That's not who I am. If things go badly for me, I'll fall to the ground without a parachute, broken beyond repair."

I take her hand. "You think I have nothing at risk? I'm risking the same thing as you. If this is about money, I'll talk to Mom and make them change it to include whatever terms you want. You can have the whole damn trust for all I care."

She pulls free and backs toward the front door. "You still think it's about the money, and that tells me you don't even get what I'm saying. You don't gamble on love. You've never even had a serious girlfriend. You want to skydive your way through life, because the physical fear of hitting the ground thrills you, but you don't risk your heart." She shakes her head. "I've already been there when someone went splat. I won't survive that again, so I can't do this."

A knock at the door prevents me from responding. "I can't believe you called Ethan."

"He's the only person here that I know."

"Uber's always an option," I mutter.

"I should have called Uber so they could give me a ride... to meet with Ethan? I still have a job to do, because I need to pay my bills." She rolls her eyes. "Goodbye, Trig."

She walks out and doesn't look back.

19
GEO

I tell Ethan I only need a ride because I have a meeting back home, and Trig's stuck in wall-to-wall meetings.

He doesn't argue with me, but when he drops me off at the airport, he hugs me tightly. "If you need to talk, call me. I've been planning to visit Atlanta for a while, and you're always welcome here."

I manage a reasonably believable smile when we part ways, but something about buckling up on my flight sets me off. I spend about eighty percent of the eight hours in the air sobbing. The Japanese businessman next to me doesn't love it and asks to change seats about ten times.

I can't really blame him. If I had the option, I'd try to distance myself from me too.

Paisley's waiting when I land. I sent her a cryptic text message asking for a ride before I left, so I can't really fault her for pouncing on me when I open the passenger side door of her shiny yellow VW Bug.

She takes one look at my puffy face and her eyes soften. "Are you okay?"

I manage to shove my bag in the back and then slump into my seat. "Not really."

"Do you want to talk about it?" She bites her lip. "Because I want to be a good friend, I swear I do, but I am drowning in curiosity here."

I close my bloodshot eyes. "Let's just say easy in, easy out."

"Oh, let's say more than that." Paisley puts the car in gear and starts to drive me home.

I hiccup and start to sob again.

"Or not, honey, that's okay. I'm sorry."

"It's fine," I say between heaving breaths. "He gave me a ring, and then a prenup."

"No he didn't." Paisley clucks. "Men are really dumb. But that was probably only because his family will make you sign one eventually."

I stare out the window at the buildings passing in a blur. My next words come out in a whisper. "He said my family didn't turn out well, and he knows because I took him with me to see Mom."

Paisley puts her hand over mine and doesn't speak another word the entire way home, moving her hand only when she needs to shift. When she stops in front of my building, I grab my bag and open the door. Before I can even stand up all the way, Paisley runs around to my side and pulls me close.

"It's going to be okay," Paisley says. "It doesn't feel like that now, but you survived Mark. You can survive this spoiled trust baby too."

I don't tell her this might feel worse. Because the more I think about what happened, the more I think this one may be entirely my fault. I think at the end of the day, nothing that's been glued together is ever quite the same, and I've been glued back together too many times. I don't even resemble the simple, mostly rational Geo who fell in love with Mark.

When I pull away, Paisley's face looks pained. "Are you okay?" I ask.

"I'm not sure if this is a good time to mention it, but, well. Delaying might be worse. I possibly did something bad."

I've already wrecked my life. How much worse could anything Pais did make things? "What did you do?"

"I saw Rob yesterday at the gym, and I might have mentioned..."

That I was engaged. I should have told Paisley that Rob confessed to being in love with me. She would probably have kept her mouth shut if she knew and saved us all some pointless angst.

I close my eyes. "How did he take it?"

"Surprisingly poorly. He acted like I told him you were dying."

"At least one person will be glad to hear my newest update," I say, not looking forward to calling him any time soon.

When I reach my own, tiny, pathetic, mortgaged condo, I beeline for the bed and collapse.

I wake up the next morning to the persistent sound of a gong ringing. I rub my eyes once before I recognize the noise. When I checked my mom into Arbor Terrace, they gave me the number for the clinical department. If there was ever an issue with my mom, I wanted a really annoying ringer. In the two years she's been there, I've never heard it.

Until now.

My heart breaks. No, not my mom. I can't take anything else right now. She needs to be fine. I stifle my fear and swipe to answer the call. "Hello?"

"Mrs. Polson?"

I wince. "Miss."

"Right. Miss Polson?"

"Yes, that's me."

"This is Fred from Arbor Terrace."

Get to the point. "My mom's a resident there, I know this number. What's wrong?"

"Nothing's wrong, but we've left you several messages. You didn't get them?"

I pull away from my phone and notice I've got twenty-one unopened voicemails. Yuck. "I'm sorry, I may be a little behind."

"Your mother's injection is in one hour. Usually the family wants to be there for it."

"Excuse me?"

"Will you be attending?" Fred asks. "If not, that's fine. I'll let her know you couldn't make it."

I look at my bedside clock. Eight a.m.

"I'll be there," I say. "Count on it."

He hangs up before I can ask anything else.

I wrack my brain for what injection it might be while I shower. I wish it was the Phineas Trial injection, but I missed the window on that, so clearly that's not it. Maybe it's for her knee pain? They talked about a cortisol injection, I think? I hope it's not too painful, but I can almost always calm her down.

I drive to the Terrace as fast as I'm willing to risk, arriving ten minutes early. I don't pray much, but I say a silent prayer from the parking lot.

"Dear God, first let me say that I am so grateful my mom's not injured or dying or anything. But then I need to ask a favor. Please let my mom be okay today. I know I don't pray to you much, and that it's selfish for me to ask for this reason, but I can't handle anything else right now. Please help my mom not to be in pain for this injection of whatever it is and not to cry, and help her to know me when she sees me. Please. That's all. Amen."

I unclench my hands from the steering wheel and drag myself inside.

"Where's Megan?" I ask the man at the desk.

"I'm Fred," he says. "We spoke on the phone? Megan has weekends off. You never come in on Saturdays, or you'd have met me already. I cover the front desk whenever Nelly's busy."

Who's Nelly? I feel a small pang of guilt that I never come on the weekend. Should I be coming more often than twice a week? Am I a bad daughter? I tell myself that my coming agitates my mother, but maybe I'm just a coward.

"Right this way," Fred says, reaching for my arm as though I'm a shuffling geriatric.

"I know where her room is," I snap. "It's not like I never visit, just not on Saturdays. I'm an event planner. Saturdays are my busiest days."

"The injections take place in the clinic bay. Do you frequent the clinic on your many visits?" He frowns at me, turns on his heel, and marches out.

I follow him without apologizing, even though I know I probably should. I'm sick of feeling crappy about everything, and Fred should be nicer to family members. Isn't that kind of elder care 101?

I can hear her from down the hall. I don't need Fred to lead me anymore, not with my mom calling out in pain. I race down the checkered tile floors ahead of him and swing around the corner. "Mom?"

She's sitting in a chair while a nurse tries to hold her arm still.

"No needles," she yells. "Get away from me, devil woman."

They're just trying to give her the medicine. I rush to her side. "It's okay Mom, I'm here. It's Geode."

Her eyes widen. "I'm not your mother. I've only been married a year."

I sigh. "Fine, you got me. I was playing a joke. Your husband sent me. He wants you to calm down and let this lady give you a shot. The flu is bad this year, and he needs you healthy. He already paid for the vaccination."

She glares at me. "Why should I believe you?"

"Daddy—I mean Clyde told me you might be worried. He knows how you hate needles. He said if you didn't believe my message came from him, to tell you how he likes your hair best."

She lifts her head and pats her hair with her free arm. "And how is that?"

"He likes it when you let it air dry, all curly and wild. He thinks you look like you belong in the woods with the sprites and the fairies." My breath catches, remembering all the times Dad told Mom the things he loved about her.

"What else did he say?" Mom grabs my hand. "My Clyde."

"He said you dazzled him from the first moment he saw you. He said he knew he wanted to marry you when he tasted your biscuits. The recipe your mom taught you. The secret ingredient is honey, just two tablespoons."

Mom beams. "He does love my biscuits."

"Not as much as he loves your smile." That might be a lie, but it's the thing I've missed the most.

Mom holds still for the injection and the nurse straightens and crosses the room to dispose of the empty syringe. She bobs her head at me. "Thanks for calming her down. It should only take ten minutes before it kicks in."

"What's it for?" I whisper. "I thought cortisol went directly into the knee."

The nurse tilts her head, clearly puzzled. "No, this is the first round of the Phineas Trial. You signed all the paperwork."

My lips move, but no words come out.

The nurse's eyes widen. "Wait, didn't you? If I injected the wrong patient they are going to fire me, and I need this job."

I choke out the words, "No, I mean. I did sign the enrollment, but then I couldn't get the fee together in time. They told me it was too late."

She shrugs. "I don't know anything about that." She points at a chart. "This is your mom though, right?"

I read the name. "Yep, that's her."

"Geode?"

My mom's eyes light up when I turn toward her. "What are you doing here? I figured you'd be at work."

"I came to see you," I say, my voice cracking. "I needed to see my mom today."

"You can take her to her room," the nurse says. "But I'm supposed to hover outside the door to monitor her reaction and take notes."

I nod. "Fine, that's fine."

Mom stands up and we walk down the hall. "It's nice outside today," she says, "for winter time. Would you like to sit in the courtyard?"

I bob my head. "I'd like that."

Mom takes my arm in hers as we walk down the hallway and my life doesn't seem quite so bleak. We exit the door, the nurse trailing a dozen feet behind us. We angle two chairs so they're out of the wind. Everything in the flower beds is dead, but the fresh air is invigorating.

My mom takes my hand. "Tell me what's going on, Geo."

"You have Alzheimer's, Mom."

She nods. "I know that, and I'm sorry. I know it's hard for you."

I gulp in air to keep from crying. "But you're in a clinical trial, the Phineas Trial. They have some injections that help stabilize patients so they have regular lucid intervals."

Her eyes take on a desperate gleam. "I don't know whether I want that," she says.

"Why not?"

She sighs. "I'm sorry. I do, of course. But when I'm lucid, I remember that he's gone." She crumples, tears rolling down her face. "I miss him. I miss your dad."

I miss you, I want to say, and you're right here next to me. But I don't want her wallowing in guilt, and I understand the feeling, all too well.

"If you want me to un-enroll you. . ." I trail off, because I don't know whether I can really follow through on my offer.

She shakes her head. "No, don't do that. You're right. I miss you just as much as your father, and you're here. And today, I'm here too." She squeezes my hand. "Tell me everything. You're planning events, right?"

I nod my head. "I am. I have a bachelor and bachelorette party next weekend, and a Casino night on Valentine's Day. I've also got a wedding for a, well, he's almost a billionaire."

Mom's eyes widen. "That sounds very exciting."

I tell her about the things we're considering. A backyard wedding on a river, or a destination wedding in Hawaii. I tell her all about the botanical gardens that overlook the beach. "I should have checked out more places while I was there," I say, "but I got in a fight with, well, he was my boyfriend."

Mom sits up. "Your what?" She narrows her eyes at me.

"Was he tall? Really tall, with full, wavy brown hair and dimples?"

I bob my head and pull out my phone. I open the photo app, knowing our photo was the last one taken, but I don't look at it. It'll make me bawl for sure. I swivel the phone to face her. "He came with me to see you Monday."

"He's so handsome. The two of you together must have stopped a lot of people in their tracks. Tell me about him."

I shake my head. "That's pointless. We broke up yesterday."

"Why?" Mom's eyes are full of concern, just like they used to be.

I don't really want to get into it, but maybe I should. Mom always gave such great advice. "He proposed, and then the next morning, he bought me a ring."

Mom's eyes dart toward my left hand.

"I gave it back," I say. "Actually, I might have kind of shoved it back at him."

"Why? Was he mean?"

I shake my head. "You and Dad had nothing at the beginning, and you grew and learned together, just the two of you against the world. That's why you were so strong."

Mom frowns. "Your dad's a wonderful man and I don't like saying anything bad about him, but he wasn't wise with money."

"I'm sorry?" I must have misunderstood her.

"Your father invested in every single Ponzi scheme ever created, I think," Mom says. "No matter how many times I begged him not to, he insisted the new one would be different. He had no business sense. Not even a business penny."

I forgot how awful my mom's puns could be.

"I mean, I stayed with him, but only because I forgave him so fast. I thought about leaving him more times than you can count." She tilts her head. "So is this handsome man of yours poor? Or rich?"

I sigh and slouch in my seat. "He's richer than Croesus, Mom, and it's family money too."

"And?" Mom asks. "I mean, it's not like people usually bemoan that their new son-in-law has loads of cash.'"

I roll my eyes. "Mom, he wanted me to sign a prenup. I had to list all my assets and then it outlines the many many things he owns to make sure when he gets tired of me, I get none of that."

"Is he a womanizer?" Mom asks.

I shrug. "No, I mean, not that I know of. I haven't known him very long."

"Your dad and I married twelve days after we met."

"Wait, what?"

She laughs. "We never really told people. But he was home from college and we couldn't bear the thought of spending a semester apart."

"Did you regret it?"

"All the time! Whenever he took every dime we had saved and invested in some cleaning supply company, or a pet food group, or once, he sank eleven thousand dollars into a company called Micro Plush. They sold tiny little stuffed animals the size of a penny. I can't really fault him there. Ty Beanie Babies were all the rage ten years later." She sighs. "The point I'm trying to make is that sometimes you meet someone and you just know. Your heart has more intelligence than your head gives it credit for. I'm not telling you that you should marry him. But I think you already know what you feel about that."

She doesn't think it's crazy I almost agreed to marry someone I had known for nine days.

She pats my hand. "Are you relieved you dumped him?"

The tears start then and I can't gulp them back, not this

time, not with all the air in the world. Mom slides her chair next to me and wraps an arm around my shoulders. I bury my face against her shoulder. "I miss his face, I miss his jokes, and I miss the way he takes care of me. I miss his boyish grin, and his mop of hair. I miss his sister, and I miss playing him at chess. I could go on and on."

"He's a chess player?" Mom asks. "That's a lucky break."

I wipe my face and sit up. "I messed it all up already. Beyond repair."

"Are you sure?" Mom asks.

I nod my head. "I freaked out on him when he showed me the prenup. He said it wasn't because he wanted one, but his family required it. Actually, he didn't even show it to me. It just fell out if his bag and I pounced on it."

"His parents signed one, I'm guessing?"

I nod. "And they're miserable. His mom hates his dad, but wants to keep running the business. It trapped them in an awful marriage, from what Trig says."

"And his dad sees other women?"

I shrug. "I think so. I don't know for sure."

"Do you think Trig would just divorce you for his next love interest, leaving you penniless?"

I try to imagine Trig ditching me for another woman. I think about him when we've been together. He doesn't even seem to notice the other women. Ivy, Megan, waitresses, hostesses.

But he sees me.

"No." But how can you ever really know what is waiting around the corner?

"If you don't suspect his care for you is feigned, why did you really get so upset and break things off?"

I close my eyes. "Maybe I'm scared. Maybe last time I almost got married, everything in my life imploded."

"More like exploded," Mom says.

I flinch.

She wraps her arm around me again. "I'm sorry sweetheart. And you lost your dad right after that. And then me too, essentially. It's been a rough few years."

Tears stream down my face again, and I wish I wasn't such a big baby.

"You can't nuke every single person who tries to love you because you're afraid of how much it might hurt. That would be my worst nightmare for my sparkly, beautiful Geode. That would be worse than if your dad and I had put you into child modeling." She kisses my forehead and brushes my hair back. "When you were born, every single person we met gushed. 'This is the most beautiful baby we've seen,' they'd say. 'Look at her eyes!' or 'Her hair is to die for!' At first your dad and I loved it. You were two-years-old the first time an agent approached us, offering us the sun, moon, and stars if we'd let you model. Your dad wanted the money. I'd be lying if I didn't admit it was an attractive offer. Your dad had just invested in a soap company I knew was doomed, and things were tight."

Mom strokes my cheek. "You've always been the most beautiful person I know and people envy that, but they don't understand. It's different than being cute. It's not the same as being pretty. It's so much harder. There's so much pressure, and all in the wrong places. Clyde and I decided that people needed to get close to see your true beauty. We turned down modeling scouts, and businesses looking for print ads. When you were fourteen, the first agent approached you instead of us. Do you remember?"

I nod.

"You were so upset we wouldn't let you go to that audition. You'd have gotten the job, I know it. But it would have ruined you. It would have transformed you, and you were too fragile inside for that. It sounds like this Trig might have seen past your face."

He did. I think he really did. And I burned it down.

"If your boy is right for you, and he might yet be," Mom says, "he'll forgive you. And if he won't, then he's not the man you need. Trust me. Anyone who lets one mistake ruin something wouldn't have lasted anyway."

"I don't think I can call him," I say. "It's too embarrassing. I was too horrible."

"Then you don't love him enough."

Or I'm not brave enough. I know Trig said he wanted me to forgive him when he made mistakes, but he didn't mention forgiving me.

Mom plays me at a game of checkers, and then Monopoly. She hates chess, so I don't even ask. My dad was the chess player.

"I'm tired of thinking," she finally confesses after I take her last property. "Maybe we could watch some TV."

We're halfway through a rerun of Gilmore Girls when I notice my mom's leaning away from me awkwardly on the sofa, her eyes darting my way now and then furtively.

"Mom, you okay?"

She glances around as though she's not sure who I'm talking to. I should be grateful for the time I had, I know I should. It's hours more than I've had in years. But somehow in that moment, it feels like someone sliced my heart in two. I didn't even get to say goodbye.

When I stand up, she breathes a relieved sigh and spreads out on the sofa, continuing to watch the show. I blow her a kiss when I'm far enough away it won't distress her. "Thanks for a great Saturday, Mom."

20

TRIG

I stare out the window at the surf for so long I'm late.

But I don't sit around and mope. That's not who I am. If Geo wants to leave, she can leave. I'm not going to make her sign paperwork she doesn't want to, and I'm not going to force her to love me back. I'm not that pathetic yet, thank goodness.

The stabilizing tech is as good as they promised. I catch some of the best waves of my life off the North Shore that day. Until I catch one that's a little too big out past the reef.

I'm knocked under and roll over several times, trying to relax through it like I've been taught. My shin catches a rock or some coral and pain rips through me. I'm numb enough from this morning that it doesn't phase me as much as it normally would, but when I head back for shore, blood trails behind me.

Derek, one of the developers, swears when he sees me. "Oh man, we've got to get you to the hospital, like stet."

"I think it's stat," I say.

He presses a towel against my shin and helps me into his jeep. "Keep pushing on that, okay?"

The beach towel's almost entirely soaked in red where I've been squeezing it by the time we reach the Wilcox Emergency Room. One of the early nurses peels back the towel and shudders. I look down at the six inch gash. I really tagged myself this time.

"We'll get you right back." She wraps my leg with gauze and compression bandages, ostensibly to slow the bleeding until I can get stitches. Derek's boss drops off my bag with my phone right as they're showing me into a room.

"I'm sorry you wiped out," Cliff says. "But those were some epic waves this morning."

I force a grin that I hope doesn't look as horrifying as I feel. "They were. I'm sure you'll be hearing from us soon, although I may send you this bill."

Cliff addresses the doc before he leaves. "Cheapest care possible for this guy, you got it? Like Band-Aids and Kleenex should be fine. Apparently I'm paying."

The ER doctor's putting in stitches when Brekka calls.

I answer. "Hello?"

"How did it go? You didn't call or text or anything. Did you get a ring? Does she like it?"

"Well," I say. "Let's review. I got her a ring. She gasped. 'Oh, Trig,' and then she gushed, 'this is just gorgeous'."

"I'm so glad she liked it."

"And then," I say, "she—ouch! Watch it down there."

The ER doc shakes her head. "No phones allowed, Mr. Thornton, but you don't see me complaining."

"Wait, where are you?" Brekka asks.

I sigh. "I hit a rock and I'm in the ER."

"Not again," she says. "How bad is it?"

"How bad is it, doc?" I ask.

"Seventeen centimeter laceration, two centimeters deep. Two layers of stitches. Should be okay to walk on regularly within two days, fine to resume normal activities within a week. I'll write you for Vicodin if you want some."

"Why do you act so stupid?" Brekka asks. "I bet you didn't take it easy at all. I'm sure Geo's upset."

"Geo's not even here." My voice sounds flat and hard, even to me.

"What? What's going on, B?"

Oh you know. Mom and her stupid paperwork ruined everything, as usual. "Geo saw the prenup and completely freaking freaked out. I swear, I stood there and like spluttered. She called Ethan and bailed. Headed home on a commercial flight—" I glance at the clock. "About now."

"Hold the phone," she says.

"Uh, it's in my hand."

"Smart aleck. I mean, wait up. That can't be the whole story. What did she say exactly?"

I close my eyes. "She might have asked me why I proposed and implied that I did it to like claim her or something. In that regard, nice suggestion on the huge ring. She called it a shackle, I think."

Brekka sighs. "Did you tell her all the reasons you loved her?"

"No, I told her I only proposed to pee on her so the other dogs would leave her alone."

"Excuse me?"

"Never mind. This whole day has royally sucked. Look, she wouldn't listen when I said I didn't care about the prenup."

"The timing was bad, but she would have had to sign it eventually," Brekka says.

"I know! I told her I didn't want it, but she had to at some point."

"Okay," Brekka says. "Focus. What really upset her?"

"She felt like she wasn't valuable, I think. Maybe."

"She said that?"

"She got all worked up that she had to list her assets. She said all she has is a lot of credit card debt from her many, many manicures."

"That's funny," Brekka says.

"Right?" I miss her scowls, her jokes, her sparkling eyes. "But then she also said she wants to have peach cobbler at our wedding—" I close my eyes. And I told her that her dad was worthless for dying penniless, leaving her holding the bag with her mom.

"Hello? Trig? I feel like I'm losing a lot in translation here."

I groan. "I kind of insulted her family."

"No you didn't. That's not like you. You're never mean. How could you have even done that? Do you even know them?"

"I met her mom," I admit. "In a nursing home."

"How old is she?" Brekka asks. "Why's her mom in a nursing home?"

"Her mom had her late, I gather, and she has early onset Alzheimer's. And her dad died of cancer. Her mom's like super nice, but Brekka. It was hard to see Geo in there. She obviously misses her, and she's only twenty six and caring for her mom alone."

"You screwed up big time."

I know. "I don't think I can fix it." A tear slips down my face, and it's not from the pain of the stitches or the throbbing in my leg.

"You can't make it worse, I don't think," Brekka says. "At least that's something. Let's review. She's upset you want a prenup because it makes her feel worthless, and what else?"

"She's mentioned that I want to take risks and she's

already gone splat," I say. "I think she hates the skydiving and skiing and surfing and dirt bikes."

"I get that."

"What do you mean you get that?" I ask.

"I hate it too."

I almost drop the phone. "Uh, you're the reason I do all that stuff in the first place."

"That makes no sense, B. What are you even talking about? I sit in this stupid chair biting my nails to the quick every time you're on one of your dumb trips."

"After the accident." I clear my throat. "After I paralyzed you, I sat around with you, day in and day out, resolved not to do anything you couldn't."

"Right," she says. "Because you stupidly blamed yourself for that semi-driver who had a heart attack. No one else faulted you, but you took the blame on yourself anyway."

"The point is, you made me promise to do every single thing you couldn't. To live life to the fullest. I can't quit." I pause. Brekka bites her nails to the quick? I'm not living for her, I'm causing her distress?

When she doesn't reply, I ask, "I can't quit living for you, doing the things you can't, right?"

"I meant go ski or run marathons, or whatever athletic dreams you have. I didn't mean you should fling yourself out of planes, you moron. Have you even seen what our corporate life insurance policy on you costs, thanks to your idiotic activities?"

"You always come watch when you're close. You take photos, and when you aren't around, you make me describe every second to you, in detail."

She practically yells into the phone. "I'm trying to be supportive, dummy. I can barely get to the bathroom to pee by myself. I don't want to be the person no one can talk to about the fun things they do, but you're next level and I hate watching it. I'm constantly terrified you'll die, or worse, end up paralyzed like me."

She thinks being paralyzed is worse than dying? Then why not risk the surgery? Why not chance getting better? I almost press her on it, but then I remember what Geo said. It's Brekka's life to live. "Well, maybe telling her I won't do stupid stuff anymore will help her feel better about not going splat."

"Unless she's worried about her heart going splat," Brekka says quietly. "She may have meant it metaphorically."

My sister's a friggin' genius.

"And there may be one more thing," I say. "She said if we sign a prenup, I'll basically be following Mom and Dad's path to misery. Do you think that's true?"

Brekka sighs. "I'm on your side with this one. I mean, what other choice do we have? All the family money is in there. It's not like *you're* asking her to sign it. And you're not our father, so you should be fine."

Brekka's not precisely correct, and when that occurs to me, so does a solution. And the more I think about it, the more it feels like shackles have fallen away from me and I can spread my wings and take flight. For maybe the first time ever.

"Geo hates Valentine's Day and that's a real shame," I say. "Do you think there's enough time to get this done before then?"

"Get what done?" Brekka asks me.

I tell her.

"I don't know. Are you sure you want to do that? It's drastic, and maybe irreversible."

"I've never been more positive." Now that I've had the idea, it's like I can't stop thinking about it. I'm doing this as much for me as for Geo. I can't follow Mom and Dad's blueprint to never-ending purgatory. I need to forge my own path, and this is the only way out of the Thornton maze.

"I hope this isn't a mistake," Brekka says. "Because I don't think you can unwind it."

"I don't think I'd ever want to. I only wish I'd thought of this years ago."

"Trig, if we're wrong and she doesn't really love you, or if Valentine's is the wrong day to spring this on her..."

Brekka's always right, but Geo mentioned the day herself. And my job from day one, even if I didn't know it then, has always been to heal what Mark broke when he died. I may as well fix it on the same day it shattered.

"I've got to go," I tell Brekka. "I have a lot of calls to make."

21

GEO

I call Rob the second I reach my car.

"Geo?"

My throat closes off and I don't know how to thank him. Rob offered to pay the Phineas Trial fee a hundred times, and I told him no every time. Pride's a funny thing. I've never been so glad someone overrode my explicit commands in my life.

"I just left the Terrace." I break down into sobs.

"Geode, are you there? Is everything okay? I'm walking to my car now."

"No," I choke out. "I'll be okay, really. I promise."

"Did you say you were at the Terrace?" he asks.

"Yeah. I had to call to say thank you. Thank you a million times over."

"Umm, I hate to do this, but I need to ask why you're thanking me."

I inhale deeply. He doesn't know why I'm thanking him, and he knows I've been to see my mom. "I got my money together too late. Mom got declined for the Phineas Trial."

"I know. You told me."

"But today I got a call. Someone got her in, and she had her first injection today."

"What?" Rob asks. "How?"

Maybe he's covering, afraid I'll be mad. "I'm so grateful, Rob. You don't have to pretend you had nothing to do with it."

"I'm not trying to be modest here, or keep you from being mad. I wish I'd been confident enough to do it now, seeing how well it's worked out, but it wasn't me, G. I swear."

I close my eyes and lean my head against the steering wheel. "It wasn't?"

"Nuh uh. If I were you, I'd call my mega rich fiancé. Maybe he did it."

"We broke up," I whisper.

"Oh G. I'm sorry."

His pity galvanizes me. "It couldn't have been him, Rob. It must have been a mix-up or something. Which means when they come asking me for the money, I may need a loan. It was a hundred and fifty grand, and Luke and Mary prepaid the first hundred. I have a little over twenty saved, but I don't get that bonus until the end."

"I've always been happy to pay for all of it," Rob says. "I told you months ago."

I know, and I don't deserve him. "I remember, but it's not a gift. It's a loan."

"Understood. I'll bring a check over later today. Name the amount."

I can't see him, not right now. I just can't. "I'll drop by the dealership next week. We need to go over the details of your Casino night anyway."

"I'm sorry that things didn't work out with that guy, but I'm glad you're out there again. Even if it's not with me."

"Thanks."

I hang up and lean back in my seat, completely emotionally drained. When I get home, I look over the paperwork I filled out and dial the number from my initial application. I get an answering machine, so I guess I'll have to call back Monday.

I want to call Trig. I should call him and ask.

I pick up my phone but before I dial, I pull up our photo. His smile is so boyish, so kind. I want to get back to this again, but I don't know whether I can. My heart contracts and I put the phone back down. I'll call him tomorrow. I won't feel so wrung out then.

Except on Sunday, Paisley comes over and insists on taking me shopping. "You need to get out of this condo," she says. "And since you just got a manicure, we're going shopping."

She makes me go to a movie too, and Rob meets us. When he sits next to me, it feels surprisingly normal. He passes me a check when the movie ends. "I'm really glad your mom got enrolled, no matter how it came about."

"Me too." I hug him and it's like coming home. I hope Rob can forgive me for not loving him the way he loves me, because I need him in my life.

"Ice cream?" The smile Paisley turns on me looks glued on.

"I don't think I can handle any more forced happiness today," I say.

"Forced? Pah. I'm an absolute delight," Paisley says. "Don't take my word for it. Lots of people have told me that."

I roll my eyes. "You can't use my own words against me."

"I absolutely can, and I will," Pais says. "Best friend prerogative."

"Fine," I say. "Ice cream in January. Why not?"

At least we have the place to ourselves.

"I heard from Ethan today," Paisley says. "You guys remember him?"

Rob grunts. He never liked Ethan or the rest of our college friends much. "What did he want?"

"He says he bumped into the fair Geo a few days ago."

"In Hawaii." I lick my mint ice cream. "He actually picked me up from the beach house right after I dumped Trig."

"Was his hair perfectly coiffed into an effortless surfer do?" Rob asks. "And his shirt unbuttoned about three buttons too far?"

As someone with a very solid, very defined chest that's always covered under a layer of fabric unless he's actively swimming, it annoys Rob when other guys flaunt their muscles.

"His hair looked exactly the same as it always has. Maybe a tiny bit blonder from all the Hawaiian sun. And he didn't ask me a single question or make things worse in any way. He was utterly professional at work, and entirely gentlemanly the rest of the time. He even offered me an amazing deal for Mary and Luke's wedding."

"Fine, maybe he's not so bad," Rob says. "Sometimes people improve with age."

"I was kind of excited when he texted," Paisley says. "I always liked him, you know."

I shake my head. "I didn't know that. Seriously? Ethan?"

"He only ever had eyes for you, though. I love you, G, but sometimes it sucks being Watson."

"Excuse me?" I ask.

She rolls her eyes. "Sherlock Holmes' best friend."

"Oh please," I say. "You're exaggerating."

Rob shakes his head. "Not really."

I throw a balled up napkin at him.

"You guys are making me feel better, and I appreciate it, but Ethan was just being nice. He felt sorry for the bird with the broken wing. That's all."

Paisley whips out her phone. "You think so, huh?" She turns her phone around so we can read the screen.

The text chain looks like this:

Ethan: I SAW GEODE YESTERDAY. SHE'S AS GORGEOUS AS EVER. THEN SHE CALLS AND NEEDS A RIDE ON A COMMERCIAL FLIGHT HOME. ALONE. ALL TRAGIC LOOKING. NOW I'M TRYING TO CONVINCE MYSELF I SHOULDN'T GO BEAT THE %&*# OUT OF THAT TRIG. WHAT HAPPENED?

Paisley: I DON'T KNOW EXACTLY. SHE SAYS IT'S HER FAULT THOUGH, SO MAYBE DON'T KNOCK HIM OUT YET.

Ethan: I'M COUNTING ON YOU TO TELL ME WHEN SHE'S OVER IT. I'LL BE ON THE NEXT PLANE TO ATLANTA. THAT GUY'S AN IDIOT. BUT HIS LOSS...

Paisley flips her phone back around. "So, Sherlock, what were you saying exactly?"

But I don't love Ethan. And I ruined everything with the guy I do love. I burst into tears, and embarrassingly, I can't stop for several minutes.

Rob offers to take me home, but I think he's relieved when Paisley insists on driving me.

I appreciate my friends' efforts, but it's time for me to face the firing squad.

I try to call, but my fingers shake so hard when I try to call that I can't press the button. I text Trig instead.

DID YOU ENROLL MY MOM IN THE PHINEAS TRIAL?

When he doesn't reply right away, I want to curl up in a

fetal ball and die. What if he's on a date? What if he thinks he dodged a bullet?

I force myself up off the floor. It's only six p.m. I will not sit around staring at my phone. I put on my workout leggings and the jacket I haven't worn in ten days and plug my phone into the wall. I probably shouldn't go on a run in the early evening without my phone, but I have to get away from it. Leaving it feels safer than running with it.

I run nearly seven miles, which might have been too ambitious on my recently sprained knee. I'm hobbling toward the park exit when I see the cutest yellow lab bounding along in front of a familiar face.

Paul Manning.

I barely know the guy, but pride's a funny thing. I force myself to jog instead of walking, and secretly hope he doesn't recognize me. I do not feel like making small talk.

"I've been jogging at night for nearly a week, and I finally catch you!"

So much for being passed without him noticing me. Sometimes I really hate my face.

"Paul." I force a smile. "You haven't been running every evening."

His dog doesn't bark, but if tails could wag right off, its tail would. I crouch down, ignoring the complaint from my knee, and pet his head. He licks my face, which I don't love. But he has a pretty face and soft fur.

"If Trig can stalk you from fifteen states away," Paul says, "I can certainly run a little later."

I snort. "Trig's not stalking me. He isn't even talking to me right now."

Paul frowns. "You're kidding."

"It's complicated I guess, but I think it's safe to say that we broke up."

His eyebrows rise. "So you were together? Because last

week I thought I witnessed him asking you on your first date."

"Trig moves fast, I guess."

Paul shakes his head. "Molasses moves faster than Trig. Tortoises do. Snails race past him. I've known him a long time, and I've never even heard him call anyone his girlfriend. The fact that you needed to break up is notable."

Tears threaten and I take a huge gulping breath.

"Are you okay?"

"It's just my knee. You haven't seen me out running because I sprained my knee last weekend skiing up in Vail. I might have run a little further than I should have."

"I parked not far from here. Need a ride?" he asks.

"Nah, my condo's around the corner. It's probably closer than your car."

"I'm happy to help you over to it, in the least creepy way I could possibly say that. I swear I'm not hitting on you, at least not when Trig's not around. I couldn't help myself earlier, and I'm sorry. He and I have a stupid rivalry neither of us can quite let go."

"He doesn't seem like the kind of guy to be competitive," I joke.

Paul chuckles. "I suppose when he and Luke hit it off, I was a little jealous."

"I could see that."

"Well, if you won't accept my assistance, I'll at least stop delaying you. Let's get together for that lunch though. I promise not to hit on you, or press you for info either. And bring the list of names. I probably know the dirt on most of Luke's half of the guest list. Maybe it'll help you with seating arrangements."

"Thanks," I say. "I really appreciate it."

I hobble the last hundred yards to my condo and ignore my phone on my way to the shower.

Only after I'm clean do I check the screen. He's replied to my question about whether he enrolled my mom, but not in a satisfying way.

NO.

That's it. Nothing else. No, "Did she get in?" or, "Why do you ask?" or "Have a good life." Not even a "How could you leave me like that, you tramp?" Just no.

Nothing else.

I type in the words, I MISS YOU. I LOVE YOU. Then I delete them.

Four times.

I flop back on my bed. I can't cry anymore, not when it's my fault I'm in this mess. He proposed. He bought me a ring. I flipped out on him when I saw some papers that he hadn't even given me himself, and then I took the slightest provocation to run, far far away. Like a bratty baby.

When Mark died, I would have given anything to get him back. Now Trig's alive, probably baffled as heck by me, and I can't bring myself to apologize and tell him I miss him. What is wrong with me?

Is it because he's such a risk? What if he keeps performing idiotic stunts and he dies too? I don't share his belief that God will shelter me from hard things. But at the end of the day, his stunts make me nervous, but he's made it this far so clearly he's pretty coordinated. And he's never made me do anything I don't want to. I chose to ski with him. And before I hurt my knee, I had fun. Quite a lot of fun, actually.

Am I afraid his interest in me won't stick? Am I worried about the prenup? Does my fear over that outweigh what I feel for him?

No. Which is why I said yes when he proposed.

So why did I freak out?

I set my phone on my nightstand and the photo there

catches my eye. Mark. I pick it up. I used to feel a sharp pain like being burned and stabbed simultaneously with a hot poker every time I saw his face. Missing him was a constant ache, a hitch in my side, a silent agony I had to push past every day to swing my feet out of bed. To brush my teeth. To call clients. To check out venues.

I made up wild excuses and drove ten miles out of the way to avoid every location I had considered for our wedding.

Now I look at the photo with a sort of dreamy fondness, the pain softened with time. I miss Mark, my first love, my protector who adored me and made me feel safe.

But I'm not gutted when I think back on Mark anymore. Because I love someone else now. Maybe I feel guilty about that, but I think that's only part of it.

Loving and losing Mark turned me into a coward.

The more time I spend with Trig, the more I'll love him. Which means the more it will hurt when he gets Alzheimer's. Or his chute doesn't open. Or he dies from cancer. Maybe that's why I never told him I loved him back. Everyone dies at some point. And the more people you love, the more people you lose, and the more pain you feel.

I can't live this way. I stand up and look in the mirror. I stare myself down. "You will tell him you love him."

I pick up my phone and text him back. I can't bring myself to say anything else, so I keep it short.

I LOVE YOU.

The text goes through and I have a sudden impulse to run another eight miles. Or drink a bottle of vodka and pass out. Or bang my head against the wall.

Because he still hasn't replied.

I check my phone to see how long it's been since I sent it. How long has this painful, awful silence stretched?

Two minutes.

It feels like a week.

I want to text Brekka. I have to delete her number and our text chain to keep from doing it.

I stare at my phone like a dog watching the door for its master's return for almost an hour. When it finally rings I drop it on the floor. I pick it up with shaking hands and look at the screen.

It's Mary. I swear and answer.

"Thanks for the stuff you sent over," she says. "Normally I wouldn't bother you on a Sunday, but since you sent it over today I figured you might not mind."

"Sure," I say.

"I've been thinking about the bachelor/bachelorette parties. I was planning to have you come with us to San Francisco, but since Paisley's coming, maybe you should be on hand for the bachelor party, in case anything goes wrong? What do you think?"

Spend the weekend with Trig after he's completely ignored my declaration? I'd rather swallow a bucket of nails. Acid dipped nails.

"I love Paisley, you know I do, but while she's great with lists, she's not level headed when something goes wrong. If the spa messes something up, I'd rather be there to handle it. Plus, I have the advantage of being the one they promised the moon to, which helps. Besides, I'll be here this week to check and double check details for the guys."

She exhales. "I'm so glad we hired you. That makes perfect sense. Thank you."

"Did you have a chance to look at the information I sent on the botanical garden in Kauai?" I ask.

"I did, and it looks heavenly. I think we need to talk to our guests and find out who could make it to Hawaii. Once we've run that down, I'll give you our final decision and we can prepare invitations. I love the pressed linen samples you sent. How long do we have to decide?"

I feel bad putting Ethan off, but he said he'd book the weekend now and hold it until the day before without a deposit. "I think I can put him off for another two or three weeks. I knew the owner back in college, so I've got a little latitude."

"You're a miracle worker," Mary says.

My phone dings in my ear, which means there's a text.

"Well, if that's everything?" I say, "I've got a conference call to hop on."

"On a Sunday night?" Mary asks. "And I thought I worked hard. I won't keep you, but Amy said she misses you. She offered to make fish sticks again if you were coming over this week, but I told her you might not want the same thing every time you come. One of her teachers at preschool told her fish is good for your arteries, and she's obsessed with it, but the only kind she likes are the fish sticks." Mary groans. "I've never been more sick of anything in my life. I actually miss the Froot Loops."

Mary's such a good mom. She reminds me of my own.

When she hangs up, I close my eyes. I hold the phone to my heart and take a deep breath in and out, and then I force myself to look.

I LOVE YOU TOO, MORE THAN YOU KNOW. BUT I NEED A LITTLE TIME.

I wasn't quite out of tears after all.

22
TRIG

DID YOU ENROLL MY MOM IN THE PHINEAS TRIAL?

When the text comes through, my heart stops dead. I can't breathe. Geo's messaging me. She walked out without a backwards glance, and I've been working on fixing my mistake for days without any idea whether she would even see me again.

I want to tell her yes. Yes, I contacted the trial and I donated two million dollars to their research and they agreed to extend the date of entry for her mother. But I can't bring myself to do it. She needs to believe that she didn't fail her mom. This needs to be her save, not mine. That clinical trial is her Hawaiian beach house. It's the reason she's planning a wedding for the first time in four years.

Geo beats herself up about enough things that aren't her fault. Besides, all I did was turn back the clock on one thing in her life and set it right. I had the ability to do it, so I took action. I wish I could mitigate the entry fee for her, but she's too smart. She'll be suspicious enough as it is.

NO, WHY DO YOU ASK? I type, my finger hovering over the send button. I desperately want her to respond to me. I'm craving interaction with her. I've been desperate for it for days. Maybe if I handle this right, she'll even invite me over.

I'd call my pilot and fly out immediately. And then she'd yell at me about the prenup again. Or I'd blurt out that I love her and she'd look at me in shock or disdain or pity, and I'll die inside a little more. I breathe in and out. I need to calm down. I know she loves me and she's just scared. I have a plan to put her fears to rest and show her how serious I am about marrying her.

That's why I can't engage with her, not yet. I have a court hearing set for Thursday. Then the bachelor party. After that, I'll be ready. After that I won't be speaking hollow words. I'll be demonstrating with action.

I delete the WHY DO YOU ASK? and send only the NO. I really hope it doesn't hurt her feelings. I hope she's not crushed. I hope she's not wondering whether I love her, like I'm wondering how she feels. I hope she knows I love her, and that I'm sorry, but in case she doesn't, I need time to do more than say the words.

When I get a text from her later, I LOVE YOU, I crumple. I have to text her back.

I LOVE YOU TOO. I'M GETTING ON A PLANE NOW. I CAN BE THERE BY MIDNIGHT.

No. That's all wrong. I delete it.

I'LL BE IN ATLANTA TOMORROW. LET'S TALK. That's not as pathetic or desperate. I can wait a bit and send that.

Except I'm back to where I was two hours ago. I'm not ready yet. I have only words to share, nothing concrete.

I clench my fists and scream in frustration.

My chef, Antonio, peeks his head around the corner. "Are you okay, sir?"

I forgot he was still here. "No, I mean, yes, I'm fine. You can go home."

"You haven't had dinner yet, sir."

Of course I haven't. "I'm not hungry."

He frowns. "Tiger Prawns sir? Just flown in? Or maybe a filet, rare?"

I shake my head. I think about asking his opinion, but I have to figure this out myself. I can't make anyone else translate for me. Besides, no one else knows Geode like I do, not even my brilliant Brekka. I need to hold the course.

How I wish I could push pause on her life for a few days until my ducks are in a row, spare her the pain I've been feeling without her here by my side.

I can ask for time, but she'll think that means I'm not ready to see her. Or that I can't forgive her. I puzzle over it for a long time, but I can't see any way around it. I need to demonstrate to her that she matters more to me than any amount of money. I need to show her I'm not my father, or my mother, but I can't do everything in a day. She'll have to be patient.

I LOVE YOU TOO, MORE THAN YOU KNOW. BUT I NEED A LITTLE TIME.

When I think of how she'll feel when she reads my text, my heart breaks. She's strong though. So strong. I hit send. She doesn't reply, and I force myself not to send anything else either.

By Wednesday, I have all the details ironed out, so I text Geo. I KNOW YOU'RE SWAMPED THIS WEEKEND. CAN I SEE YOU MONDAY?

Dots. I hate the infernal dots. But it does tell me she's live and has seen my message. I love the dots. I can't look away from them. Until a message pops up.

CLIENT EVENT THAT NIGHT.

What the heck?

I text Luke. ANY IDEA WHAT GEO HAS GOING ON MONDAY NIGHT?

He's always quick to reply. HER BIGGEST CLIENT OWNS SOME CAR DEALERSHIPS OR SOMETHING. THEY HAVE SOME BIG BLACK TIE CASINO NIGHT.

ON VALENTINE'S DAY?? I ask.

APPARENTLY IT'S AN ANNUAL THING. IT STARTED AS A WAY TO IGNORE VALENTINE'S. HE INVITES A LOT OF BIG BUYERS IN ATLANTA. NOW IT'S LIKE AN ATLANTA FIXTURE. IT'S CALLED LIKE HOT FOR HONDA OR SOMETHING. GEO KNOWS WHAT SHE'S DOING, AND SHE MARKETED THE HECK OUT OF IT.

Of course she did. Her big client has got to be Rob. Maybe that's why she didn't consider her Monday night dinners a date. Rob's her client. That makes sense.

I hate the idea of him spending Valentine's Day with her. That ruins all my plans. Geo says he's a good guy, so I look him up and take a calculated risk. I dial his office and wait patiently when his secretary puts me on hold. He might refuse to talk to me. I probably would, if our situation was reversed. I'm betting on him being a better man than me.

"Rob Graham," he says, his voice deeper than I remember from Macaroni Grill.

"Rob, this is Trig Thornton. I'm in love with your best friend, Geode Polson."

"I know who you are." And he hasn't hung up on me yet. I don't hate him as much as I did.

"Thanks for taking my call. I'm sure you considered refusing to talk to me. I'll cut to the chase. I have a favor to ask." I hate when people act all chummy and fake, trying to butter me up. When I have a favor to ask, which isn't often, I get right to it. "It's a big ask. I know you have a Casino Night Monday. I know Geo's going to be there. I could have just bought tickets through a shell company, but I don't play that way. I'd like to see her, and I'd like it to be on Valentine's Day."

"I broke my back four years ago," he says. "But it's healed now, and once a Marine, always a Marine. I'll end you on Monday if Geo leaves my party without a smile on her face. I don't care the reason."

"Fair," I say. "I'll see you Monday."

"You'll be on the list." He hangs up.

I still detest him, but he's exactly the kind of guy I want Geo to have around if things don't go my way. I wonder what his best friend Mark was like. I'm sure he didn't deserve Geo, but I'm beginning to think he was probably a decent guy.

Luke loves his bachelor party, I think. And I manage not to spend the entire time looking at the photo of Geo and I on my lock screen like a dope. Paul only mocks me for it about six million times. How he knew we broke up, I don't know, and I don't even care.

I'm a ball of nerves on Monday. I send Brekka fifteen photos before I settle on a plain black tuxedo with a sapphire blue tie. I slide the ring I bought in Hawaii into my pocket. I consider buying her a different one, but it's part of our story. Her bad reaction that day wasn't to the ring I chose. I think I got that right. My screw-up came later. I think she'll want the original ring, if I'm not way off base. And if I am, well, maybe I don't know Geo as well as I think I do. But I think I know Geo better than she knows herself, at least in the ways that really matter.

I hope.

I valet my Vantage exactly half an hour after the Casino night starts. She would have arrived early, checked on everything, dealt with any issues and she should be in a lull, according to the event planner we use for Nometry. I hope Victorine's right. If not, I know who I'll hire to replace her.

My heart's racing a mile a minute when I walk into the huge ballroom, decorated like the casino from Ocean's Eleven. Geo did an amazing job.

At first I don't see her, which is strange because she'd stand out in every crowd I've ever walked into.

Then she enters the room from the back, talking to one of the bus boys as she walks. He's clearly smitten with her, and it's easy to see why. I've never seen her look more breathtaking. She's wearing a hot pink sheath dress and tall pink wedges. Her hair falls down her back like a waterfall of shimmering ebony. She's wearing an onyx necklace surrounded by sapphires. Whoever gave her that had a good eye. The black for her hair, set off by the blue of the sparkling stones.

Even though I wasn't referring to her appearance when I said it, she really does shine. It's hard to look away. I stare at her for a good minute before she glances my way, and then I freeze in place.

She walks toward me with a look in her eyes I can't interpret. "Trig?"

"Geo?"

She reaches my side and looks up at me. "What are you doing here?"

"I'm a potential client," I say. "What are you doing here?"

She puts a hand on her hip. "You're never going to buy a Honda."

Rob walks up alongside her, and I hate to admit it, but

he looks pretty decent in a tuxedo. Not as good as me, but okay.

"Trig," he says calmly.

Geo spins around to face him. "You knew he was coming?"

Rob nods. "He cleared it with me, yes."

Her eyes flash. "You didn't think to pass that information along to me?"

"I'm sorry," he says. "Next time I'll be sure to send you a full list of all my potential new customers. I didn't realize you were wanting that level of review."

She practically pulses with light when she's angry. When it's not directed at me, I love watching it.

But she turns on me next. "So you're buying Hondas now?"

"We have a great line of products you might love as company cars, and we're happy to ship to Colorado or anywhere else," Rob says. "I can put my people in touch with yours."

Well played, Rob. "Absolutely."

When Geo turns to grab a glass from a tray, Rob points two fingers at his eyes, and then turns one finger toward me in a very *Meet the Parents* way. I roll my eyes, after he's not facing me anymore, of course.

Geo takes a sip and when she looks back up at me, her heart's in her eyes. I want to scoop her up and carry her out of here in a bubble.

"Why are you here?"

"For you," I say. "I messed everything up last time, but I want to try and get it right. Will you talk to me for a minute?"

Her lower lip trembles and I touch her chin. She leans toward me. I've practiced this speech a hundred times today. I practically have it memorized. I contemplated dozens of different ways this could have gone. But none of my ideas prepared me for her reaction.

She turns away from me to set her drink on a table, and then she leaps toward me. I almost drop her, but luckily my arms react faster than my brain. The feel of her in my arms again is better than waking up on Christmas morning, or shredding down a perfect run, or the first bite of ice cream in July.

"I'm glad you came," she says. "I'm sorry I didn't say this before. I think I was too afraid of—well. Of everything. But I love you, Trig. I love your lopsided grin. I love your dimples. I love your hair." She reaches up to muss it. "I love your gentleness, your sense of humor, your cunning, your business acumen. I love your generosity, and how forgiving you are. I love that you're open and willing to try new things. I love your devotion to your sister and your patience with your difficult mother. Basically, I love everything about you."

My mouth drops open and I stare at her dumbly. "Uh. I have a whole speech ready."

"I don't need a speech." She shakes her head. "Not if you love me too. I just needed you to show up. I'll sign the prenup, and I'll grit my teeth while you're dropped out of helicopters or you leap from airplanes or whatever else you need to do. I might even try parasailing. Or maybe not. I'm not sure."

I laugh. "You're crazy. In the very best way."

"I'm crazy about you," she says. "I had no idea how much I was giving up by sitting on the sidelines of life. It felt safer, but I was wrong. But thanks to the right motivation, I'm finally wearing my football gear or whatever, and ready to go out on the field."

I laugh and shake my head. "Been practicing your speech too?"

"Clearly not." She bites her lip and I kiss her then, unable to wait. She tastes like moonlight. Like sugary moonlight and champagne bubbles.

When I hear giggles behind us, I set her down. "I really did prepare a speech. I'd love to walk you to the corner of the room or something and share it with you."

"I could do that." She winks at me and my knees go wobbly.

Walk, Trig. You can walk. I follow her like a baby duck. She sits down and points at a chair. I take it gratefully and slide it closer to her.

"Let's hear this epic speech," she says.

I gulp. I wasn't expecting quite so much build up. "Well, I guess first I wanted to tell you that you were right, completely right. I don't want a marriage like my parents, and if their personalities contributed to their mess, certainly the Thornton Trust didn't help, with all its contracts and documents and whatnot." I pull the rumpled prenup out of my pocket. "I wanted to burn this, but." I point at the ceiling fire alarms. "Fire code. I figured being the event's planner, you might not want to deal with the fallout."

"Courteous of you."

"Pretend I'm burning it though, because that's a more dramatic gesture." I try to tear the prenup in half, but it's surprisingly hard to tear sixty pages. This whole thing is not going well. I force a chuckle and split out ten or so pages and tear them. Then the next ten. And so on.

Geo's looking at me like I'd look at a ten year old playing the violin at his first concert. This is painful, and she pities me.

I should have bagged the whole speech.

"I told you I needed time," I say. "But not for the reasons you probably thought. Brekka helped me sort through everything I screwed up within an hour or so. Basically, I thought I'd made her a promise to do risky, exciting things, and I liked some of it, but if it makes you nervous, I'll never ski again. I'll never surf. I'll get a subscription to the home shopping network, or some Hallmark movie channel and we'll sit in front of the TV every night. I don't care."

She shakes her head. "A little excitement is good for me. How about we meet in the middle? No more skydiving, but a little more skiing? Preferably without Natalie along."

I beam at her. "I think we could work that out, but maybe without putting it in writing."

She giggles.

I'm doing better. Thank goodness. "But I should probably tell you that my mom would never have ever agreed to me tearing up the prenup."

She frowns. "Then why bother?"

I take the plunge. "Because, fair warning, I disclaimed my inheritance. Brekka's twice as rich now as she was when you met her. I went before a judge and had him remove me as a beneficiary of the Thornton Family Trust."

"What?" she asks.

I translate. "I'm poor now."

Geo shakes her head. "Why would you do that, you idiot?"

Uh. What?

"I don't want to be responsible for you giving up your inheritance. And if I'm being honest, I don't think you'll be very happy as a poor person."

I am an idiot. I thought she'd be delighted. "So you're mad."

She stands up and then sits down on my lap and brushes her full, pink lips against mine. "I'm unreservedly, beyond belief, beyond sanity, in love with you. You could owe a million dollars and I'd help you file for bankruptcy and find a job as a checker at the grocery store. But I don't want you to be miserable. I'm worried you might be, and I'll feel like it's my fault."

"Remember how I said Brekka and I sold our graduation gift to start Nometry?"

She nods.

"That means my company isn't part of the trust, and I still own fifty-one percent. Plus whatever house and cars I've gotten as gifts or bought with my own money. Basically anything that wasn't a trust asset is still mine."

"You're saying your version of poor isn't really the same as mine?" she asks.

I nod. "Something like that. I opened a joint account in your name and mine, and I've come up with a list of houses I want us to look at. Hand me your phone." She complies and I install an app for my bank.

I type in the numbers and turn the interface around. "The password is peachcobbler1+1=2. Think you can remember that?"

Her eyes water and I wipe her cheeks. "I'm almost done. Just one more minute, okay?" I reach into my other pocket and pull out a document. "I had my lawyer draw this up. Turns out Georgia is an 'equitable division' state or something like that. Basically, whatever we each have when we get married stays our own property."

She shrugs. "I don't care."

I shake my head. "I do. Peach cobbler, baby." I hand her the papers. "This is my prenup. It makes my shares in Nometry evenly owned by both of us. We're in this together all the way. And don't worry, I ran it past Brekka. She says it's fine, and welcome to the family."

I shift her into the chair next to me and get down on

one knee again. "Geode Marie Polson, will you marry me? Pretty, pretty please?"

A tear rolls down one cheek and she nods. "Of course I will. You had me at peach cobbler."

I stand up and swing her around. Twice. Then I kiss her until I can't breathe anymore.

After that we dance. And dance. And then I play a little poker, which I'm pretty decent at after years of dealing with bluffing business men and women.

"Wow," Geode says when I cash in my chips. "You cleaned up. I almost feel bad for the people you played. Except I hear we need it now."

I shrug. "That's the word on the street."

"How poor are we as a result of your little temper tantrum, anyway?"

I take her hand in mine. "Nometry was worth about one point three billion when we had it valued last year, give or take. It goes up and down, but mostly up."

She stops in her tracks. "So even though you quit-claimed your inheritance or whatever, we're still almost billionaires?"

I nod. "I guess you could say that."

She swallows. "How much money was in that trust?"

I laugh. "You don't want to know."

She leans against me and sighs. "You're right. I really don't."

I kiss her on the forehead. "Even if it had been double what it was, you'd still be worth it."

***

The next book in my Almost a Billionaire Series is out!
Check out Finding Spring here!

Also, if you want a FREE BOOK from me, go sign up for my newsletter at: www.BridgetEBakerWrites.com. You will get Already Gone for free!!

If you enjoyed Finding Cupid, please leave me a review on Amazon (and Good Reads)! It helps more than you can imagine.

Keep reading for a sample of Finding Spring!

23

BONUS: FIRST CHAPTER OF FINDING SPRING

I barely survived the burning pile of garbage that was my first marriage. I marvel every single day that I emerged from that nightmare with something as beautiful as my son Troy. Sometimes I catch myself staring at him: the curve of his chubby baby face, the delicate bones in his arms, and the curlicues in his hair.

I'm staring at him and thinking about how quickly he's growing, when he knocks his cereal bowl onto the floor. Milk sprays in directions my high school physics teacher wouldn't have even believed possible.

My sense of wonder evaporates in the heat of frustration.

"Troy, sweetie!"

He turns wide, shining eyes toward me, eyes that could have inspired an anime character. "I'm sorry Mommy."

I sigh and grab two hand towels. I dampen one of them and hand the other to Troy. "Clean up the mess, and I'll wipe it all down for you after you're done."

I'm a firm believer that kids need to try to clean up their own messes, but Troy isn't very effective yet. My knees ache by the time I finish wiping the bottom of the cabinets on the far side of the kitchen. That's when I notice Troy's curly head bobbing up and down toward the front door. He's dragging the tin watering can behind him, sloshing water over the side onto the tile.

I sigh dramatically. "I'm just finishing cleaning up the last mess. What are you doing?"

"I forgot yesterday, Mom."

I shake my head. "We're supposed to be getting ready for your party. Besides, we've talked about this. It's pointless."

He sets his jaw and huffs. "It needs water."

Troy turns four today. His dad won't be at his party, which is both a relief and a sorrow. I'm the one who took out the restraining order, so I can't really fault Chris for not coming. Troy and I are stronger without him, but the absence of his dad has made Troy a little obsessive. His latest hang-up centers on a dead plant in a pot on the front porch.

"I looked it up honey, remember? Gerbera daisies are annuals here in Atlanta. That means they die when the weather gets cold and they don't come back. Once spring comes, we can buy some more, but this little plant is completely dead. Watering it won't help."

Troy opens the door and doggedly hoists the watering can a few inches off the ground to pour water over the blackened stems and leaves of the former daisy. "Plants need water and sun and dirt."

I wait for him to finish and usher him back inside, taking the much lighter watering can from his hands. In Troy's mind, everything can be fixed. Broken toy? Mom can glue it. Hole in his jacket? Mom will sew it up. One day he'll learn that some things can't be saved, but for now, I don't put up more than a token protest.

I'm totally the mom I swore I'd never become, the kind who secretly flushes a dead goldfish and replaces it before my son wakes up. Not that we have a fish, thankfully. I'm at capacity on the total number of living things I can preserve right now with just Troy and myself.

Guests should be arriving any minute. I only invited a handful of people, but Troy won't know it's a pathetically small party. I survey the family room, breakfast room and kitchen. My homemade Lightning McQueen cake sags in the middle and the frosting has slid down in a few places, forming bunchy piles. But the price was right—$4.75 for all the ingredients combined.

Red and gold balloons are taped to the back of each chair, and streamers dangle from the ceiling. His gift from me rests in the center of the table. I stayed up way too late last night making car shaped sugar cookies for party favors, which now sit in clear plastic baggies, all piled in a bowl. I've got a stack of crustless peanut butter and jelly sandwiches in the fridge, along with a bowl of apple slices.

Sadly, this pitiful party still cost more than I should've spent. I need a job so bad.

I cross the room to the built-in desk between the laundry room and the kitchen to check my email before the party starts. Maybe someone has replied to a job application and there's an email inviting me for an interview. It could happen, right? Except it doesn't.

My inbox is as empty as my bank account.

A bright red piece of paper on the fridge catches my eye and I snatch it down and stuff it in my pocket, grateful I remembered to hide it before Mary shows up.

She would not understand the importance of my list. Not that I really need the list taped to my fridge. I know the three things on it by heart.

Trudy Will Not Date Anyone Until:

1. She graduates.
2. She finds a dream job.
3. She repays Troy's medical expenses.

I've been officially divorced for barely more than a month, and Mary's already raring to set me up. Clearly her newfound happiness in love has nowhere to go and is spilling over on her family and friends.

In Mary's defense, lots of women in my place might be dating already. Chris did leave me more than six months ago, even if I didn't want to admit it was real for a while. But I did things wrong the first time around, and I'm not going to screw up again. No dating or even flirting until my three tasks are complete. Graduation hovers right around the corner, but finding a dream job seems like a long and possibly unrealistic trip I won't ever be able to take. And repaying the enormous sum Mary paid for me feels like a distant island only imagined in fairy tales.

Mary loaned me a huge pile of money when Troy was diagnosed with type one diabetes to cover medical costs, and I will pay her back if it kills me. Unless I die of old age first, which seems like a possibility. After all, right now I can't even come up with any money to pay her rent for her house I'm living in. Which means my debt is increasing, not decreasing.

The doorbell rings and Troy races to answer it. He nearly trips over his own feet. "Honey, wait for me. You're too young to be answering—"

Troy doesn't even pause, but he swings the door wide enough that I can see Mary's smiling face. Her grin always lifts my spirits. Her fiancé Luke follows her through the door, and Amy and Chase dart past the adults. Chase and Troy immediately shoot around the corner headed for Troy's room. I almost call them back to interact with the rest of us, but I stop myself. If Troy and Chase want to play boy stuff on Troy's birthday, I should let them. Besides, only three other kids are coming. I'll call them back to greet the other guests when they arrive.

"Trudy, everything looks great," Mary says. "I can't believe you made that cake."

I lift one eyebrow. "You can't?"

Luke shakes his head. "I can't either. It looks amazing, seriously. If you weren't about to graduate in computer stuff, I'd say go find a job at a bakery."

This is exactly why I can't trust a word they say. "I really am looking for jobs. I'll pay you rent as soon as I can."

Mary flinches. "That's not what Luke meant." She crosses the room and pulls me against her for a hug. "You don't need to rush. Troy needs you. You're welcome to stay here for as long as you want."

Tears threaten and I inhale deeply to head them off. The income I earn each month selling handmade home decor on Etsy barely covers the cost of groceries. I moved in with Mary around Christmas, but when she got engaged, Luke bought a new house for her. Mary's been kind enough to keep paying the utility bill on this place so that I have somewhere to live with Troy. She's never once complained, but I feel guilty about it every day.

"I know you're not pushing, and I appreciate it. I swear to you though, I will be able to pay rent soon."

"Aunt Trudy," Amy says.

I glance down at her. She's got one hand on her hip, and the other around a box. "Where should we put Troy's presents?"

She's only holding one, but I don't point that out. "The kitchen table is great. Thanks for being so polite about asking."

Amy glances at our four-person table and raises one eyebrow skeptically. "They definitely won't fit there."

I crouch down and hold out my hands. She's clearly not accustomed to parties with only a handful of guests. "I think we'll be okay. Here, if you give it to me, I'll make room for it."

Amy shakes her head. "No, this is just the one Chase picked. The rest of the presents are in Dad's truck."

I frown. Surely Mary and Luke wouldn't have brought something huge. I told Mary I bought Troy a remote control Mickey car, and my sister wouldn't upstage my gift. Right?

Amy reaches out with her free hand and pushes on the corners of my mouth. "Don't frown. Dad said you might have forgotten how you couldn't fit the surprise for Troy in your car, but we brought it for you." She leans close and whispers. "*Did* you forget? Because sometimes old people forget things, and Dad says that's really normal. It's the train table Troy loves to play with when he comes to Mom's house, like Chase's."

This time I can't blink back my tears, so I stand up and wipe at my face. "I did forget. Thanks for reminding me, Amy. And you're right, it didn't fit in my car."

Amy claps her hands. "I helped wrap all the trains. I thought Troy would like to open each one." Her eyes sparkle. "I'll go help Dad bring them inside if that's okay."

I point. "Maybe put them over there by the window."

Amy races back toward the door with Luke on her heels. He glances back at me, his eyebrows drawn together quizzically. "I hope you don't mind."

How could I mind that I have such generous family? It's exactly the kind of thing Mary would have done herself before she met Luke. Of course, she and I would have stayed up late the night before putting it together one dumb piece at a time.

I smile at him. "Of course not. Thanks."

He bobs his head and steps out.

"He's a really, really good guy," I say.

Mary beams. "I know he is. And your guy is out there too, I can feel it."

I roll my eyes. "If you mention Paul's name one more time, I may duct tape your mouth shut."

Mary puts her arm around me. "I didn't say it this time. And you can't be too cranky about it. You haven't even met him yet."

"I've been divorced for one month," I say.

"But you've been entirely alone for five. Most women would be looking around by now."

"You're just in the engagement haze. I'm not in a rush. I'll meet Paul at your wedding, and I don't need you guys to make things unbearably awkward before then. I wouldn't even want to go on a date with Bradley Cooper if he knocked on my door. I'm not ready to date."

"I said something similar not too long ago." Mary drags me into the kitchen and lets go of my hand to sink down onto a chair. "Then I met Luke and realized I'd been lying to myself. Everyone wants to fall head over heels, if they meet the guy they trust to catch them."

"My heart's deader than those daisies Troy keeps watering. Dating anyone would be grotesque, trust me. Let's all agree to spare poor Paul the miserable experience."

Mary lifts her eyebrows. "I'll do no such thing."

My door bangs open and I'm glad I didn't bother sitting down myself.

Paisley flies through the door in front of Luke, sliding along my tile in an unnatural way. "What's up party people!?" She pulls up short and barely avoids toppling right into me. Meanwhile, Luke singlehandedly hefts a huge table through my doorway sideways.

I maneuver around Paisley and rush over to help guide

Luke. Amy follows after her dad with an armful of small packages.

"Thanks guys," I say.

Amy and Luke head back down to grab the rest of the trains and track, all wrapped up individually. Troy unwraps presents slower than an arthritic snail, so this is going to be painful. Before I can follow them out and offer to help, Paisley zooms over to the family room with two more boxes under her arm.

"What in the world is wrong with you?" I squint at her feet. No wonder she practically knocked me over when she came inside. "Please tell me you don't have wheels on your shoes."

Paisley plops both boxes onto the top of the train table. "My rolly footwear is literally the coolest thing ever invented. I can't believe I hadn't tried them before now."

"I'm pretty sure they never made them in big people sizes before now," Mary says.

"Very funny." Paisley leans close to me, her eyes twinkling. "Don't worry, Trudy. I got you and Troy matching pairs. You're going to *love* these, I swear."

I groan. "You better be kidding. I need a broken ankle about as much as Troy needs a double shot of caffeine."

"What you need is more excitement in your life," Paisley says. "You can't find it unless you look, and maybe I should specify. I mean you need to look somewhere outside of this house."

"Speaking of excitement, how did you get up the porch stairs?" I ask. "Without breaking your neck, I mean?"

Paisley's grin splits her face and she lifts one foot up. "That's the beauty of these. They're shoes on the front. I walked up."

Mary and I share a glance, but before we come up with anything witty enough to say about the oddity of Paisley's brain, a boy from Troy's Sunday school class shows up. The other boy and the girl arrive moments after. The next hour and a half is full of squeals, games, and far too many juice box spills for only six kids.

Amy takes it upon herself to enforce all house rules. She follows the four-year-olds around and orders them not to write on anything but paper. She makes them wash their hands before leaving the kitchen area to play. And when one of the little boys dashes over to the table to snatch a handful of grapes, she stops him with a firmly outstretched palm.

"Graham," she says imperiously, "you're welcome to eat those, but in this house, food stays in the kitchen."

Mary and Luke watch it all with identical indulgent half-smiles on their faces. If it wasn't so cute, it might be a little alarming. My sister's been replaced. Now she's half of a couple that seems to communicate silently in smirks and loaded looks.

"Amy has turned into quite the little lieutenant, hasn't she?" I ask Mary.

"We're spending more and more time at Mary's place," Luke says. "So that it won't be such a big transition when we move in after the wedding. Amy's happy not to be outnumbered anymore, and she may be taking her job as Mommy's helper a little too seriously."

Mary shrugs. "I think it's harmless. For now."

Luke rolls his eyes. "You would think that. She didn't imperiously order you to take your shoes off and leave them by the front door yesterday."

"You were tracking mud inside," Mary says.

Amy approaches, arms folded across her chest. "Aunt Trudy, I think the kids are getting a little bored with the beanbag game. I keep having to stop them from opening Troy's presents. It might be time for cake."

Mary shoots me a sheepish look.

"Why little Miss, I think you're right. Why don't you call everyone over?"

Amy herds the kids toward the table like a well-intentioned border collie. Chase bristles a little at his sister's officious commands, but Troy and his friends don't seem to mind. After one look at the cake, even Chase happily stands near the table with his small hands folded in front of him.

"Thank you all for coming," I say to the kids and their parents. "We are so happy that Troy's four years old!"

Troy hugs my leg. "I'm finally big!"

My heart contracts and I crouch down in front of him. "All I asked for this Christmas was for you to stay little."

Troy raises his chin. "But I gave you something different. A stuffed teddy bear. Which means I can be big now."

I pick Troy up. He may be big, but he still fits on my hip. "Now everyone wants to sing to you, okay? And then we can cut this cake."

Troy claps, and Paisley lights the candles.

I choke back tears during the song, not ready to acknowledge that my baby's a little boy. But he blows out all four candles without help, and I have to admit it. He's growing up.

We open presents next, and he loves the train table. Even so, a tiny part of my heart soars when he proclaims that the Mickey remote controlled car is his favorite toy. One day I'll be able to afford fancy gifts, but for now I'm glad my boy likes simple things.

After the other three guests have left, Mary calls for Chase and Amy. "Time to go, kids."

"You can stay as long as you want," I say. "No big rush on our end."

"I've got fifty million emails to wade through." Mary sighs.

"And I have to sign off on all the launch plan details." Luke shakes his head. "I know you're actively searching, but jobs are overrated."

"You might have a different opinion if you were in my shoes," I say. "I've filled out eighty-six applications and not gotten one interview."

Mary's eyebrows draw together. "I wish you'd come work for me. I don't understand why you won't."

Mary has always been a genius, and laser focused on top of it. She put herself through college and took care of me at the same time. She found her own job right out of school and worked her way to the top by the age of thirty. She never had a leg up from anyone, so she doesn't get why I won't accept one when she's offering it.

"I need to find a place myself," I say.

"Just apply for a position at LitUp Applied Science," Luke says. "I won't even tell anyone to pick you, I swear."

I roll my eyes. "*Sure* you wouldn't. You guys are amazing, but I'm graduating in two months and I need to do this on my own." Plus, there's no way I want to work at Luke's office, where he will awkwardly try to shove me at his little brother daily. Blech.

"If you change your mind, just say the word," Mary says. "Being the boss should have some perks, right?"

A terrible thought occurs to me. What if they're offering me jobs because they're sick of me not contributing? Mary's too nice to complain, but the idea of her grumbling to Luke about how I'm such a freeloader when I could be earning something to pay them makes me dizzy.

I bite my lip. "If I still can't find anything in the next two weeks, I'll apply for a job at both of your companies. I know I'm sponging off you right now so I shouldn't be too picky, but I'd really like to try and do this myself."

Mary puts her hand on my arm. Her voice is soft when she says, "Trudy, you are not sponging. You're caring for my beautiful nephew. You watch Chase and Amy all the time, and you're finishing up your degree. I don't even know how you'll find time to work between now and graduation."

"I watched my friend Pam's son Benson for free for two years while she was getting her beautician's license. She's too nauseated by the smell of hair products during her second pregnancy to work. Plus her husband got a promotion, and told her to take some time off. Troy and her son are the same age and they play beautifully, so she's going to watch Troy for free while things level off around here."

"What about school?" Luke asks. "You only had four classes between you and graduation, but that's still a full load."

"Yeah I was so close. I was such an idiot not to finish. Luckily, the university has a new program that lets me take the computer classes mostly online, which means I could go at whatever pace I wanted. The reason I started looking for jobs is that I'm essentially done."

"How's that even possible?" Paisley asks. She's been wiping down the counters, and I almost forgot she was still here.

"I've been working on them every single time Troy takes a nap, and after he goes to bed. I'm finished, other than taking my finals, which I can't do until the first week of May."

Paisley whistles. "Well folks, Mary and Trudy may not look an awful lot alike, but it turns out, Trudy's just as big of a nerd. Good luck living with a Wiggin girl, Luke, that's all I have to say."

"I can't wait." Luke kisses Mary's forehead.

Mary beans Paisley in the head with a grape.

"Nice shot," I say. "See? We're not too nerdy. We can still lob a grape well enough to leave a welt."

Luke's phone buzzes and he checks it. "That's Paul. He needs my feedback in the next hour on the supply chain revisions." He slides his phone into his pocket. "Sorry we can't stay longer."

"If you guys are super busy, leave the kiddos," I say. "They can spend the night."

Luke's head whips toward Mary's so fast, I worry about whiplash. "That's not a bad idea."

Mary shakes her head. "We can't, not tonight. They have dentist appointments in the morning, remember?"

Luke grunts. "Fine, fine. Thanks for the offer, Trudy."

Once they've gathered all their things and extricated both kids, they head out the door. Luke turns back toward me before he heads down the steps. "I'm going to hold you to your promise," Luke says. "Not because we care whether you're paying rent. We couldn't care less, I swear. But you're too great an asset to be wandering around undiscovered. You can keep sending resumes into slush piles for two more weeks, and if no-one bites, then you're going to come work for me."

He hugs me, and I close the door behind him.

Paisley's sweeping now. I cross the room and take the broom from her. "I didn't invite you over to be my maid."

"There were only six kids, right? How come it looks like a tornado went through the house?" she asks.

"It looks almost this bad before I put Troy to bed every night." He's watching Mickey Mouse on TV right now, but I glance at the clock. "Which I have to do in an hour or so, anyway."

"Maybe I'll stick around for a movie, then. Do you have time?" she asks.

"You don't have other plans?" I'm giddy about having some girl time, but I feel bad keeping her here on a Sunday night. I'm sure she has other things to do. "It's a weekend and you're single and flirty and fun."

Paisley laughs. "It's cute that you think I have plans. I had a horrible date on Friday. It was so bad I deleted the dating app from my phone."

"Whoa! No more internet dating for you?" I ask.

She giggles. "Let's not get too carried away. I have about ten other apps, but that particular one's toast."

"I don't even want to think about all that," I say.

"You never used apps before you married Chris?" Paisley asks.

"I mean, they existed, but I met him through a friend. After that..."

Paisley nods. "Yeah, Mary told me. He kind of took over your life."

I shrug. It's been so strange making decisions on my own, now that he's finally been eliminated from my life. Strange, but also liberating. "Anyhow, I have a while before I need to worry about it."

She narrows her eyes at me. "Do you now?" She snatches my phone and starts poking at buttons.

"Hey," I say. "Give that back."

"I'm bringing you into the twenty-first century."

I snatch my phone back. "I'm not dating at all."

Paisley's jaw drops. "Why not?"

I pull the crumpled list out of my pocket. "Last time I started dating someone and got excited, I got married and pregnant and didn't finish my last semester of college."

"Not everyone is Chris," Paisley says. "In fact, most people aren't anywhere near that narcissistic."

"Thank goodness for that," I say, "but I need to worry about getting my ducks in a row. Besides, right now I don't even want to date." I plop down onto one of the kitchen chairs. "I think my heart died."

"I didn't realize you were so upset over the divorce." Paisley collapses next to me. "I'm sorry. I'm a lousy friend."

I shake my head. "It's not the divorce, or even Chris. My overwhelming feeling about that was just relief."

Paisley leans toward me. "Then what's with the vampire situation?"

"Huh?" I ask.

"Your undead heart?"

Paisley's such a goober. "I don't know. I haven't wanted to watch rom coms, or any kind of love stories. I don't ever catch myself checking out hot guys. If my heart isn't dead, it's broken beyond repair. I don't even think about all that stuff."

"When would you go see a movie if you wanted to? Do you ever leave the house anymore?"

I whap her on the arm. "I leave the house."

"I'm not actually kidding. Other than shipping your Etsy signs and like, grocery shopping, when do you go anywhere?"

My cheeks heat up. "I don't have enough money to pay for a gym membership—I only have one because Mary added me to her account for a Christmas present." My voice drops to a whisper. "I really do need a job."

Paisley's face crumples. "Oh Trudy, I'm sorry. I didn't even think about that. Look, the last year has been a rough one."

"Try the last five."

She slides her chair close and puts her arm around me. "This year is going to be your best yet, then."

A tear slides down my cheek. "Why would you think that? I haven't got a single lead for a job. Not one."

"That's how it works. When life gets horrible enough,

we make changes. It takes time to course correct, but once we do, that's when things improve. I've been watching. You're headed the right way again, so things will come around for you."

I hope she's right.

"Hey what jobs are you applying for, anyway?" she asks.

"What do you mean?"

"You're graduating in computer science, right?"

I nod. "I'm applying for IT jobs, if that's what you're asking. But they all require experience. I don't know how I'm supposed to get any, since none of them will take me without it."

She taps her lip and stands up. "You should search for jobs where the company is looking for an assistant *and* an IT person."

I tilt my head. "Why, exactly?"

"First of all, you have experience as an assistant and you have a reference, too. You've helped with Sub-for-Santa several times. You list that and then you put me down as a reference. I'll give you a glowing recommendation."

"But I don't want to be an assistant," I say. "No offense." I still have no idea what Paisley likes about being Mary's go-fer.

She rolls her eyes. "You might like it once you try it, but even if you don't, it would get your foot in the door, Trudy. Once they meet you and see how smart you are, you'll be a shoo-in for their IT position."

Sly like a fox. My kind of plan.

With Paisley's help, I add to my resume. When she wants me to change Trudy to 'Gertrude,' I balk. "It makes me sound a hundred years old."

"You're applying for assistant jobs. The older, the more competent, right?"

I suppose she would know. We work on applications

until Troy gets sick of Mickey, which is about eleven applications in. Frankly, I was surprised to even find that many places looking for both assistants, and IT personnel.

"An assistant spy," I say. "I like it."

She grins and helps me put Troy to bed. Afterward, she insists on watching *Kate and Leopold*. I almost enjoy it.

The next day, I check my email after my morning walk with Troy. I definitely enjoy seeing not one, not two, but three emails from companies interested in interviewing me. Maybe Paisley's right and things are turning around for me. I'm smiling when I call them one-by-one and set up interviews.

ACKNOWLEDGMENTS

Thanks as always to my husband, my mom and my kids. I could never write without the support of all of them.

Thanks to my beta readers, my ARC team and my fans. You have no idea how much your positive reviews and words of encouragement mean.

Thanks to the Writing Gals for helping me learn so much by your generous and open sharing of knowledge!

Thanks to Esther for checking in with me every day and keeping me excited to write. And I'd be remiss not to thank Susannah, for being an amazing cheerleader!

ALSO BY BRIDGET E. BAKER

The Almost a Billionaire clean romance series:

Finding Faith (1)

Finding Cupid (2)

Finding Spring (3)

Finding Liberty (4)

Finding Holly (5)

The Birthright Series:

Displaced (1)

unForgiven (2)

Disillusioned (3)

misUnderstood (4) -March 15, 2020

Disavowed (5)- May 15, 2020

unRepentant (6)- coming spring 2020

Destroyed (7) - coming spring 2020

The Sins of Our Ancestors Series:

Marked (1)

Suppressed (2)

Redeemed (3)

A stand alone YA romantic suspense:

Already Gone

Made in the USA
Monee, IL
12 May 2020